AN OLD-FASHIONED ARMY FOR A NEWFANGLED WAR . . .

A motion caught Mauser's eye and he let off a short burst of machine-gun fire, bringing down two men who had darted from a building across the plaza. To their right, one of the cavalrymen screamed agony as he took a hit. Several of the horses whinnied nervously. Their force was melting away, despite the comparative strength of their position.

A wounded man was pulled into the sanctuary; Mauser caught a glimpse of a bloodied face, an eye drooling from its socket.

The Vickers up in the bell tower chattered, chattered again, spewing hot lead at a group of mounted soldiers moving into town. "If we can hold 'em here for another hour or two, the old man will come up and trim their pants," Jim Hawkins said. "Then we'll both make Middle Caste."

MACK REYNOLDS
WITH
MICHAEL BANKS

JOE MAUSER
MERCENARY FROM TOMORROW

BAEN
SCIENCE FICTION
BOOKS

JOE MAUSER, MERCENARY FROM TOMORROW

This is a work of fiction. All the characters and events portrayed in this book are fictional, and any resemblance to real people or incidents is purely coincidental.

A Baen Books Original

Baen Publishing Enterprises
260 Fifth Avenue
New York, N.Y. 10001

First printing, May 1986

Parts of this novel have appeared in substantially different form as the novellas "Mercenary" and "Frigid Fracas."

ISBN: 0-671-65570-1

Cover art by Jael

Printed in the United States of America

Distributed by
SIMON & SCHUSTER
TRADE PUBLISHING GROUP
1230 Avenue of the Americas
New York, N.Y. 10020

To Mack . . .
  with Compounded Interest

And to Rosa!

CHAPTER ONE

Joseph Mauser spotted the recruiting lineup from two blocks down the street, shortly after driving into Kingston. Perhaps three hundred men stood in a ragged line that terminated at a monolithic structure sporting a decorative facade. That would be the local office of Vacuum Tube Transport. Baron Haer would be recruiting there for the fracas with Continental Hovercraft if for no other reason than to save on rents.

The baron was watching his pennies on this one and that was bad, very bad.

So bad, in fact, that as Mauser let his hovercraft sink to a parking level and vaulted over its side he found himself questioning his decision to sign up with the vacuum tube outfit, rather than with their opponents. Joe was an old pro, and old pros do not get to be old pros in the Category Military without developing an instinct to stay away from the losing side, no matter what the opportunity.

Fine enough for Low-Lowers and Mid-Lowers to sign up with this outfit as opposed to that, motivated by nothing more than the stock shares offered and the snappiness of the uniform, but an old pro considered carefully such matters as budget. Skimping on

1

equipment, provisions, or the quality of soldiers and officers could get a lot of good men killed, and he'd heard that Baron Haer was watching every expense, even to the point of calling upon relatives and friends to serve as his staff. Continental Hovercraft, on the other hand, was heavy with variable capital and in a position to hire old Stonewall Cogswell himself as their tactician.

However, the die was cast. You don't run up a caste level, not to speak of two at once, by playing it careful. Joe had planned this out; and for once, old pro or not, he was taking risks. Big risks, but with an eye toward a bigger payoff. His plan, properly timed and properly carried out, would win him Upper status—the final goal of his career. Everything he had was riding on its success.

He made a beeline for the offices ahead, striding past the line of potential soldiers. Recruiting lineups were not for such as he, not for a man of officer rank.

Mauser glanced over the lineup as he walked. Among these men were the soldiers he'd be commanding in the field. He calculated the general quality of these would-be mercenaries. The prospects looked grim; there were few veterans among them. Their stance, their demeanor, their . . . well, you could tell a veteran even though he be Rank Private, and few here could claim even that status.

He knew the situation, and why such as these were here. The word was out among those in the know: Vacuum Tube Transport and Baron Malcolm Haer had been set up for the defeat. You weren't going to pick up any lush victory bonuses signing with him; the odds were too heavy against it. The baron was equipped to mount an army for a regional dispute, but not to handle what he'd been maneuvered into this time.

In short, no matter what Haer's past record, the word was that Continental Hovercraft would take this fracas. Continental Hovercraft and old Stonewall Cogswell, who had lost so few engagements that most telly buffs could not remember even one.

Individuals among these men did show promise. Mauser spotted a few possibles as he walked. But promise means little if you don't live long enough to cash in on it. Combat odds dictated that you'd lose eight to ten of these bright-faced first-timers for every veteran. It was a safe bet that most of them didn't even have such basic knowledge as how to take cover. A fold in the terrain had to be ten inches or a foot high before they even noticed it.

But, Mauser told himself, you still kept your eye open for those who showed promise. He noticed one such, dead ahead—a small fellow who'd obviously gotten himself into a hassle trying to keep his place in line against two or three heftier men. The little guy wasn't backing down a step. Mauser liked to see such spirit. It could mean the difference between life and death when you were in the dill.

He wasn't particularly interested in the argument, beyond breaking up a situation that might cause trouble in the ranks later on. As he drew abreast of the men he assumed an attitude of authority and snapped, "Easy, lads! You'll get all the scrapping you want with Hovercraft. Wait until then."

He'd expected his tone to be enough, even though he was in mufti. A veteran would have recognized him as an old-timer and probable officer, and heeded automatically.

These were obviously not veterans.

"Says who?" one of the Lowers growled back at him. "You one of Baron Haer's kids or something?"

Mauser stopped and faced the Lower. He was

irritated now, largely with himself; he didn't want to be bothered. But he'd committed himself. He had no alternative but to see the matter through. He expected to be in command of some of these men by tomorrow; in as little as a week he would go into combat with them. He couldn't afford to lose face. Not even at this point, when all, including himself, were still effectively civilians. When matters pickled in a fracas you had to have men who respected you, who had complete confidence in you.

An expectant hush fell over those nearby, all Lowers so far as Mauser could see. Their long wait had been boring. Now something would break the monotony.

The man who had grumbled the surly response was a near physical twin of Joe Mauser, which put him in his early thirties, gave him five-eleven of altitude and about one hundred and eighty pounds. There the resemblance ended. Mauser bore himself with the quiet dignity of he who had faced death over and over again, and had handled himself under such conditions as to satisfy himself. He was a moderately handsome man, his face marked but not particularly disfigured by two scars—one on forehead, one on chin—which cosmetic surgeons had not been able to eradicate completely.

The pugnacious Lower was surly in manner as well as voice, and his shoulders slumped in a way that seemed to proclaim that fate had done him ill through no fault of his own. His clothes marked him a Low-Lower—a man with nothing to lose. Like many who have nothing to lose, he was willing to risk all for principle. His face now registered that ideal. It also registered the fact that Joe Mauser had no authority over him, nor his friends.

Mauser's gaze flicked to the Lower's allies. They

weren't quite so aggressive, and their rapidly shifting eyes indicated that they had come to no conclusion about their stand. Still, Mauser recognized them for what they were: bullies. Let there be a moment of hesitation and all three of them would be on him.

That in mind, Mauser wasted no time on verbal preliminaries. In a lightning move, he closed on the belligerent Lower. His right hand darted out, fingers close together and pointed. An instant later his fingers sank into the other's abdomen, immediately below the rib-cage, and found their target—the solar plexus. The man jerked, doubled over, and sank silently to the ground.

It was then that Mauser discovered he had underestimated the other two. Even as his opponent crumbled, they came at him from both sides. And at least one of them had been in hand-to-hand combat before, probably in the prize ring. Another pro like Mauser himself, though from a somewhat different field.

Mauser took the first blow, rolling with it, then automatically dropped into the stance of the trained fighter. He retreated slightly to erect defenses, plan attack. They pressed him strongly, reading victory in his withdrawal.

The one to his left mattered little. Mauser could have polished him off in a matter of seconds, had there been seconds to devote. The other, the experienced one, was the problem. He and Mauser were well matched, and with the oaf as his ally the Lower really had the best of it.

Just then the source of the problem waded in, delivering sudden, unexpected support. As big as any of the men there so far as spirit was concerned, the little man advanced on the veteran, fists before him in typical street-fighting fashion.

His attack proved a bit hasty, however. He took a crashing blow to the side of his head which sent him sailing back into the recruiting line, now composed of excited, shouting onlookers.

That small wrangle bought what Mauser needed most—time. For a double second he had the oaf alone on his hands, and that was enough. As the man swung on him, Joe sidestepped, caught a flailing arm, turned his back and automatically went into that spectacular wrestling hold called the Flying Mare. Just in time he recalled that his opponent was a future comrade-in-arms and twisted the arm so that it bent at the elbow rather than breaking. He hurled the other over his shoulder and as far as possible to take the scrap out of him, then twirled to meet the attack of his sole remaining foe.

That phase of the combat failed to materialize.

A voice of command bit out, "Hold it, you lads!"

The situation that had originally started the fight was being duplicated. But while the three Lowers had failed to respond to Mauser's tone of authority, there was no similar failure now.

The owner of the voice, beautifully done up in the uniform of Vacuum Tube Transport complete to kilts and the swagger stick carried by ranks of colonel or above, stood glaring at them. Age, Mauser estimated as he came to attention, somewhere in his late twenties. An Upper in caste—a born aristocrat, born to command, his face holding that arrogant, contemptuous expression once common to the patricians of Rome, the Prussian Junkers, the British ruling class of the 19th century. Joe knew the expression well. How well he knew it—on more than one occasion, he had dreamed of it.

Mauser said, "Yes, sir."

"What in Zen goes on here? Are you lads over-tranked?"

"No, sir," Mauser's veteran opponent grumbled, eyes on the ground, a schoolboy before the principal.

The Upper glared at Mauser. Mauser said evenly, "A private disagreement, sir."

"Disagreement?" The Upper snorted. His eyes went to the two fallen combatants, now beginning to recover. "I'd hate to see you lads in a real scrap."

That brought a strong response from the men in the recruiting line. The *bon mot* wasn't that good, but caste has its privileges; the laughter was just short of uproarious.

This seemed to placate the kilted officer. He tapped his swagger stick against his leg while he ran his eyes up and down Mauser and the others, as though memorizing them for future reference.

"All right," he said, "get back into line, and you troublemakers quiet down. We're processing as quickly as we can." Then he added insult to injury with an almost word-for-word repetition of what Mauser had said a few minutes earlier. "You'll get all the fighting you want from Hovercraft, if you can wait until then."

The Lowers who had been in the original altercation resumed their places sheepishly. The little fellow, rubbing what had to be an aching jaw, made a point of taking up his original position. None challenged him. He darted a look of thanks to Mauser, who remained at attention.

The Upper looked at him. "Well, lad, are you interested in signing up with Vacuum Transport or not?" There was a fine impatience in his voice, just a touch of extra emphasis on "lad."

"Yes, sir," Mauser replied. Then, "Joseph Mauser, sir. Category Military, Rank Captain."

"Indeed." The officer looked him up and down all over again, his nostrils high. "A Middle, I assume. And brawling with recruits." He held a long silence.

"Very well, come with me." He turned and marched off.

Mauser shrugged inwardly. This was a fine start for his fling—a fine start. He had half a mind to give it all up, here and now, and head on north to Catskill to enlist with Continental Hovercraft. He was almost sure to win at least a junior position on Stonewall Cogswell's staff, although that would mean that his big scheme would have to wait for another day.

But, at the thought of his plan, he set his lips and fell in behind the aristocrat. A few hundred steps brought them to the offices which had been Joe's original destination.

Two Rank Privates, carrying 45-70 Springfields and wearing the Haer kilts in a manner that indicated permanent status with Vacuum Tube Transport, came to the salute as they approached. The Upper flicked his swagger stick to his cap in easy nonchalance. Mauser felt envious amusement. How long did it take to learn to answer a salute with just that degree of arrogant ease?

They passed through double doors into a large room. Office furniture, terminals, and other pieces of equipment were scattered about, apparently at random. Counters and desks trailed long lines of recruits. The sound of printers humming, keyboards clicking, sorters and collators flicking, merged into an annoying hum as Vacuum Tube Transport office workers, mobilized for this special service, processed volunteers for the company forces. Harried noncoms and junior-grade officers buzzed everywhere, failing miserably to bring order to the chaos. To the right, a door sported a newly-painted medical cross. When it occasionally popped open to admit or emit a recruit, white-robed doctors, nurses, and half-nude men could be glimpsed beyond. Joe gave the scene a cursory glance; he had seen it all a hundred times over.

He followed the Upper through the press and into an inner office at which door the Upper didn't bother to knock. Instead he pushed his way through, waved in greeting with his swagger stick to the single occupant, who looked up from a paper-strewn desk.

Joe had seen the face before on telly, though never so worn and haggard as this. Bullet-headed, barrel-figured Baron Malcolm Haer of Vacuum Tube Transport: Category Transportation, Mid-Upper, and strong candidate for Upper-Upper upon retirement. However, few expected retirement of the baron in the immediate future. Hardly. Malcolm Haer found too obvious a lusty enjoyment in the competition between Vacuum Tube Transport and its stronger rivals. A roly-poly man he might be physically, but his demeanor reminded one of Bonaparte rather than Humpty Dumpty.

Mauser came to attention and bore the sharp scrutiny of his chosen commander-to-be. The older man's eyes left him to go to the kilted Upper. "What is it, Balt?" he said.

Balt gestured with his stick at Mauser. "Claims to be Rank Captain. Looking for a commission with us, Dad. I wouldn't know why . . ." The last sentence was added lazily.

The older Haer shot an irritated glance at his son. "Possibly for the usual reasons mercenaries enlist for a fracas, Balt." His eyes, small and sharp, returned to Mauser.

Still at attention, Mauser opened his mouth to give his name, category and rank, but the older man waved his hand negatively. "Captain Mauser, isn't it? Right. I caught the fracas between Carbonaceous Fuel and United Miners, down on the Panhandle Reservation. Seems to me I've spotted you once or twice before, too."

"Yes, sir," Mauser said, somewhat relieved. This was some improvement over the way things had been going.

Now the older Haer was scowling at him. "Confound it, what are you doing with no more rank than captain? On the face of it, you're an old hand, a highly experienced veteran."

Old pros, we call ourselves, Mauser thought to himself. *Old pros, among ourselves.*

Aloud, he said, "I was born a Mid-Lower, sir."

There was understanding in the old man's face, but the younger Haer said loftily, "What's that got to do with it? Promotion in Category Military is quick, and based on merit."

Mauser frowned. At a certain point, if you are good combat officer material, you speak your mind no matter the rank of the man you are addressing. On this occasion, Joe Mauser spoke his mind, and needed few words to do so. He let his eyes go up and down Balt Haer's immaculate uniform, taking in the swagger stick, then said simply, "Yes, sir."

Balt Haer flushed with quick temper. "What do you mean by your attitude? What . . .?"

But his father was chuckling. "You have spirit, Captain. I need spirit now. You are quite correct. My son—though a capable field officer, I assure you—has probably not participated in a fraction of the fracases you have to your credit. However, there is something to be said for the training available to Uppers in the military academies. For instance, Captain, have you ever commanded a body of men larger than a company?"

Mauser frowned. "In the McDonnell-Boeing versus Lockheed-Cessna fracas we took a high loss of officers when McDonnell-Boeing rang in some fast-firing French *mitrailleuse* we didn't know they had.

As my superiors took casualties I was field-promoted, first to acting battalion commander, then to acting regimental commander, and finally to acting brigadier. For three days I held rank of acting commander of brigade." He took a breath. "We won that fracas, sir."

The other's brow creased, as if in thought. Apparently the incident was familiar to him. Joe certainly remembered it . . . how well he remembered. Now, bringing it back, he would be lucky if it didn't come to him in his dreams this night. That was where Jim, his comrade in arms for six years and more, had taken a burst in his guts that all but cut him in two.

Balt Haer snapped his fingers. "I remember that. Read quite a paper on it." He eyed Mauser almost respectfully now. "Stonewall Cogswell got the credit for the victory and received his marshal's baton as a result."

"He was one of the few other officers that survived," Joe said dryly.

"But, Zen! You mean you got no promotion at all?"

Joe said, "I was upped to Low-Middle from High-Lower, sir. At my age, at the time, it was quite a promotion."

The older Haer nodded. "That was the fracas that brought on the howl from the Sovs. They claimed those *mitrailleuse* were post-1900 and violated the Universal Disarmament Pact. Yes, I recall that. McDonnell-Boeing was able to prove that the weapon was used by the French as far back as the Franco-Prussian War." He eyed Joe with new interest now. "Sit down, Captain. You too, Balt. Do you realize that Captain Mauser is the only recruit of officer rank we've had today? If only we could bring in a few more of his mettle . . ."

"Yes," the younger Haer said dryly. "However, I

doubt that we'll see more officers, if you want my opinion, and it's too late to call the fracas off now. Hovercraft wouldn't stand for it, and Category Military would back them. Our only alternative is unconditional surrender, and you know what that means."

"It means our family would probably be forced from control of the firm," the older man rumbled. "But nobody has suggested surrender on any terms. Nobody, that is, until now." He glared at his son, who took it with an easy shrug as he swung a leg over the edge of his father's desk.

Taking advantage of the baron's invitation, Mauser found a chair and lowered himself into it. Evidently, the foppish Balt Haer had no illusions about the spot his father had gotten the family corporation into. And the younger man was right, of course.

But the baron wasn't blind to reality any more than he was a coward. He appeared to dismiss his son's defeatism with a shake of his head. He eyed Joe Mauser speculatively. "As I say, you're the only officer recruit today. Why?"

"I wouldn't know, sir," Mauser replied. "Perhaps most of the freelance Category Military men are occupied elsewhere. There's always a shortage of trained officers."

Baron Haer was waggling a finger negatively. "That's not what I mean, Captain. You are an old hand. Why are *you* signing up with Vacuum Tube Transport, rather than Hovercraft? Where is the benefit in signing with a smaller outfit, for a man of your caliber?"

Mauser looked at him for a moment without speaking. He knew what the other was thinking. Theoretically, there was no espionage between rival outfits in the fracases, but in actuality, commanders as wily as Stonewall Cogswell might deliberately infiltrate the enemy force with a knowledgeable officer in an attempt to ferret out information. And Mauser was known to have fought under Cogswell before.

"Come, come, Captain," the baron prompted. "I am an old hand too, in my category, and not a fool. I realize there is scarcely a soul in the West-world expecting my colors to have an easy time of it. Nor is it expected that I can attract the cream of the crop; pay rates have been widely posted. I can offer only five common shares of Vacuum Tube for a Rank Captain, win or lose. Hovercraft is doubling that, and can pick and choose from the best officers in the hemisphere."

"I have all the shares I need," Mauser said softly.

Balt Haer had been looking back and forth between his father and the newcomer, his puzzlement obvious. "Well," he broke in, "what in Zen motivates you if it isn't the stock we offer?"

Mauser glanced at the younger Haer to acknowledge the question, but he spoke to the baron. "Sir, like you said, you're no fool. However, you've been sucked in this time. When you took on Hovercraft, you were thinking in terms of a regional dispute. You wanted to run one of your vacuum tube deals up to Fairbanks from Edmonton. You were expecting a minor fracas, involving possibly five thousand men all told. You never expected Hovercraft to parlay it up, through their connections in the Category Military Department, to a divisional-magnitude fracas which you simply aren't large enough to afford. But Hovercraft was getting sick of your competition; you've been nicking away at them too long.

"So," he went on relentlessly, "they decided to do you in. They've hired Marshal Cogswell and the best combat officers in North America, and they're hiring the most competent veterans they can find. Even the fracas buffs figure you've had it. They've been watching you come up the aggressive way, the hard way, for a long time, but now they're all going to be waiting for you to get it."

Baron Haer's heavy face had hardened. He growled, "Is this what everyone thinks?"

"Yes. Everyone intelligent enough to have an opinion." Mauser nodded toward the outer offices. "Most of those men out there are rejects from Catskill, where Baron Zwerdling is recruiting. Either that or they're inexperienced Low-Lowers, too stupid to realize they're sticking their necks out. Not one man in ten is a veteran. And when things pickle, you want veterans."

Baron Malcolm Haer sat back in his chair and stared coldly at Captain Joe Mauser. He said, "At first I was moderately surprised that an old-time mercenary like yourself should choose my uniform rather than Zwerdling's. Now I am increasingly mystified about motivation. So again I ask you, Captain— why are you requesting a commission in my forces— which you seem convinced will meet disaster?"

Now they had reached the critical point. The old man was suspicious, and Mauser couldn't blame him. He had to tread carefully, or he might fail to convince the baron of his sincerity when he offered his plan. A plan that was, on the face of it, outrageous. But now was not the time to reveal that plan, lest it be quashed before he could implement it. He had to get in good with these people, to win their confidence, if he was going to have a chance to make his fling.

He wet his lips carefully. "I think I know a way you can win."

Baron Haer leaned back in his chair. "Ah, now I see. I can appreciate your self-confidence, Captain Mauser, considering your past record. But what you are really after is to be a part of the underdog's victory, and pick up a share of the glory, eh? And perhaps you'll be a little more visible on this side than working under Cogswell. After what happened to you in the McDonnell-Boeing fracas, that would seem reasonable—"

"Uh, father . . ." the younger Haer cleared his throat. "Are you sure that this is a wise decision? Perhaps we should take another look at the options."

"You're looking at the options, Balt!" the baron roared. "Certainly, the potential exists for Captain Mauser to be a plant, working undercover for Cogswell—I'm not blind. If that is the case, then we've lost the war before the first battle."

He stood then. "But, as you well know, without competent, *experienced* officers, we're lost in any event. We've few enough of them, and Captain Mauser is the best of the lot."

Balt Haer glared for a moment, then nodded, lips pressed tightly together.

Baron Haer extended a hand. "Welcome to Vacuum Tube Transport, Captain Mauser."

CHAPTER TWO

His permanent military rank—decided upon by the Category Military Department—the Haers had no way to alter, but they were short enough of competent officers that they gave him the acting rating and pay scale of major.

They also gave him command of a squadron of cavalry. Joe Mauser wasn't interested in a cavalry command for this fracas, but he said nothing. It wasn't time as yet to reveal the big scheme, and he didn't want to buy trouble by complaining. Besides, he could be of use in whipping the Rank Privates into shape.

After they'd finished discussing the preliminaries, Mauser left to unsnarl the red tape involved in signing up with Vacuum Tube's forces. He reentered the confusion of the outer offices just in time to run into a telly team doing a live broadcast.

Joe Mauser recognized the reporter who headed the team, although the man's name escaped him. Mauser had run into him more than once in fracases, and knew the man to be a cut above the average newscaster. As a matter of fact, although Mauser held the military man's standard prejudices against telly, he had a basic respect for this particular newsman. When he'd seen him before, the fellow had been hot in the midst of the action, hanging on even when things were in the dill—he and Mauser had even shared a foxhole at one point. He took as many chances as did the average combatant, and you couldn't ask for more than that. Undoubtedly, he was bucking for a bounce in caste.

The other knew him too, of course. It was part of his job to be able to spot the celebrities and near celebrities. He zeroed in on Mauser now, directing the cameras with flicks of his hand. Mauser was glad to co-operate—like any old pro, he was fully aware of the value of telly to one's career, even though he was at best ambivalent about the telly coverage of fracases.

"Captain! Captain Mauser, isn't it? Joe Mauser, who held out for four days in the swamps of Louisiana with a single company while his ranking officers reformed behind him."

That was one way of putting it, but both Mauser and the newscaster knew the reality of the situation. When the front collapsed, his commanders—of Upper caste, of course—had pulled out, leaving him to fight a delaying action while their employers mended their fences with the enemy, coming to the best terms possible. That had been the United Oil versus Allied Petroleum fracas, and Mauser had emerged with little either in glory or pelf.

What happened behind the scenes meant nothing to the buffs, though. The mind of the average fracas buff didn't operate on a level that could appreciate anything other than victory. The good guys win, the bad guys lose—that's obvious, isn't it? Not one fracas fan out of ten was interested in a well-conducted retreat or holding action. They wanted blood, lots of it, and they identified with the winning side. What mattered the tactics and strategies that brought the blood? One might as well wonder at the workings of telly itself.

It was the *fiesta brava* of Spain and Latin America all over again. The crowd identified with the matador, never the bull. Invariably, the cheers went up when finally the wounded, bedeviled, and bewildered animal went down to its death, its moment of truth. In the fracases, fans might start out neutral, but as the action developed and it became obvious that the victors-to-be were going in for the kill, the fans' loyalty was totally with the winner.

Mauser wasn't particularly bitter about this aspect. It was part of his way of life. His pet peeve was the *real* buff. The type of fan, man or woman, who could remember every fracas you'd ever been in, every time you'd copped one, and how long you'd been in the hospital. Fans who could remember, even better than you could, every time the situation had pickled on you and you'd had to fight your way out as best you could. They'd tell you about it, their eyes gleaming, sometimes even with a slight trickle of spittle at the sides of their mouths.

They usually wanted an autograph, or a souvenir such as a uniform button. And there seemed to be no end to the tactics these fanatics would employ in consummating their adoration. Once a fan had maneuvered his way into the hospital where Mauser was laid up with a triple leg wound from a Maxim gun and begged for a piece of bloody bandage. It was one of the great regrets in Mauser's life that he'd been in no shape to get up and kick the cloddy down the stairs.

Now he said to the telly reporter, "That's right, Captain Mauser. Acting major in this fracas, ah—"

"Freddy. Freddy Soligen. You remember *me*, Captain—"

"Of course I do, Freddy." Mauser spoke rapidly, to cover his embarrassment over his slip in memory. "We've been in the dill together more than once, and even when I was too scared to use my sidearm, you'd be scanning away with your camera."

"Ha ha, listen to the captain, folks." Freddy's voice was smooth, his words practiced. "I hope my boss is tuned in. But seriously, Captain Mauser, what do you think the chances of Vacuum Tube Transport are in this fracas?"

Mauser looked earnestly into the camera lens. "The best, of course, or I wouldn't have signed up with Baron Haer. Justice triumphs, Freddy, and anybody who is familiar with the issues in this fracas knows that Baron Haer is on the side of true right."

Freddy said, holding any sarcasm he might have felt, "What would you say the issues were, Captain?"

"The basic right of free enterprise to compete. Hovercraft has held a near monopoly on transport to Fairbanks. Vacuum Tube Transport wishes to lower costs and bring the consumers of Fairbanks better service through running a vacuum tube to that area. What could be more in keeping with the traditions of the West-world?" He paused, wondering whether the fans would even consider the issues. "Although Continental Hovercraft stands in the way of free enterprise in this dispute, it is they who have demanded of the Category Military Department a trial by arms. On the face of it, justice is on the side of Baron Haer."

Freddy Soligen addressed the camera. "Well, all you good people of the telly world, that's an able summation the captain has made, but it certainly doesn't jibe with what Baron Zwerdling said this morning, does it? However, as the captain says, justice will triumph, and we'll see what the field of combat will have to offer. Thank you very much, Captain Mauser. All of us, all of us tuned in today, hope that you personally will run into no dill in this fracas."

"Thanks, Freddy. Thanks all," Mauser said into the camera before turning away. He wasn't particularly keen about this part of the job, but you couldn't underrate the importance of pleasing the buffs. In the long run your career was aided by your popularity— and that meant your chances for promotion both in military rank and in caste, since the two went hand in hand. The fans took you up, boosted you, idolized you, even worshiped you if you really made it. He, Joe Mauser, was only a minor celebrity, and as such appreciated the chance to be interviewed by such a popular reporter as Freddy Soligen.

Even as he turned, he spotted the men with whom he'd had his spat earlier. The little fellow was still to the fore. Evidently the others had decided the one place extra that he represented wasn't worth the trouble he'd put in their way to defend it.

On an impulse he stepped up to the small man, who grinned in recognition. The grin was a revelation of an inner warmth beyond average in a world which had lost much of its human warmth.

Mauser said, "Like a job, soldier?"

"Name's Max. Max Mainz. Sure I want a job. That's why I'm in this everlasting line."

"First fracas for you, isn't it?"

"Yeah, but I had basic training in school."

"What do you weigh, Max?"

Max's face soured. "About one twenty."

"Did you check out on semaphore in school?"

"Well, sure. I'm Category Food, Sub-division Cooking, Branch Chef, but like I say, I took basic military training like most everybody else."

"I'm Captain Joe Mauser. How'd you like to be my batman?"

Max screwed up his not overly handsome face. "Gee, I don't know. I kinda joined up to see some action. Get into the dill. You know what I mean."

Mauser said dryly, "See here, Mainz, you'll probably find more pickled situations next to me than you'll want—and you'll come out alive, or at least have a better chance of it than if you go in as infantry."

The recruiting sergeant looked up from the desk. "Son, take a good opportunity when it drops in your lap. The captain is one of the best in the field. You'll learn more, get better chances for promotion, if you stick with him."

Mauser couldn't remember having run into the sergeant before, but he said, "Thanks, Sergeant." Evidently realizing Joe didn't recognize him, the other said, "We were together on the Chihuahua Reservation in the jurisdictional fracas between the United Mine Workers and the Teamsters, sir."

It had been almost fifteen years ago. About all that Joe Mauser remembered of that fracas was the abnormal number of casualties they'd taken. His side had lost, but from this distance in time Mauser couldn't even remember what force he'd been with. But now he said, "That's right. I thought I recognized you, Sergeant."

"It was my first fracas, sir." The sergeant returned to a businesslike manner. "If you want me to hustle this lad through, Captain—"

"Please do." Mauser turned back to Max. "I'm not sure where my billet will be. When you're through all this, locate the officer's mess and wait there for me."

"Well, OK," Max said doubtfully, still scowling.

"That's 'sir'," the sergeant added ominously. "If

you've had basic, surely you know how to address an officer?"

"Well, yes sir," Max said hurriedly.

Mauser began to turn away, but then spotted the man immediately behind Max Mainz. He was the one with whom he had tangled earlier, the one with previous combat experience. He pointed the man out to the sergeant. "You'd better give this lad at least temporary rank of corporal. He's a veteran and we're short of veterans."

The sergeant said, "Yes, sir. We sure are. Step up here, lad." Mauser's former foe looked properly thankful.

Mauser finished with his own red tape and headed for the street to locate a military tailor who could do him up a set of the Haer kilts and fill his other dress requirements.

As he went, he wondered vaguely just how many different uniforms he had worn over the years. In a career as long as his own one could take, from time to time, semi-permanent positions with bodyguard services, company police, and the permanent combat troops of this corporation or that. Such positions held an element of security, but if you were ambitious you signed up for the fracases and that meant into a uniform and out of it again in as short a period as a couple of weeks.

At the door he tried to move aside, but was too slow for the quick-moving young woman who caromed off him. He caught her arm to prevent her from stumbling. She looked at him with less than thanks.

Joe took the blame for the collision. "Sorry," he said. "I'm afraid I didn't see you, Miss."

"Obviously," she said coldly. Her eyes went up

and down him, and for a moment he wondered where he had seen her before. Somewhere, he was sure.

She was dressed as they dress who have never considered cost, and she had an elusive beauty which would have been even the more had her face not projected quite such a serious outlook. Her features were more delicate than those to which he was usually attracted, her lips less full, but still—he was reminded of the classic ideal of the British Romantic Period, the women sung of by Byron and Keats, Shelley and Moore.

She said, "Is there any particular reason why you should be staring at me, Mr. . . ."

"Captain Mauser," Joe said hurriedly. "I'm afraid I've been rude, Miss—well, I thought I recognized you." He hoped that she wouldn't think he was running a tired old line on her.

She took in his civilian dress, typed it automatically, and came to an erroneous conclusion. She said, "Captain? You mean that with everyone else I know drawing down ranks from lieutenant colonel to brigadier general, you can't make anything better than captain?"

Joe winced. "I came up from the ranks. Captain is quite an achievement, believe me. Few make it beyond sergeant," he said humbly.

"Up from the ranks!" She took in his clothes again. "You mean you're a Middle? You neither talk nor look like a Middle, Captain." She used the caste rating as though it was not *quite* a derogatory term.

Not that she meant to be deliberately insulting, Joe told himself wearily. It was simply born in her. As once a well-educated aristocracy had, not necessarily unkindly, named their status inferiors *niggers*— or other aristocrats, in another area of the country, had named theirs *greasers*—so did this aristocracy use derogatory labels in an unknowing manner.

"Mid-Middle now, Miss," he said slowly. "However, I was born in the Lower castes."

An eyebrow went up, half cynical, half mocking, as though amused at a social climber. "Zen! You must have put in many an hour studying. You talk like an Upper, Captain." With a shrug, she dropped all interest in him and turned to resume her journey.

"Just a moment," Mauser said. "You can't go in there, Miss—"

Her eyebrow went up again. "The name is Haer," she said. "And just why can't I go into my father's offices, Captain?"

Now it came to him why he had thought he recognized her. She had basic features similar to those of that overbred ass, Balt Haer. With her, however, they came off superlatively.

"Sorry," he said. "I guess you can, under the circumstances. I was about to tell you that they're recruiting, with men running around half clothed. Medical inspections, that sort of thing."

She made a noise of derision and said over her shoulder, even as she sailed on, "Besides being a Haer, I'm an M.D., Captain. At the ludicrous sight of a man shuffling about in his skin, I seldom blush."

She was gone.

Mauser watched her go. Her figure was superlative from the rear, as Grecian classic as her face. "I'll bet you don't," he muttered.

Had she waited a few moments, he could have explained his Upper accent and his unlikely education. When you'd copped one and spent days or weeks languishing in a hospital bed, you had plenty of time to read, to study. And Mauser had decided early on in life that any bit of knowledge he might gain was precious, potentially useful. His career had verified that belief on numerous occasions, and his natural curiosity and intelligence made it easy for him to follow his program of self-education. Had he been born an Upper, he might have been an Academician, but as it was . . .

Yes, time in the hospital had given him time to study, and more. Time to contemplate—and fester away in his own schemes of rebellion against fate. And Mauser had copped many in his time.

CHAPTER THREE

By the time Mauser called it a day and retired to his quarters, he was exhausted to the point where his occasional dissatisfaction with the trade he followed was heavily upon him. Such was the case increasingly often these days. He was no longer a kid. There was no longer romance in the calling—if there ever had been for Joe Mauser.

He had met his immediate senior officers, largely dilettante Uppers with precious little field experience, and been unimpressed. And he'd met his own junior officers and been shocked. By the looks of things at this stage, Captain Mauser's squadron would be going into this fracas both undermanned and with junior officers composed largely of temporarily promoted noncoms. If this was typical of Baron Haer's total force, then Balt Haer was right; unconditional surrender was to be considered, no matter how disastrous to the Haer family fortunes.

Mauser had no difficulty securing his uniforms. Kingston, as a city on the outskirts of the Catskill Reservation, was well populated by tailors who could turn out uniforms on a twenty-four-hour delivery basis. He had even been able to take immediate delivery of one kilted uniform. Now, inside his quarters, he began stripping out of his jacket. Somewhat to his surprise, Mainz, the small man he had selected earlier to be his batman, entered from an inner room, resplendent in the Haer uniform.

IIe helped his superior out of the jacket with an ease that held no subservience but at the same time was correctly respectful. You'd have thought him a batman specially trained.

Mauser grunted, "Max, isn't it? I'd forgotten all about you. Glad you found our billet all right."

Max said, "Yes, sir. Would the captain like a drink? I picked up a bottle of applejack. Applejack's the drink around here, sir. Makes a topnotch highball with ginger ale and a twist of lemon."

Mauser looked at him. Evidently his tapping this man for orderly was sheer fortune. Well, Joe Mauser could use some good luck on this job. He hoped it didn't end with selecting a batman.

He said, "Sounds good, Max. Got ice?"

"Of course, sir." Max left the small room.

Vacuum Tube's officers were billeted in what had once been a group of resort cottages on the old road between Kingston and Woodstock. Each cottage featured full amenities, including a tiny kitchenette. That was one advantage to a fracas held in a civilized area where there were plenty of facilities. Such military reservations as the Little Big Horn in Montana and some of those in the Southwest and Mexico were another thing.

Mauser lowered himself into the room's easy chair and bent down to untie his laces, then kicked his shoes off. He could use that drink. He began wondering all over again if his scheme for winning this fracas would come off. The more he saw of Baron Haer's inadequate forces, the more he wondered. He simply hadn't expected Vacuum Tube to be in *this* bad a shape. Baron Haer had been riding high for so long that one would have thought his reputation for victory would have lured at least a few freelance veterans to his colors. Evidently they hadn't bitten. The word was out, all right.

Max Mainz returned with the drink.

Mauser said, "You had one yourself?"

"No, sir."

"Well, go get yourself one and come on back and sit down. Let's get acquainted."

"Yes sir." Max disappeared back into the kitchenette to return almost immediately. The little man slid into a chair, drink awkwardly in hand.

His superior sized him up all over again. Not much more than a kid, really. Surprisingly forward for a Lower who must have been raised from childhood in a trank-bemused, telly-entertained household. The fact that he'd broken away from that environment at all was to his credit. It was considerably easier to conform—but then it is always easier to conform, to run with the herd, as Mauser well knew. His own break hadn't been an easy one.

He sipped at his drink. "Relax," he said.

Max nodded and cleared his throat. "Well, this is my first day."

"I know. And you've been seeing telly shows all your life showing how an orderly conducts himself in the presence of his superior." Mauser took another pull and yawned. "Well, forget about it. I like to be on close terms with any man who goes into a fracas with me. When things pickle, I want him to be on my side, not nursing a grudge brought on by his officer trying to give him an inferiority complex."

The little man was eyeing him in surprise.

Mauser finished his drink and came to his feet to get another one. He said, "On two occasions I've had an orderly save my life. I'm not taking any chances but that there might be a third opportunity."

"Well, yessir. Does the captain want me to get him—"

"I'll get it," Mauser said.

When he'd returned to his chair, he said, "Why did you join up with Baron Haer, Max?"

The other shrugged. "Well, besides the fact that Continental Hovercraft's recruit roster was full, the usual. The excitement. The idea of all those fans watching me on telly. The shares of common stock I'll get. And, you never know, maybe a bounce in caste. I wouldn't mind making Upper-Lower."

Mauser said sourly, "One fracas and you'll be over the desire to have the buffs watching you on telly while they sit around sucking trank. And you'll probably be over the desire for the excitement, too. Of course, the share of stock is another thing."

"You aren't just countin' down, Captain," Max said, an almost surly overtone in his voice. "You don't know what it's like being born with no more common stock shares than a Mid-Lower."

Mauser held his peace, nursing his drink. He was moderately fond of alcohol, but could count on the fingers of one hand the number of times he had really overindulged. And he never used trank, that government-approved and -promoted narcotic. An old pro in the Category Military doesn't foul up his reflexes, certainly not on the eve of a fracas. He let his eyebrows rise to encourage the other to go on.

Max said doggedly, "Sure, they call it People's Capitalism and everybody gets issued enough shares to insure him a basic living from the cradle to the grave, like they say. But let me tell you, you're a

Middle and you don't realize just how basic the basic living of a Lower can be."

Mauser yawned. If he hadn't been so tired, he might have found more amusement in the situation. If nothing else, it was ironic.

He decided to let Mainz continue to think he was talking to one with no knowledge of life as a Lower. "Why don't you work? A Lower can always add to his stock by working."

Max stirred, indignant. "Work? Listen, sir, mine's just one more field that's been automated right out of existence. Category Food Preparation, Sub-division Cooking, Branch Chef. I'm a junior chef, see? But cooking isn't left in the hands of slobs who might drop a cake of soap into the soup." That last was delivered with an angry sarcasm. "It's done automatic. The only changes made in cooking are by real top experts, almost scientists, like. And most of them are Uppers."

Mauser sighed inwardly. Mainz's story was like that of millions of others. The man might have been born into the food preparation category from a long line of chefs, but he knew precious little about his field. Mauser might have suspected. He himself had been born into Clothing Category, Sub-division Shoes, Branch Repair. Cobbler—a meaningless trade, since shoes, like so many other items, were no longer repaired but discarded upon showing signs of wear. In an economy of complete abundance, there is little reason to repair basic commodities.

That was the result of social evolution. Decades of reckless experimentation during the previous century had led to this: a utopia in which almost no one had to work and in which—typical of such societies—a small fraction of the population held the true power and wealth. In an attempt to make everyone equal, inequality had been intensified. It was high time the government investigated category assignment and reshuffled and reassigned half the nation's population. But there would still be the question of what to do with the technologically unemployed.

Max was saying, "The only way I could figure on a promotion to a higher caste, or the only way to earn stock shares, was by crossing categories. And you know what that means. Either Category Military or Category Religion, and I sure as Zen don't know nothing about religion."

Mauser chuckled at the unintentional humor in Max's statement. "Theoretically, you can cross categories into any field you want, Max," he said mildly.

Max snorted. "Theoretically is right . . . sir. But have you ever heard of a Lower, or even a Middle like yourself, crossing categories to, say, some Upper category like banking?"

Mauser chuckled again. He liked this peppery little fellow. If Max worked out as well as Joe thought he might, there was a possibility of taking him along to the next fracas. He had once had a batman for a period of almost three years, until the man had copped one that led to an amputation and retirement.

Max was saying, "I'm not saying anything against the old-time way of doing things, or talking against the government, but I'll tell you, Captain, every year goes by it gets harder and harder for a man to raise his caste or earn some additional stock shares."

The applejack had worked enough on Mauser to bring out one of his pet peeves. He said, "That term, 'the old-time way,' is strictly telly talk, Max. We don't do things the old-time way. No nation in history ever has—with the possible exception of Egypt.

Socio-economics are in a continual flux, and here in this country we no more do things in the way they did a hundred years ago than a hundred years ago they did them the way American Revolutionists outlined back in the 18th century."

Max was staring at him, completely out of his depth. "I don't get that, sir."

Mauser said impatiently, "Max, the politico-economic system we have today is an outgrowth of what went earlier. The welfare state, the freezing of the status quo, the Frigid Fracas between the Westworld and the Sov-world, industrial automation until useful employment is all but needless—all these things could be found in embryo more than a century ago."

"Well, maybe the captain's right, but you gotta admit, sir, that we mostly do things the old way. We still got the Constitution and the two-party system and—"

Joe was tiring of the conversation now. You seldom ran into anyone, even in the Middle caste—the traditionally professional class—interested enough in such subjects to be worth arguing with. He said, "The Constitution, Max, has reached the status of the Bible and other religious books. Interpret it the way you wish, and you can find anything. If not, you can always make a new amendment. That trend started in the middle of the 20th century, when the old U.S. Supreme Court took it upon itself to intervene in matters best settled by lower courts, or disputes that were already covered by existing laws. The idea of 'equality' got pushed to the limit, Max, and our ancestors tried to legislate equality among unequals. That is, they figured that if they *said* all people were equal, it would make it so. Didn't work—just gave those who were at the bottom an excuse to stay there, while getting a free ride. And it paved the way for our current system."

Max started to interrupt, but Joe ignored him. "So far as the two-party system is concerned, what effect does it have when the Uppers are in control of both? What is the difference if *two* men stand for exactly the same thing? It's a farce."

"A farce?" Max blurted, forgetting his servant status. "That means not so good, doesn't it? Far as I'm concerned, election day is tops. The one day a Lower is just as good as an Upper. The one day when how many shares you got makes no difference. Everybody has everything."

"Sure, sure, sure," Mauser sighed. "Election day in the West-world, when no one is freer than anyone else. The modern equivalent of the Roman Baccanalia."

"Well, what's wrong with that?" The other was all but belligerent. "That's the trouble with you Middles and Uppers, you don't know how it is to be a Lower, and—"

Suddenly Mauser snapped, "I was born a Mid-Lower myself, Max. Don't give me that nonsense."

Max gaped at him, utterly unbelieving.

Mauser's irritation fell away. He held out his glass. "Get me another drink, Max, and I'll tell you a story."

By the time the fresh drink came, he was sorry he'd made the offer. He thought back. He hadn't told anyone the Joe Mauser story in many a year. And, as he recalled, last time had been when he was well into his cups—on an election day at that—and his listener had been a Low-Upper, one of the hereditary aristocrats comprising the top one percent of the nation. Zen! How the man had laughed. He'd roared his amusement till the tears ran.

However, now he said, "Max, I was born into the same caste you were—average father, mother, sisters, and brothers. My family subsisted on basic income, sat and watched telly for an unbelievable number of hours each day, did trank to keep themselves happy. And thought I was crazy because I didn't. Dad was the sort of man who'd take his belt off to a child of his who questioned such school-taught slogans as *What was good enough for Daddy is good enough for me*.

"They were all fracas fans, of course, even the girls. As far back as I can remember, they were gathered around the telly, screaming excitement as the lens zoomed in on some poor cloddy bleeding his life out on the ground." Joe Mauser sneered, uncharacteristically. "That's something the Roman arena never provided the mob, a close-up of the dying gladiator's face."

Max missed the reference to the ancestor of the modern-day fracas, but Mauser's attitude was not lost on him. "You don't sound much like you're in favor of your trade, Captain," Max said.

Mauser came to his feet, setting his half-full glass aside. "I'll make this epic story short, Max. As you said, the only valid routes for rising above your caste are through the Military and Religious Categories. Like you, even I couldn't stomach the latter."

He hesitated, then finished it off. "Max, there have been few societies evolved by man that didn't allow in some manner for the competent or sly, the intelligent or the opportunist, the brave or the strong, to work his way to the top. I don't know which of these categories I fit into, but I rebel against remaining in the lower categories of a stratified society. Do I make myself clear?"

"Well, no sir, not exactly."

Mauser said flatly, "I'm going to fight my way to the top, and nothing is going to stand in the way. Is that clearer?"

"Yessir," Max said, obviously taken aback by the vehemence in his superior's voice.

Having worked himself into an unusual state of agitation with his lecture on the state of the world, Mauser found that he wasn't quite ready for sleep. The applejack offered a cure for that problem, although he was loathe to use it. Still, by the time he went to bed, the bottle was long empty.

After routine morning duties, Joe returned to his billet and mystified Max Mainz by not only changing into mufti himself but having Max do the same.

In fact, the new batman protested faintly. He hadn't nearly gotten over the glory of wearing his kilts and was looking forward to parading around town in them. He had a point, of course. The appointed time for the fracas was getting closer, and buffs were beginning to stream into Kingston to bask in the atmosphere of pending death. Everybody knew what a military center on the outskirts of a fracas reservation was like immediately preceding a clash between rival corporations. The high-strung gaiety, the drinking, the overtranking, the relaxation of what mores existed. Even a Rank Private had it made. Admiring civilians to buy drinks and hang on your every word, and—more important still to Max—sensuous-eyed women, their faces slack in thinly suppressed passion. It was a recognized phenomenon, this desire on the part of certain female telly fans, to date a man and then watch him later, killing or being killed.

"Time enough to wear your fancy uniform later," Joe told him. "In fact, tomorrow's a local election day. Combine that with all the fracas fans gravitating into town and you'll have a blowout the likes of nothing you've seen before."

"Well, yes, sir," Max begrudged. "Where're we going now, Captain?"

"To the airport. Come along."

Outside, Mauser led the way to his hovercraft. As soon as the two were settled into the bucket seats, he hit the lift lever with the butt of his left hand. Once they were air-cushion borne, he pressed down on the accelerator.

Max Mainz was impressed. "You know," he said, "I never been in one of these swanky jobs before. The kinda car you can afford on the income of a Mid-Lower's stock isn't—"

"Oh, come off it, Max!" Mauser said wearily. "People are always griping, but in spite of all the beefing in every strata from Low-Lower to Upper-Middle, I've yet to see any signs of organized protest against our present politico-economic system."

"Hey," Max said. "Don't get me wrong. What was good enough for Dad, is good enough for me. You won't catch me talking against the government."

"Hmm," Joe murmured. "And all the other clichés taught to us to preserve the status quo, our People's Capitalism." They were reaching the outskirts of town, crossing the Esopus. The airport lay only a mile or so beyond.

The sarcasm was too deep for Max, and since he didn't understand, he said, tolerantly, "Well, what's wrong with People's Capitalism? Everybody owns the corporations. Damnsight better than what the Sovs have."

Mauser said sourly, "We've got one optical illusion; they've got another. Over there they claim the proletariat owns the means of production, distribution, and communication. Great. But the Party members are the ones who control it, and as a result, they manage to do all right for themselves. The Party hierarchy over there is like the Uppers over here."

"Yeah." Max was being particularly dense. "I've seen a lot about it on telly. You know, when there isn't a good fracas on, you tune to one of them educational shows, like."

Joe winced at the term "educational," but held his peace.

"It's pretty rugged over there," Max continued, "but here in the West-world the people own a corporation's stock and they run it and get the benefit."

"Makes a beautiful story," Joe said dryly. "Look, Max. Suppose you have a corporation that has two hundred thousand shares out and they're distributed among one hundred thousand and one persons. One hundred thousand of these own one share apiece, and the remaining stockholder owns the other hundred thousand."

"I don't know what you're getting at," Max said.

Joe sighed. "Briefly," he said, "we are given the illusion that this is a People's Capitalism, an improvement over democracy, with all stock in the hands of the people—evenly distributed. Actually, the stock is in the hands of the Uppers, all except a mere dribble. They own the country and then run it for their own benefit.

"True democracy—and true freedom—was allowed to die at the end of the 20th century, thanks in large part to so-called Socialists who, it was largely thought, gained no little support from the Communist world."

Max shot a less than military glance at him. "Hey, you're not one of these Sovs yourself, are you?"

They were coming into the parking area near the

airport's Administration Building. "No," Mauser said, so softly that Max could hardly hear his words. "Only a Mid-Middle on the make."

Followed by Max, he strode quickly to the Administration Building, presented his credit identification at the desk, and requested a light aircraft for a period of three hours. He made it clear that he required a specific type of aircraft. The clerk, hardly looking up, began going through motions, keying codes into a terminal and speaking into a telescreen.

The clerk said finally, "You might have a short wait, sir. Quite a few of the officers involved in this fracas have been renting out taxi-planes as fast as they're available." He paused as the terminal spat out a printed slip, then handed it over along with Mauser's credit card. "And I don't know whether you'll get the kind of deal you're after; it's first come, first served today. You'll be paged when your aircraft is ready."

The delay didn't surprise him. Any competent officer made a point of conducting an aerial survey of the battle reservation before going into a fracas. Aircraft, of course, couldn't be used *during* the fray, since they postdated the turn of the century and hence were regulated to the cemetery of military devices—along with such items as nuclear weapons, tanks, and even powered vehicles of sufficient size to be useful.

Use an aircraft in a fracas, or even *build* an aircraft for military use, and you'd have a howl go up from the military attachés of the Sov-world that would be heard all the way to Budapest. Not a fracas went by but there were scores if not hundreds of foreign military observers, keen-eyed to check whether or not any really modern tools of war were being illegally utilized. He sometimes wondered if the Sov-world armies were as strict in their adherence to the rules of the Universal Disarmament Pact. Probably, since West-world observers were breathing down their necks, as well. But they didn't have the same system of fighting fracases over there. The Neut-world, of course, didn't figure into the equation, and Common Europe was another matter entirely. Still, observers from those blocs were to be found at every major fracas, as well.

Mauser and Max took seats while they waited, and both thumbed through the ubiquitous fracas fan magazines. Joe sometimes found his own face in such publications, probably more as a result of having been around so long than anything else. He was a third-rate celebrity; luck hadn't been with him as far as the buffs were concerned. They wanted spectacular victories, murderous situations in which they could lose themselves in vicarious thrills. Mauser, unfortunately, had reached most of his peaks while either in retreat or while commanding a holding action. His fellow officers and superiors appreciated him, as did a few ultra-knowledgeable fracas buffs, but he was all but unknown to the average dimwit whose life was devoted to blood and gore.

On the various occasions when matters had pickled and Mauser had fought his way out against difficult odds, he was almost always off camera. Purely bad luck. On top of skill, determination, experience, and courage, you had to have luck to get anywhere in Category Military. But then, that was true of life in general.

This time, Mauser reminded himself, he was going to make his own luck.

A voice said, "Ah, Captain Mauser."

Joe looked up, then came to his feet quickly. He

started to salute out of sheer reflex, then caught himself; he was not in uniform. He said stiffly, "My compliments, Marshal Cogswell."

The other was a smallish man, but strongly built, with a strikingly narrow face. His voice was clipped and clear, the air of command etched into it. He, like Mauser, wore mufti. He now extended his hand to be shaken.

"I hear you have signed up with Baron Haer, Captain. I was rather expecting you to come in with me. Had a place for a good aide-de-camp. Liked your work in that last fracas we went through together."

"Thank you, sir," Mauser said. Stonewall Cogswell was as good a tactician as ever free-lanced, and more. He was an excellent judge of men and a stickler for detail. And right now, if Joe Mauser knew Marshal Cogswell as well as he thought he did, Cogswell was smelling a rat. There was no reason why an old pro should sign up with a sure loser like Vacuum Tube when he could have earned more shares taking a commission with Hovercraft, especially in view of the fact that as an aide-de-camp it was unlikely he would run much chance of getting into the dill.

He was looking at Mauser brightly, the question in his eyes. Three or four of his staff stood a few paces back, looking polite, but Cogswell didn't bring them into the conversation. Mauser knew most by sight. Good men all. Old pros all. He felt another twinge of doubt.

He had to cover. At last he said, "I was offered a particularly good contract, sir. Too good to resist."

The other nodded, as though inwardly coming to a satisfactory conclusion. "Baron Haer's connections, eh? He's probably offered to back you for a bounce in caste. Is that it, Joe?"

Mauser avoided the marshal's eyes, but Stonewall Cogswell knew what he was talking about. He'd been born into Middle status himself and made it to Upper the hard way. His path wasn't as long as Mauser's was going to be, but long enough and he well knew how rocky the climb was.

Mauser said stiffly, "I'm afraid I'm in no position to discuss my commander's military contracts, Marshal. We're in mufti, but after all . . ."

Cogswell's lean face registered one of his infrequent grimaces of humor. "I understand, Joe. Well, good luck. I hope things don't pickle for you in the coming fracas. Possibly we'll find ourselves allied again at some future time."

"Thank you, sir," Mauser said, once more having to catch himself to prevent an automatic salute.

Cogswell and his staff strolled off toward the reservation desk, and Mauser looked after them thoughtfully. Even the marshal's staff members were top men, any one of whom could have conducted a divisional magnitude fracas. Joe felt the coldness in his stomach again.

Even though the fracas must have looked like a cinch, the enemy wasn't taking any chances. Cogswell and his officers were here at the airport for the same reason as Mauser. They wanted a thorough aerial reconnaissance of the battlefield before the issue was joined.

Max was standing at his elbow. "Who was that, sir? Looks like a real tough one."

"He *is* a real tough one," Joe said sourly. "That's Stonewall Cogswell, the best field commander in North America."

Max pursed his lips. "I never seen him out of uniform before. Lots of times on telly, but never out of uniform. I thought he was taller than that; he's no bigger than me."

"He fights with his brains," Mauser said, still looking after the craggy field marshal. "He doesn't have to be any taller."

Max scowled. "Where'd he get that nickname, sir?"

"Stonewall?" Mauser was turning to resume his chair. "He's supposed to be quite a student of a top general back in the American Civil War—Stonewall Jackson. Uses some of the original Stonewall's tactics."

Max was again out of his depth. "American Civil War? Was that much of a fracas, Captain? It musta been before my time."

"It was quite a fracas," Mauser said dryly. "Lots of good lads died. A hundred years after it was fought, the reasons behind it seemed about as valid as those we fight fracases for today. Personally, I—"

The public address system blared his name. His aircraft was ready.

Max in tow, Mauser crossed the administration building's concourse and exited via a small door through which, Joe noted, Cogswell and his men had disappeared earlier. Rank hath its privileges, he reminded himself; doubtless Cogswell had phoned ahead and someone had been bumped off the reservation lists in his favor.

They exited into bright sunlight and followed a concrete walkaway to the hanger area, where Mauser quickly spotted what had to be the aircraft assigned him—a small two-seater. He crossed the tarmac, hailed an attendant, and quickly took care of the necessary formalities of handing over his reservation slip and identifying himself.

As he and Max climbed into the cockpit of the

single-engine mini-jet, Joe chuckled inwardly at how surprised old Stonewall would be to know just what Joe Mauser was looking for on this flight. Even greater would be his surprise when he was presented, so to speak, with the results of Mauser's research.

CHAPTER FOUR

The mini-jet banked sharply as it began its descent to the airfield below. Joe Mauser's face was thoughtful. He had requested a slow, wide-winged aircraft, but the clerk hadn't been able to do much for him. The others hiring rental craft had also been interested in hoverability and low speed, albeit for reasons different than Mauser's. He'd had to settle for what was available.

Max, seated next to him, gulped, "Hey, Captain, take it easy."

Mauser looked at him.

"I ain't never been up in anything this small before."

"Oh," Mauser grunted. He leveled out and continued the descent, less steeply now. "When we get around to it, we'll have to check you out on flying, Max."

His batman was taken aback. "You mean *me*? A pilot?"

Mauser said, "One of the things you want to learn early in the game, Max, is that the mercenary's life isn't exactly as portrayed on the telly screens. What the fracas buff mainly sees is the combat, and not very much of that, since most combat is on the drab and colorless side. Most of your time is spent crouched in some hole, or face down behind whatever cover you can find. The lens concentrates on the hand-to-hand stuff. The buff isn't interested in such matters as artillery laying down a barrage. He's not even interested in a cavalry squadron making a sweep around a flank to execute some bit of strategy that might decide the fracas. He wants action and blood."

Max, holding to a grab-bar as the small aircraft dropped, managed to get out, "I don't think I know what you're talking about, sir."

Mauser's hands moved over the controls expertly, straightening the craft for the runway rising to meet them. He had already received his landing instructions from the control tower.

He said, "The more you know about subjects seemingly remote from your trade, Max, the better off you'll be. Any medical knowledge that you might have, for instance, is priceless. It won't show on the telly screen, but it sure as hell helps for you to be as near an M.D. as you can make yourself. It also helps to be as good a swimmer as you can, as good a horseman, as competent a mountain climber.

"You've got to be a survival expert who can find a meal in a swamp, a desert, a forest, or on top of a seemingly barren mountain. And you want to be a mechanical wizard, capable of repairing not only every weapon allowable under the Universal Disarmament Pact, but any other gadget that might be used in war—from a telegraph to a mechanical semaphore. You even want to be a better ditch digger than the most competent Low-Lower who ever spent his life making with a shovel."

Max was staring at him. "Ditch digger? Who wants to be a ditch digger? I didn't cross categories to become any ditch digger!"

Mauser interrupted him mildly. "We call them

trenches, Max. And the sooner you learn to burrow like a mole, the better off you'll be, particularly when they ring mortars in on you."

"Oh," Max said weakly. "Yeah, sure."

"And you better learn to climb trees faster than any lumberjack, and to shore up a shaft better than any miner." The two braced themselves as the small craft jolted, its tires squealing as they touched the runway. "Over the years, such skills are more important than being a crack shot, or an expert with a knife in close personal combat. The fact of the matter is, you might go through a half-dozen standard fracases and never get into personal combat, but I've never been in one that didn't involve digging entrenchments."

Mauser concentrated for a moment on braking the mini-jet.

"Do you understand what I'm saying? That being a mercenary has very little to do with what you see on telly? The sooner you realize that, the better your chances of surviving."

"Well, yeah," Max said doubtfully. "But what good's flying? Nobody's allowed to use aircraft in action, Captain. Even I know that."

Mauser was taxiing toward the hangers.

"Max, even as a Rank Private you've got to stack the cards in your favor—any way you can! When you're in there, if you've managed to swing percentages your way just one percent—just one percent, Max—it might be the difference between copping the final one and surviving.

"Every old pro who's going to be in this fracas has been studying the terrain, Max. Stonewall Cogswell has fought this reservation three times that I know of, and probably more. But where is he, right this minute? He and his whole field staff are up in a transport going over the whole reservation, again and again. Why? Because possibly he's forgotten the exact layout, although that's not very likely with the marshal. But maybe, since he fought this reservation last, a new road has been cut from one point to another. Possibly the streams are so high this month that fords he's used before can't be utilized, or maybe the streams are so low that new fords are practical. Maybe a forest fire has leveled some clumps of trees that were formerly suitable for gun emplacements. Maybe a lot of things, Max, and Stonewall Cogswell is going to have every bit of information he can cram in, before the fracas proper."

"Zen!" Max muttered. "I was thinking Military was one category where education didn't make much difference. Way you sound, Captain, you gotta be like an Education Category professor in every field there is before you make even Rank Sergeant."

They came to a halt before the hangers, and Mauser cut the exchange short. He turned the craft over to the field's employees, gathered up the charts and the papers on which he'd scribbled notes. His face was thoughtful. The morning had been profitable, but he wanted to take at least one more flight over the reservation. What he had been telling Max was all too true. You became a real pro, an old pro, by taking infinite pains with every detail.

But for Mauser it was more than just the old survival bit, this time. This was his big fling.

He was walking toward the administration building to wind up his account for the mini-jet's rental when a male voice behind him whined, "Captain Mauser, could I have your autograph?"

He began to turn, wearily bringing a smile to his face for the sake of the fracas buff, fumbling in his jerkin pocket for a stylus.

But then the man laughed.

It was Freddy Soligen. Back in the shadow of one of the hangers Mauser could see the little man's crew, taking advantage of the shade and relaxing between interviews of the notables that were coming and going.

Mauser grinned. "Hello, Freddy. It works both ways. Could I have yours? Somebody ought to collect the autographs of telly reporters who've been in the dill as much as you have."

Freddy Soligen must be out here at the airport getting preliminary material, as he had been in the recruiting offices in Kingston. Mauser knew it was all part of the game. The buffs couldn't expect to see a top fracas every day, nor even every week—a major conflict such as this one would only develop, say, ten or a dozen times a year. In between the buffs had to be happy with telly war dramas, or with the sort of thing Freddy was doing now—building up to the fracas to come, or following it, rehashing and commenting on the action.

Of course, true buffs ate it up. Interviews, especially, since these allowed the buffs to see their favorite warriors live, and any hints about the personal affairs of star-level fighters were most valued.

He didn't expect Soligen to want to interview him again just now. It was too soon after yesterday, and Joe Mauser wasn't a top fracas star. Somebody like Stonewall Cogswell or Jack Altshuler, the cavalryman, you could interview as often as they would submit, which wasn't too often in some cases; in fact, the marshal was notoriously uncooperative with the telly men. He could afford to be; he was as high in the Category Military as it was possible to get, and he needed publicity like he needed a head wound.

But on Joe Mauser's level, the better his in with the combat lensmen the more likely the lenses would be on him for his moments of glory—and Mauser could certainly use that in this fracas. This was his big fling, and it would not do to have what he had planned pass notice.

"That'll be the day," Freddy said, his voice sour with cynicism, "when somebody asks a telly reporter for an autograph. The stupid cloddies don't even realize that somebody has to be there in the middle of the action, directing the cameras."

Mauser chuckled. "Face it, Freddy—your colleagues aren't usually as near as all that. That's why they have pillboxes for the cameras! Some of you boys are as safe as the buffs sitting in front of their idiot boxes watching the show, and the buffs know it."

Freddy frowned slightly. "A lot of my friends might be interested to hear what you say, Captain—if they hadn't copped the final one."

Mauser nodded. "I'll take that. I wasn't talking about you, Freddy, nor all of the others. I haven't forgotten the time the two of us were pinned down in a foxhole on that damn knoll."

"Yeah. Hotter 'n' hell, and me with a mini-ball through my camera—right in the middle of it, and I couldn't get any footage! We were thirsty enough to drink a river, and nothing to drink but that little half pint of whatever you had."

"Tequila," Mauser said. "Mexican tequila." He shook his head. "That's the last time I ever took anything stronger than water into combat. It tasted all right for the minute, but Kipling was right."

"Kipling?" Freddy's eyes were automatically scanning the tarmac, checking to see if he was missing anyone he might approach for some telly footage.

Mauser said, "Old-timer British poet. He used to write about the fighting in India—

"When it comes to slaughter,

"You'll do your work on water,
"And you'll lick the bloomin' boots
"Of 'im that's got it."

The reporter's eyes came back to him, speculatively. "Where'n Zen did you learn to quote poetry?"

Mauser laughed it off. "In hospital beds, Freddy. In hospital beds."

Soligen was looking at him as though for the first time. "You know," he said, "now that I think about it, I've known you about as long as anybody I can think of in Category Military, and my memory must go back at least fifteen years. I haven't seen a great deal of you, perhaps, but over the years you've always been around. What in Zen are you doing, still a captain?"

Mauser couldn't completely repress the flush that came to his face. He said, "What are you doing still in charge of a combat camera crew after fifteen years? By this time, you ought to at least be in charge of covering this whole fracas."

Freddy shook his head. "You know better. There's precious little promotion in Category Communications; it's frozen. The jerk in charge of this coverage sits back in Kingston in an air-conditioned office giving commands to units like me. He's never been in the dill in his life and doesn't expect to be—he's an Upper. But it's different in Military. If you're on the ball, you can get bounced in rank."

Joe shrugged it off. "Maybe I'm not photogenic, Freddy. The buffs don't take to me."

The telly reporter cocked his head to one side and peered up at Joe. "No, it's not that," he said seriously. "As a matter of fact, that beautiful withdrawn air of yours . . ."

Mauser's eyebrows went up.

Soligen snorted. "Don't you even know about it?

Most of the phonies I come in contact with cultivate
this craggy, military dignity that you come by natu-
rally. You look like the kind of officer a bunch of
Lower riflemen would *love* to have in command when
the situation pickles. I'm just wondering why you've
never hit the big time. What you ought to do is pull
something out of the hat that'd give us cameramen a
reason to zero in on you." He grinned. "Capture old
Stonewall Cogswell, or something."

For a moment, Mauser wondered if Soligen suspected that he was about to do exactly that. That is,
pull something out of the hat that would focus the
attention of every fracas buff in the West-world on
Joe Mauser. But no, that was ridiculous. Mauser had
confided in no one—he couldn't. Oh, had Jim still
been alive, yes, Joe would have told him. But as it
was, no. It might take no more than a hint to blow
the whole plan.

But still . . . here was the man who could bring
the results of that plan to the attention of the world.
Without thinking it through, Mauser said, "Freddy,
possibly you're right. Can you keep something under
your hat?"

Freddy Soligen tilted his head to one side again
and cocked an eye at Joe. "I've kept so many items
under my hat in my time, Captain, that sometimes
there's been damn little room for my head."

"I'm sure you have. In your own field, Soligen,
you're an old pro. As much as I am in mine."

"Okay. Okay. There're no violins handy, but I'll
accept the compliment. So what do I keep under my
nonexistent hat?"

Mauser said slowly, "If there's any way you can
swing it, have that camera crew of yours as near my
vicinity as possible."

The telly reporter frowned in anger. "This is the

big deal to keep under my hat? For crissake, Captain, you're not that green. You must know that every Category Military cloddy on the make tries to suck up to telly teams. You'd think most of them were Tri-Dee stars, trying to get their faces on lens as much as possible." He snorted again. "This is the first time *you've* braced me, though!" There was contempt in his voice; that and a certain disappointment.

Joe now realized he'd made a mistake. He couldn't put it over this way. He either had to tell Freddy Soligen now or forget it. But he had no intention of telling Freddy Soligen a thing. He couldn't afford to.

He said, "Forget about it. To hell with it, Freddy. See you there, later." He turned and walked off. Max Mainz, who had been standing off a few feet, followed.

The telly reporter started after him, then stopped and called out, "Yeah. See you, Captain. Hope you run into no personal dill."

"Same, Freddy," Mauser called over his shoulder.

Soligen continued to scowl after him. His reporter instinct told him something was off. It wasn't like Captain Joe Mauser to be sucking up to a telly man, trying to get on lens for a moment or two for the publicity value. Of course he, Soligen, had possibly precipitated it with his crack about Mauser pulling something out of the hat just to become newsworthy. But still . . .

Just then Freddy Soligen noted the landing of Stonewall Cogswell's transport. He started off to round up his crew, but his tight little face still registered suspicious thoughts.

They drove back to their billet in silence, Max Mainz respecting Mauser's desire to mull over the morning's developments, whatever they were. Max still wasn't quite sure what had been accomplished by the flight over the military reservation. From several thousand feet of altitude, he had been able to make out precious little below, and couldn't understand why they so completely covered the mountain ridges, hovering at this point or that for five or ten minutes at a time.

His captain pulled up the sporty little air cushion car before their cottage and left Max to bring their things in.

Mauser entered the front door, pulled his jerkin off, and threw it over the back of a chair. He went on through the front room and into the kitchenette. There were several bottles standing on the cabinet; he picked up one and scowled at it. Tequila. It brought to mind what Soligen had said about the knoll they'd been pinned down on, years ago, down on the Chihuahua Military Reservation in what had once been Mexico.

He'd been a top sergeant at that time, and had picked up a taste for the fiery Mexican spirits. He remembered how they drank it there. You put a little salt on the back of your hand and a quarter of a lime on the bar before you. After licking the salt, you picked up the shot glass of tequila and tossed its contents back over your tonsils. You then grabbed the lime and bit into it, by way of a chaser.

He didn't have any limes here in Kingston, nor the patience to go through the routine. He poured a glass of the colorless potable and tossed it off, stiff-wristed. He started to pour another, but caught himself. At this time of day? He put the bottle back and went back to the living room, scowling.

He didn't think of himself as a drinker. He knew the drinkers, and what happened to them. You didn't remain one in Category Military; if you did, you didn't last long. You needed your reflexes at top peak.

Back in the living room, he noticed the message light glowing on the terminal. He flicked the playback.

The screen lit up with the expressionless face of a girl clerk clad in the Haer uniform. Probably an office worker, drafted for special work during the fracas. It wasn't the best thing in the world for Baron Haer to be doing. Even clerks in the military should be old hands. Silly mistakes made by tyros could lose a fracas.

She said, "Captain Mauser, please report soonest to the offices of Reconnaissance Command." The screen blanked; a recording.

There were no other messages. He shrugged and went into his bedroom to get back into his cavalry major uniform. He was sorry now he had taken the drink; it would be on his breath when he showed up at headquarters. But then he shrugged impatiently at himself. Why should he give a damn? For that matter, every officer in the Haer forces was probably doing a bit more drinking than usual. They had something to drink about, to be sure.

As he dressed, he called through the door to Max, "I've got to go into Kingston. Take the rest of the day off, if you want. Believe me, you can use the rest. Tomorrow we'll start whipping this outfit into a unit." He added, *sotto voce*, "If possible."

Max said, "I guess I'll get into my own kilts and go into town to see what's jelling, sir."

Joe grinned, remembering his own first days in the Category Military and the glory of wearing combat attire. He had been lucky to survive the first year or so as a mercenary. You had a very good chance of becoming a casualty long before you learned the tools of your trade. He shrugged into his tunic and left the motel, still buttoning it.

Let poor Max have his moment of glory, strutting the streets of downtown Kingston in his spanking new Haer kilts under the admiring gaze of the fracas buffs who were pouring into town to get as near as possible to the Category Military officers and soldiers. Men who all too soon would be spilling their blood on the Catskill hills.

Yes, Max should enjoy it while he could. Soon enough he would know what being a mercenary was really about.

CHAPTER FIVE

He had no trouble finding the offices of Reconnaissance Command. They were immediately across the street from the building where fracas recruiting was still going on. This, Mauser reflected, was another indication of just how bad things were for Vacuum Tube. Any normal recruiting campaign would have been concluded by now; obviously, they were going to be signing men up until the last moment, with all that meant in terms of time available to get the force into some sort of unity.

He answered the salute of the two kilted Haer guards who stood before the entry to the office he had been instructed to report to, then strode into a small anteroom.

A harried captain of cavalry sat at a desk that was hopelessly strewn with papers.

Joe said, "Major Mauser, reporting as instructed."

The other nodded. "Go right in, Major. The colonel is expecting you."

Joe went through the indicated door and came to the salute. He might have known. The officer commanding reconnaissance turned out to be none other than Balt Haer, natty as ever, arrogantly tapping his swagger stick against his leg. He answered the salute, all but insultingly, by tapping the stick to his head.

"Zen! Captain," he complained. "Where have you been? Off on a trank kick? We've got to get organized."

Joe failed to take umbrage; he was too old a hand to be baited. "No, sir, I went to the airport and rented an aircraft to scout out the terrain. I might mention to the colonel that I noticed Marshal Cogswell and his whole field staff there, doing the same."

"Indeed. And what were your impressions of the terrain, Captain?" There was an overtone which suggested it made little difference what impressions an acting major of cavalry might have gained.

Mauser shrugged. "Largely mountains, hills, woods, small streams. No rivers worthy of the name. Good reconnaissance is going to make the difference in this one, sir. And in the fracas itself, cavalry is going to be more important than either artillery or infantry. A Nathan Forrest-type fracas, sir. A matter of getting there fustest with the mostest."

Balt Haer said in amusement, "Thanks for your opinions, Captain. Our staff has already come to largely the same conclusions. Undoubtedly, they'll be glad to hear your wide experience bears them out."

He took this as it came, having been through it before. The dilettante amateur's dislike of the old pro. The amateur in command who knew full well he was less capable than many of those below him in rank.

He wondered what the veteran Parmenion had thought when the news was brought him that the twenty-year-old Alexander had taken over the Macedonian host from his father, the murdered Philip. Parmenion who, shoulder to shoulder with Philip of Macedon, had whipped together the Macedonian phalanx, the most efficient military machine the world had ever seen. A military machine conceived and created, first, to unite Greece into one force, and then to take on the Persian Empire which extended from the Mediterranean to the Indus Valley and beyond. Parmenion—who except the historian even knew that general's name? Little about him had come down through the ages, other than the snide rumors that he and the other veteran field officers of the Macedonian army made a practice of getting the youthful Alexander drunk so that he would be out of the way. That—and the fact that later Alexander the Great had him killed on a trumped-up conspiracy charge.

Balt Haer's grating tone brought him suddenly back to the present. ". . . your squadron," Haer was saying, "is to be deployed as scouts under my overall command. You've had cavalry experience, I assume?"

"Yes, sir. In various fracases over the past fifteen years. Both cavalry and infantry. Some artillery, too, for that matter, but largely cavalry and infantry."

"Very well. Now then, to get to the reason I have summoned you. Yesterday, in my father's office, you intimated that you had some grandiose scheme which would bring victory to the Haer colors. But you managed to dodge divulging just what the scheme might be."

Mauser looked at him unblinkingly.

Balt Haer said, "Now, I'd like to have your opinion on just how Vacuum Tube Transport can extract itself from what would seem a poor position, at best."

Mauser's eyes went about the room. It, like the other military offices of the Haer forces, had been improvised from rented business quarters only a week or so before. The walls sported military charts of the Catskill Reservation. In a mild effort to create a military decor, two sets of crossed sabers hung above the entrance along with a battle flag which had obviously seen action, being torn and rent. In all, there were four others in the office: two women clerks fluttering away at typers and two of Balt Haer's junior officers. They seemed indifferent to the conversation between Balt and Mauser, and continued about their own affairs as the two talked.

Mauser wet his lips carefully. The Haer scion was his commanding officer, after all, but something bothered Joe about him. Something more than just the man's pompous attitude. Mauser couldn't put his finger on it, but he knew that Balt Haer was not to be trusted, not even in matters concerning his own side in the fracas.

He said, "Sir, what I had in mind is a new gimmick. At this stage of the game, if I told anybody and it leaked, it'd never be effective, not even this first time."

Haer observed him coldly. "And you think me incapable of keeping your secret, ah, *gimmick*, I believe is the idiomatic term you used?"

Joe looked about the room again, taking in the other four who were now looking at him. The men, at least, were taking their cue from their commanding officer and reflecting his hauteur.

Balt Haer rapped, "These members of my staff are all trusted Haer employees, Captain Mauser. They are not fly-by-night freelancers hired for a week or two."

Mauser said, "Yes, sir. But it's been my experience that one person can hold a secret. It's twice as hard for two, and from there on it's a decreasing probability in a geometric ratio."

The younger Haer's stick rapped the side of his leg impatiently. "Suppose I inform you that this is a

command, Captain? I have little confidence in a supposed trick that will rescue our forces from disaster
and I rather dislike the idea of an acting major of one
of my squadrons dashing about with such a bee in his
bonnet when he should be obeying my commands."

Mauser kept his voice respectful. "Then, sir, I'd
request that we take the matter to the commander in
chief, your father."

"Indeed!"

"Sir, I've been working on this a long time. I can't
afford to risk throwing the idea away."

Balt Haer glared at him. "Very well, Captain. I'll
call your bluff. Come along, we shall see the commander in chief."

He turned on his heel and stalked from the room.

Mauser shrugged in resignation and followed him.
Behind, he heard a low titter of laughter. More
amateurs, all done up in their pretty uniforms for
this fracas. He doubted strongly that the two men
would see any action, any more than would the two
women.

The old baron wasn't much happier about Joe Mauser's secrets than his son had been. It had only been
the day before that Joe had seen him, but already
the baron seemed to have aged in appearance. Evidently, each hour that went by made it increasingly
clear just how perilous a position he had assumed.
Vacuum Tube Transport had elbowed, buffaloed,
bluffed, and edged itself into the big time in the
transportation field. The baron's ability, his aggressiveness, his flair, his political pull, had all helped,
but now the chips were down. He was up against
one of the biggies, and this particular biggy was tired
of ambitious little Vacuum Tube Transport.

He listened to his son's words, listened to Joe's dogged defense.

He said, looking at Joe, "If I understand this, your scheme promises to bring victory in spite of what seems to be a disastrous situation."

"Yes, sir."

The two Haers looked at him, one impatiently, the other in weariness.

Joe said, "I'm gambling everything on this, sir. I'm no Rank Private in his first fracas. I deserve to be given some leeway."

Balt Haer snorted. "Gambling everything! What in Zen would *you* have to gamble, Captain, in comparison to what we are gambling? The Haer family fortunes are tied up. Hovercraft is out for blood. They won't be satisfied with a token victory and a negotiated compromise. They'll devastate us. Thousands of mercenaries killed, with all that means in indemnities. Millions upon millions in expensive military equipment, most of which we've had to hire, will have to be paid for. Can you imagine the value of our stock after Stonewall Cogswell's veterans have finished with us? Why, every two-by-four trucking outfit in North America will be challenging us, and we won't be able to raise the forces to meet even a minor skirmish."

Joe reached into an inner pocket of his tunic and brought forth a sheaf of papers. He laid them on the desk of Baron Malcolm Haer. The baron scowled down at the documents.

"What's this?"

Mauser said simply, "I've been accumulating stock since the age of eighteen and I've taken good care of my portfolio, in spite of taxes and the various other pitfalls which make the accumulation of capital practically impossible. Yesterday I sold all of my portfolio

I was legally allowed to sell and converted to Vacuum Tube Transport." He added dryly, "Getting it at a very good rate, by the way."

Balt Haer snatched up the papers and flipped through them, unbelievingly. "Holy Jumping Zen!" he exploded. "The fool really did it. He's sunk a small fortune into our stock."

Baron Haer growled at him, "You seem considerably more convinced of our defeat than the captain. Perhaps I should reverse your positions of command."

His son grunted, but said nothing.

Old Malcolm Haer's eyes came back to Joe. "Admittedly I thought you on the romantic side yesterday, with your hints of some scheme which would lead us out of the wilderness, so to speak. Now I wonder if you might not really have something. Very well, I respect your claimed need for secrecy. Espionage is not exactly an outdated military field, and it's quite possible that your idea, whatever it is, might be leaked if you revealed it."

"Thank you, sir."

But the baron was still staring at him. "However, there's more to it than that. Why not take this great scheme of yours to Marshal Cogswell? I understand that you have served with him in the past. And yesterday you mentioned that the telly sets of the nation would be turned in on this fracas, and obviously you are correct. The question becomes, what of it?"

The fat was in the fire now. Mauser avoided the haughty stare of young Balt Haer and addressed himself to the older man. "You have political pull, sir. Oh, I know you don't make and break presidents. You couldn't even pull enough wires to keep Hovercraft from making this a divisional-magnitude fracas—but you have enough pull for my needs."

Baron Haer leaned back in his chair, his barrel-like body causing that article of furniture to creak. He crossed his hands over his stomach. "And what are your needs, Captain Mauser?"

Joe said evenly, "If I can bring this off, I'll be a fracas-buff celebrity. I don't have any illusions about the fickleness of the telly fans, but for a day or two I'll be on top. If at the same time I had your all-out support in pulling what strings you could reach—"

"Why, then, you'd be bounced up in caste to the ranks of the Uppers, wouldn't you, Captain?" Balt Haer finished for him, amusement in his voice.

"That's what I'm gambling on," Joe said evenly.

The younger Haer grinned at his father supercili-ously. "So, our Captain Mauser says he will defeat Stonewall Cogswell in return for you sponsoring his becoming a member of the nation's elite."

"Good Heavens, is the supposed cream of the nation now selected on no higher a level than this?" There was sarcasm in the words.

The three men turned. It was the girl Mauser had bumped into the day before. The Haers didn't seem surprised at her entrance.

"Nadine," the older man growled. "This is Captain Joseph Mauser, who has been given a commission as acting major in our forces."

Mauser went through the routine of a Middle of officer's rank being introduced to a lady of Upper caste. She smiled at him, somewhat mockingly, and failed to make the standard response. In fact, she responded not at all to his amenities.

Nadine Haer said, "I repeat, why is this service the captain can render the house of Haer so impor-tant that pressure should be brought to raise him to Upper caste? It would seem unlikely that he is a noted scientist, an outstanding artist, a great teacher—"

Mauser said uncomfortably, "They say the military is a science, too."

Her expression was about as haughty as that of her brother. "Do they? And who are *they*? I have never thought so."

"Really, Nadine," her father grumbled. "This is hardly your affair."

"No? In a few days I shall be repairing the damage you have allowed, indeed sponsored, to be committed upon the bodies of possibly thousands of now healthy human beings."

Balt said nastily, "Nobody asked you to join the medical staff, Nadine. You could have stayed in your laboratory, figuring out new methods of preventing the human race from replenishing itself."

The girl was not the type to redden, but her anger was manifest. She spun on her brother. "If the race continues its present maniac course, possibly more effective methods of birth control would be the most important development we could make. Even to the ultimate discovery of preventing all future conception."

Mauser caught himself in mid-chuckle.

But not in time. She spun on him, in his turn. "Look at yourself in that silly skirt. A professional soldier! A mercenary! A killer! In my opinion, the most useless occupation ever devised by men. Parasite on the best and most useful members of society. Destroyer by trade!"

Joe began to open his mouth, but she overrode him. "Yes, yes. I know. I've read all the nonsense that has accumulated down through the ages about the need for, the glory of, the sacrifice of the professional soldier. How they defend their country. How they give their all for the common good. Zen! What garbage!"

Balt Haer was smirking at her. "The theory today is, Nadine, old thing, that professionals such as the captain are gathering experience in case a serious fracas with the Sovs ever develops. Meanwhile, his training is kept at a fine edge fighting in the inter-corporation or inter-union fracases of our free-enterprise society."

She laughed her scorn. "And what a theory! Limited to the weapons which prevailed before 1900. If there was ever a real war with the Sov-world, does anyone really believe either would stick to such arms? Why, aircraft, armored vehicles—yes, and even nuclear weapons and rockets, would be in production overnight."

Joe was fascinated by her furious attack. He said, "Then what would you say was the purpose of the fracases, Doctor . . .?"

"Circuses," she snorted. "The old Roman games all over again, and a hundred times worse. Blood-and-guts sadism. The quest of a frustrated person for satisfaction in another's pain. Our Lowers of today are as useless and frustrated as the Roman proletariat, and potentially they're just as dangerous as the mob that once dominated Rome. Automation, the second industrial revolution, has eliminated for all practical purposes the need for their labor. So we give them bread and circuses, but they're a time bomb. And every year that goes by the circuses must be increasingly sadistic, death at an ever-increasing magnitude, or they aren't satisfied. Once it was enough to have fictional mayhem: cowboys and Indians, gangsters, or G.I.'s versus the Nazis, Japanese or Commies, but that's passed. Now we need *real* blood and guts."

Baron Haer snapped finally, "All right, Nadine. We've heard this lecture before. I doubt if the captain is interested, particularly since you have yet to get beyond the protesting stage and come up with an answer."

"I have an answer!"

"Yes?" Balt Haer raised his eyebrows mockingly.

"Yes! Overthrow this absurd status society. Resume the road to progress. Put our people to useful endeavor, instead of sitting in front of their telly sets stoned on trank."

Joe had been listening to the argument with half an ear, but now, really interested, he said, "Progress to where?"

She must have caught in his tone that he wasn't needling. She frowned at him. "I don't know man's goal, if there is one. I'm not even sure it's important. It's the road that counts. The endeavor. The dream. The effort that is now wasted can be expended to make a world a better place than it was at the time of your birth."

Balt Haer said mockingly, "That's the trouble with you, Sis. Here we are, rolling in Utopia, and you don't admit it."

"Utopia!"

"Certainly. Take a poll. You'll find nineteen people out of twenty happy with things just the way they are. They have full tummies and security, lots of leisure, and trank pills to make matters seem even rosier than they are—and they're rather rosy already."

"Then what's the necessity of this endless succession of bloody fracases, covered to the most minute bloody detail on the telly?"

Baron Haer cut things short. "We've hashed and rehashed this before, Nadine, and now we're too busy to debate further." He turned to Mauser. "Very well, Captain, you have my pledge. I wish I felt as optimistic as you do about your prospects. However, if through your efforts this coming fracas is seriously affected to our benefit, I shall—ah, as you put it—pull what strings I can in your behalf toward a double bounce in your caste rating."

Joe took a deep breath, saluted, and executed an about-face.

In the outer offices, when he had closed the door behind him, he rolled his eyes upward in mute thanks to whatever powers might be. He had somehow gained the enmity of Balt, his immediate superior, but he had gained the support of Baron Haer himself, which counted considerably more.

He thought about Nadine Haer's words. She was a malcontent—but, on the other hand, her opinions of his chosen profession weren't too very different than his own. However, given this victory, this upgrading in caste, and Joe Mauser would be in a position to retire, with all goals won in the game of life.

The door opened and shut behind him and he half turned.

Nadine Haer, evidently still angry over the hot words between herself and her relatives, glared at him. This merely emphasized the beauty Mauser had noticed the day before. She was an almost unbelievably pretty young woman, particularly when flushed with anger.

It occurred to him suddenly that, if his caste was raised to Upper, he would be in a position to woo such as Nadine Haer.

He looked into her furious face and said, "I was intrigued, Dr. Haer, with what you had to say, and I'd like to discuss some of your points. I wonder if I could have the pleasure of your company at some nearby refreshment."

"My, how formal an invitation, Captain. I suppose you had in mind sitting and flipping back a few trank pills?"

Joe looked at her. "I don't believe I've had a trank in the past twenty years, Dr. Haer. Even as a boy I didn't particularly take to having my senses dulled with drugs."

Some of the fury was abating, but she obviously remained critical of the professional mercenary. Her eyes went up and down his uniform in scorn. "You seem to make pretenses of being cultivated, Captain. Then why your chosen profession?"

He had the answer to that waiting. "As I told you, I was born a Lower. I doubt if you can realize just what that means, in view of the fact that you were born in the highest ranks of our culture. Having been born a Lower, little counted until I was able to fight my way out. Had I been born into a feudalistic society, I would have attempted to better myself into the nobility. Under classical capitalism, I would have done my utmost to accumulate a fortune, enough to reach an effective position in society. Had I been born in a communist nation, I probably would have done all I could to become a member of the party bureaucracy. But as it is, under People's Capitalism—"

She interrupted, "Industrial Feudalism would be the better term."

He ignored that and continued his sentence. "—I realize I can't even start to fulfill myself until I am a member of the Upper caste."

Her eyes had narrowed, and her anger was largely gone. "But you chose the military field in which to better yourself? Why not something more worthy? The medical category, one of the arts. Almost anything except the military."

"Government propaganda to the contrary, Dr. Haer,

it is practically impossible to raise yourself in fields other than military or religion. I didn't build this world, possibly I don't even approve of it, but since I'm in it I have no recourse but to follow the rules."

Her eyebrows arched at that, and she said, "Why not try to change the rules?"

Mauser blinked at her. Was she getting at something, or just toying with him?

Her eyes turned speculative and, in an affected mannerism, she took her lower lip in her teeth as she considered him. Then, evidently reaching some sort of a conclusion, she said, "Let's look up that refreshment you were talking about. In fact, there is a small coffee shop around the corner where it would be possible for one of Baron Haer's brood to have a cup with one of her father's officers of Middle caste."

CHAPTER SIX

At the exact moment that Acting Major Joseph Mauser was seating himself across the table from Dr. Nadine Haer, Freddy Soligen was sipping his second drink at the bar of the Upper Officer's Club in the town of Saugerties.

Saugerties was located halfway between Kingston, center for the Haer forces, and Catskill, base of the Continental Hovercraft mercenaries, and enjoyed a unique status thereby. It functioned as a common ground, a meeting place, for participants in a fracas. Of course, there was nothing to keep a man of one force from the staging city of the other, but there was an unwritten law which made it bad form for one to enter an enemy camp.

But men in any trade like to talk shop, be they mechanics or writers, farmers or artists—or professional soldiers. The Upper Officers' Club in Saugerties offered a geographically and politically convenient meeting place for officers from both sides. Thus, senior officers spent many of their leisure hours at the Officer's Club in Saugerties. It was considered unseeming to discuss the fracas immediately upcoming, but there were no restrictions on discussing the combats of years gone by, nor ones to come.

Freddy Soligen was present by the sufferance traditionally awarded the newsman, for not even a member of the Upper caste was apt to be free of the lure of publicity. At least it was so among the lesser-ranking officers. When one reached the rarified altitudes occupied by such as Field Marshal Stonewall Cogswell, one could at least pretend immunity.

But Freddy Soligen was not merely suffered to enter the Upper Officer's Club; he was normally the center of attention of several officers, and found himself hard put to pay for his own drinks. Officers there were aplenty to treat a combat reporter who, the following week, might jockey his camera about to put an ambitious man on lens when he was in there looking good—or, more important still, keep him off lens when the going was rough.

But Soligen was not interested in the fawnings of even a colonel this evening. Stonewall Cogswell had entered the room, for once unaccompanied by even a single member of his staff. He marched toward his favorite table, which traditionally remained unoccupied whenever the marshal was in the vicinity of the Catskill Reservation. He walked stiff-legged, knees unbending, as a man walks who has spent long years in cavalry boots—the marshal had won his early successes in that service. In his time, Cogswell had been an even more celebrated cavalryman than General Jack Altshuler, the current darling of the fracas buffs.

Freddy watched as Cogswell paced across the room. Officers of brigadier rank and higher were bold enough to greet the celebrated strategist, but the older man answered, if at all, with the merest flick of his marshal's baton.

He sat down at his table and a waiter scurried up

with a glass, a dark bottle, and the ancient siphon which was an affectation of the marshal.

Freddy Soligen knew the story. The marshal drank old-fashioned bourbon, supposedly such a purist that there was only one type he would accept—that produced by a small distillery, located near the Kentucky River. It was practically a handicraft operation, in a day when handicrafts were unknown.

On impulse, Soligen put down his own half-finished drink—a vodka sour—and made his way to the seated marshal. He stood there until Cogswell looked up.

"Beg your pardon, sir," Freddy said. "I wonder if I could have a word with you."

The marshal typed him immediately; the lack of an educated tone in his voice branded him less than an Upper. Not being an Upper, there was only one other reason he could be here. "I don't give interviews," he replied, irritated.

"No, sir. I know you don't, not ordinarily. But I haven't got my equipment along anyway."

"Then what in Zen do you want?"

In fact, Freddy Soligen didn't exactly know. He'd approached the famous strategist on the spur of the moment, on the off chance that the marshal might drop some hint about the upcoming fracas.

He thought fast. "Well, Marshal, I thought maybe something off the record. Something that might give me a fresh angle for this fracas. A man likes to have something besides just straight shots of the action. You know, kind of a theme."

It had never occurred to Marshal Cogswell that there were any particular angles involved in covering a fracas. It was simply out of his field, something he thought about as little as possible. The telly reporters had always been more of a nuisance than anything else, and he had the standard military man's contempt for them and the fans they represented.

Still, there was something about this one. He said suddenly, "Sit down. Don't I recognize you?"

Freddy Soligen, somewhat surprised, sat. "Yes, sir," he said. "Maybe you do at that. I've covered several of your fracases, sir."

Cogswell was nodding. "Yes, I do remember. You were at that Lockheed-Cessna deal. I was commanding the right flank. Your camera crew got caught up in the cross fire of those damned *mitrailleuse* and took several casualties."

"Yes, sir," Freddy said. "Three of them were killed."

The marshal took a pull at his bourbon. "Oh? Too bad. You lads aren't supposed to get into the dill."

"Sometimes we do, though," Freddy said softly.

"Have a drink?" Cogswell pointed to his bottle.

Mildly surprised, Freddy Soligen took up the bottle proffered and looked about for a waiter. The Upper Officer's Club affected live waiters. One materialized, glass on tray. Freddy poured a slug, applied the siphon as he had seen the marshal do.

Stonewall Cogswell was evidently in a nostalgic mood. He said, "That was a long time ago."

"Sir?"

"The Lockheed-Cessna, McDonnell-Boeing fracas. You have to be long in the game to remember that far back. On an average, this isn't a category you remain in for that many years. The weaklings are weeded out—get killed or quit early on. The strong ones stick with it, but the odds are against them in the long run."

Freddy Soligen tried the whiskey and found that he didn't particularly like it. He wondered vaguely if this was one of the endless eccentricities perpetuated by so many of the Category Military pros who were on the make. Something to draw the attention of the buffs. Like the swashbuckling Captain Robert Maynard, prancing around on the beautiful palomino which was his trademark. Like Colonel Tom Clark, who had his boots built so that they gave him a romantic-looking limp, although he had never copped a wound in his life. But no, Marshal Stonewall Cogswell didn't need any gimmicks. He didn't want publicity, nor the plaudits of the buffs. He had *worked* his way to the very top, which was more than passingly offbeat in itself.

More to keep the conversation alive than anything else, Freddy said, "Come to think of it, I saw another veteran of that fracas today. Another old pro. Let's see . . . you were on the Lockheed-Cessna side. So was Joe."

"Joe?" Cogswell asked politely.

"Captain Joe Mauser."

Cogswell nodded, smiling in his fearsome way. "That's right, he was there. A second lieutenant at the time, as I recall." He pulled at his glass. "Rather surprised that Mauser didn't sign up with me for this one, since he was available. Damn good man. One of the old breed."

Freddy Soligen was feeling his drinks, but the opportunity that now presented itself didn't escape him. He had precious little information to offer Cogswell, but it just might be enough, enough to get him an in with the marshal . . .

He took a breath, then said, "Funny thing, today at the airport. Mauser isn't one of the lens hogs. I've never known Joe Mauser to suck up to us telly crewmen."

"So?" Cogswell looked at him.

Freddy shrugged his shoulders. "Today he told me

to keep an eye on him. You know, have the camera handy in his vicinity."

Cogswell poured himself another drink, carefully. He made it a practice never to take more than two on the eve of a fracas. "Hmm . . ." he said now, "What did you mean, earlier, when you said you needed an angle for shooting this fracas?"

Freddy Soligen shifted in his chair and leaned forward hopefully. "Well, sir, this one is such a setup for Continental Hovercraft that unless there's something to hang it on, some kinda departure, it's gonna be just short of boring to watch. I thought maybe there'd be some special angle you might think of. Should I devote full time, maybe, to the cavalry? Or should I kinda stick around you an' your staff? I don't know, I need something to *hang* on, a gimmick."

"A gimmick," Stonewall Cogswell said distantly, thoughtfully.

"Yes, sir."

Cogswell shook his head. "I can't offer you much, lad, but I would say that cavalry is the lookout on this one. It's going to be where you'll see the main concentration of action."

"I see," said Soligen, nodding. "Thanks, sir!"

Afterwards, after the telly reporter had left, the head of Continental Hovercraft's forces thought about it. He hadn't been able to help Freddy Soligen. The remark about the cavalry was just a throw-away line, to please the man. Frankly, he was of much the same opinion that the reporter held. This fracas should be one of the easy ones, if any fracas was easy. However, you won the easy ones only by sticking to your standards. It wasn't genius that counted—would-be military experts to the contrary—but endless attention to tedious detail; it was only after Bonaparte got fat and began taking naps in the middle of the day that he lost Waterloo.

No, he hadn't been able to help Soligen. But, aware of it or not, Soligen had given *him* something. Just a hint, but . . .

He looked about the hall, located the man he had noticed earlier, and made a motion to him with his head.

Lieutenant Colonel Fodor came over and stood at easy attention before his commanding officer's table. There was, in Fodor's mind, no need for formal military courtesy here. After all, they were in the informal atmosphere of the Officer's Club. Besides which, Michael Fodor was born a Low-Upper in caste, and although Stonewall Cogswell carried the same status, the old man had come up from the ranks of the Middles, and was thus eligible to be regarded with a slightly supercilious air—just so long as the marshal wasn't aware of it, of course.

"Yes, sir?" Fodor said.

Cogswell looked up at him thoughtfully. Lieutenant Colonel Fodor wasn't one of his regular staff but had been wished on him by Baron Zwerdling, who had, of course, a small standing military staff of his own. However, the man had a fairly good reputation as an intelligence officer.

The marshal said, "Are you acquainted with a Captain Joseph Mauser?"

"I know *of* him, sir."

Lieutenant Colonel Fodor might have added, but didn't, that his contacts with Captain Joseph Mauser had not been happy ones. To the contrary. On one occasion, the captain had captured him under somewhat ludicrous conditions. Ludicrous, that is, as it had appeared on the telly screens. Fodor had had to suffer the ribbing of his colleagues for some months after, and he still hadn't lived it down.

And there was another occasion on which Mauser, with an inferior force, had held the colonel up for long hours, leading to a complete upset of the plans of Fodor's commanding officer. Happily, on that occasion, the telly crews had not been near enough to reap for Joe Mauser the glory, nor for Lieutenant Colonel Fodor the ignominy, of the confrontation.

The marshal nodded. "I want you to put a man on him." He thought about it some more, then added slowly, "Mauser's an old-timer. It had better be a tough operator."

Lieutenant Colonel Fodor was mildly surprised. This was the first time he had served under Stonewall Cogswell, but the marshal had his reputation; it didn't include strong-arm tactics. But considering his own opinion of Captain Joseph Mauser, Fodor found the assignment somewhat gratifying.

It didn't occur to Michael Fodor that he might have misunderstood the marshal.

Mauser had returned to his billet that evening in a state of near-euphoria and thus was only mildly surprised and irritated when he found his batman absent. After all, he had given Max Mainz the rest of the day off.

He shrugged it off and went into the kitchenette. He hadn't eaten in Kingston, being too caught up in his relationship with Nadine Haer. Well, relationship wasn't quite the word, although his thoughts were certainly moving in that direction. With his *conversation* with Dr. Haer.

He sat at the tiny auto-chef table and stared down at the limited menu. He didn't feel particularly hungry, but he made a point of eating regularly during the days preceding a fracas. You wanted your reflexes to be as good as possible, and that meant taking care of all of your body's needs.

He punched in an order for a steak and was surprised when the auto-chef failed to produce it.

He grunted in disgust. Evidently, this motel had already shut down its facilities for the fracas. During a fracas, no facilities were allowed that hadn't existed prior to the year 1900. That would include auto-chefs, of course.

He came to his feet and opened the small refrigerator set into the wall.

He might have known. The only thing it contained was the makings of drinks. With a grimace, he fished out the bottle of applejack and a plastic of ginger ale. That drink Max had made had been excellent.

Joe duplicated it as best he could, forgetting the lemon twist, and carried it back into the living room. He had a lot to think about and worked away at the drink as he did. Later, he got up and made another.

An hour or so on, Max still hadn't shown. It occurred to Mauser that the little man might have found himself some fracas-buff mopsy to shack up with for the night. Oh well, let his batman enjoy it while he could. Immediately before a fracas, the Category Military was composed of gods; during it, they were entertainment stars, in the ultimate entertainment thrill; after it, they were nothing—until the next fracas.

He made himself a final drink, then went off to bed, having forgotten his rule against drinking after supper, and after having forgotten that he hadn't had supper.

As they so often did, one of the old dreams came. One of the bad ones.

It had been down on Guanajuato Reservation, in what was once called Mexico. They were involved in a regimental magnitude fracas between Pemex, the petroleum complex concern, and Texas Oil. He and Jim had been with the latter outfit under a Colonel Ed Bomoseen, a supercilious Upper who was later lost in a fracas on the Little Big Horn Reservation. At the time, Jim had out-ranked his long-time buddy slightly, holding a master sergeant's rating to Joe's staff sergeant.

It had been one foul-up after another from the beginning. The Guanajuato Reservation was much too large, even for divisional-magnitude affairs. With no more than regimental forces involved, the commanders were hard put to operate—it was just impossible to keep track of the enemy in so large an area. They had spent the better part of a month in feints and small-scale skirmishes, while trying to find and keep track of each other. At the same time, both commanders were under pressure from their principals to join the action and bring to an end the drain on resources.

Jim and Joe had been sent out on a patrol with a troop of sixteen cavalry men, veterans all, to feel out the enemy presence. Up to the point where they entered the ruins of a Spanish Colonial town nestled high in the hills of Guanajuato, they had drawn a blank.

Jim Hawkins, in command, was an old pro, and took no chances. The patrol carried their weapons ready, and double watches were posted during every stop.

They had entered the town, avoiding the main streets, and proceeded in the direction of the *Zocalo,* the central plaza which dominated practically all Mexican towns. Jim and eight of the men rode cautiously along one side of the street, hugging the buildings; Joe and his eight along the other side.

They were armed with 30-30 Winchesters, that carbine of the Old West which had seen so much use in the 19th-century development of both the United States and Mexico.

Jim Hawkins had sensed trouble in the situation right away. The town was too damned quiet. Even though they hadn't flushed any of the Pemex forces in two days of patrol in this direction, it was possible that they could run into hostile fire at any moment. On the other hand, had there been enemy in the vicinity, there should have been some telly crews. There was no sign of either.

Joe held his carbine in his hands, directing his horse by knee pressure alone. His eyes were kept busy trying to see everywhere at once, and he wished earnestly for another set in the back of his head. He shared Jim's premonition; it was mid-day and too quiet.

It was Jim who caught a flicker of sun on something in the church tower ahead and, in a blur of movement, raised his rifle and snapped off a shot. A cry of pain from the top of the tower vindicated Jim's unseemly action.

The squad scurried into doorways by reflex, seeking shelter in the large, half-ruined buildings—the mansions and palaces of the silver-rich Spaniards of another era.

But Jim called, "On the double! Hit the church!"

Joe didn't immediately get his plan of action, but Jim was in command. He dug heels into his animal's side and led his squad forward in a rush.

A high side door lay open; Jim in the lead, they galloped in, flung themselves to the floor, and opened fire before even looking around. The large room held a dozen men or more, gathered around some low tables; this was some sort of field headquarters. The Pemex men were cut down even as they looked up from their work. Joe's ears rang in the silence that followed the hail of gunfire.

At most, five seconds had passed from when Jim Hawkins had first shot the man in the tower. Some of the Pemex men hadn't even had guns at hand; they certainly hadn't been prepared for the attack. Without orders, the troop moved on through the building, finishing off the enemy detachment before it had time to reform, or be reinforced, if reinforcements were available.

Jim Hawkins hesitated only momentarily, then snapped orders, right and left. "Creager, Amshof— get those horses under cover. Somewhere in the back. Someplace with a roof. Johnson, Galloway— get up into the tower."

A Vickers gun was set up on a tripod at one of the windows.

"Joe! You and one of your men, get on that gun!"

Johnson complained, "The tower? Sarge, there's no cover up there. We'll get our asses shot off." But already he and Galloway were on their way, pounding up the wooden stairs two at a time.

Jim stood at the window, next to Joe and his gun assistant. His combat-wise eyes were drawn. He called out further orders to the remaining men, spotting them around the building. The Pemex force had numbered eighteen. All were dead. Jim Hawkins had lost two men: one dead, one with a revolver slug in his side. The wounded man, swearing, was bandaging himself as best he could, for the time being not expecting aid from his comrades in arms.

Joe said, "What do you think?"

Jim started to say something, but Johnson yelled

down from the tower, "Hey, Sarge, there's another Vickers up here!"

Jim yelled, "Get on it, and keep your eyes open. There's bound to be more of them around here."

And there were. They came spilling across the *Zocalo* in a disorganized rush. Evidently, they had been attracted by the sound of the gunfire, and didn't realize that all of their comrades were gone, their headquarters held by their enemy.

Joe began firing short bursts, and the Pemex men went down, two, three at a time. The other Vickers echoed from the bell tower.

Jim stayed at the window, carbine to shoulder, snapping out fire as fast as he could lever. He laughed down to Joe. "What a bunch of clowns! They act like we caught them with their pants down."

As Jim finished his remark, Joe's machine gun fell silent; aside from those who had been mowed down in the plaza, none of the enemy could be seen. Those remaining had taken cover, though there was precious little cover in the *Zocalo*.

Joe looked up at Jim and said, "You know what happened? They were out to lunch. Look around. This is where they were bivouacked. But they're the same as us. Haven't seen anybody in days. They got lazy. You must've winged their only lookout, up in the tower. The rest of them were off eating, except those we caught here. Their mess must be across the square."

Desultory shooting started up from across the plaza.

Galloway yelled from the tower. "Hey, Sarge, there's damn little cover up here."

"What do you see?" Jim yelled back. His eyes were alive with the spark of combat. Unlike Joe, Jim was in his glory in action. He lived for it.

"This is the center of town," Galloway yelled down.

"There's four main streets. You can see a couple miles in any direction."

"That sentry must've been sleeping," Jim muttered. "Great institution, the siesta." He looked around the ruined church. He and Joe's gun crew were in an apsidal chapel jutting from a passage leading off from the main room. Here were stacked guns and a considerable amount of gear and ammunition, as well as other supplies.

"You know," he grinned, obviously still feeling the rush of the initial victory, "we've taken their base!"

The fire outside increased.

"I'll bet there's fifty of them out there," Joe said.

Joe heard a muffled grunt from the bell tower. Johnson yelled, "Sarge! Galloway's copped one!"

Jim snapped out, "Fowler, get up there."

The Rank Private named Fowler looked over at him from where he lay, firing out of a door. He licked his dry lips unhappily, but slid backward, out of line of fire, came to his feet and headed for the steps to the tower.

Jim left, returning in a few moments with a military chart of the Guanajuato Reservation. He said to Joe, "You know where we are?" He put the map down on the floor, and began tracing with his finger.

"This is San Miguel de Allende. You're on historic ground, lad."

"Great," Joe rumbled. "Look out there—forget fifty. There must be a hundred men out there. But if we're on historic ground, I guess it's all right. And what the hell makes it so historic?"

Jim laughed. "This is the town where Ignacio Allende started the Mexican revolution against Spain. Over there"—he stabbed his finger against the map—"that's Celaya, where Pancho Villa met his Waterloo. A good commander of horses, but cavalry shouldn't charge barbed wire and trenches backed with Maxim guns. And over here"—he stabbed again at a point a few miles from where they were—"is Queretaro, where the Emperor Maximilian fought his last battle, was captured and shot."

A motion caught Joe's eye, and he let off a short burst through the window, bringing down two men who had darted from a building across the *Zocalo*.

"So . . .?" Joe said. To their right, one of the cavalrymen screamed agony as he took a hit. Several of the horses whinnied nervously. Jim's force was melting away, in spite of the comparative strength of his position.

The wounded man continued screaming, obviously in shock. Joe knew the man had to be quieted one way or another; before he could move, though, someone else went to him, pulled the wounded man into the sanctuary. Joe caught a glimpse of a bloodied face and an eye missing from its socket.

For the first time, Jim Hawkins looked worried. He started to speak to Joe, hesitated, then said, "It's getting tough, ain't it, Joe?"

Joe nodded. "Yeah, but that's what we signed up for, wasn't it?" His attempt at lightness rang hollow.

Jim seemed to come to a decision. "We need help," he said, then, over his shoulder, "Perkins, Amshof, get your mounts and make a break for it. Get back to Colonel Bomoseen and tell him it looks as though the Pemex outfit is coming through the pass from Queretaro. If we can hold them here, he'll have them caught before they can deploy out into the valley."

"Not Amshof," Perkins called back. "He's copped one."

"Then you go, Hazelton," Jim called. "Get moving, men!"

From the tower, the machine gun chattered once, twice, fell silent.

Johnson yelled, "Sarge! Fowler's bought it!"

Joe looked at his friend. "It's too exposed up there, Jim."

Jim Hawkins' face worked, but he was grinning still. "We've got to keep check on that street leading up the hill. If the main body comes, that's where they'll come from." He called, "Creager! Up into the tower."

"What? You think I'm drivel-happy?"

Jim went over to the man. "Up in the bell tower. We've got to keep that gun going. And we've got to keep our eyes on that street."

"*Our* eyes, he says," Creager muttered, glaring. However, he scurried over to the steps.

The fire from the area across the plaza was intensifying and the foe was beginning to infiltrate to both the right and left flank—some of the shooting was coming from two new directions.

Jim, hunkered down next to Joe and his helper at the belt of the Vickers gun, squinted out through the atrium at the square.

He said, "They don't know how many of us there are. For all they know, more of us are coming up. If their main body is around, they won't dare enter town until they've eliminated us."

"The way we're taking casualties, they'll know pretty damn quick there's only a dozen of us left," said Joe.

Jim thought about that, the happy gleam still in his eye. He called over his shoulder, "Corporal, take three of the men and pick out some rifles from those stacks in there. Scoot around the whole damn church and shoot through every window. Try to make enough noise to make it sound like there's two or three times as many of us. If you hit anything, so much the better, but make those bastards keep their heads down!"

He pulled his own revolver from its holster and emptied it at random across the square, then his carbine. As he reloaded, he called out, "Everybody keep up a heavy fire. If you run out of ammo, there's plenty more in their supplies. If you can't find our caliber, pick out one of their guns."

The Vickers up in the bell tower chattered, chattered again.

"Hey, Sarge," one of the men up in the tower called, "Twenty or thirty horses, up the street, coming into town."

"Let 'em have it!"

The Vickers spewed hot lead.

Hazelton and Perkins made their dash for it in a clattering of hooves.

Creager called down a running commentary. "They're edging up the north side of the plaza." He stopped as the Vickers fired three short bursts. "Almost to the first side street, and—damn! Hazelton's horse took a hit, Sarge. Dick is pinned under him." Then, "One of those Pemex bastards finished him."

Jim Hawkins called, "Perkins get through?"

"I think so," the other yelled back. "He's up the side street. OK, so far."

"Keep that damn street clear! Keep up the heavy fire. We want them to think there's a million of us."

Joe fired, fired again. He wished the gun was a Maxim rather than a Vickers. The German guns had a better cooling jacket than the British. With the Vickers he had to watch the length of his bursts, and their frequency.

His companion, feeding the belt into the Vickers, flinched, yelped. "I'm hit!" he gurgled. The man was clutching at his chest. Joe could see blood welling up from around his hand at an impossible rate.

Jim hauled him back into the corridor, returning shortly with two new canisters of Vickers rounds. He took over feeding the belt himself.

Between bursts, Joe said to him, "What do you think, Jim? Should we make a run for it? They're being reinforced by the minute. We can't hold out at this rate. Half the men are already gone, and the whole building's going to be surrounded."

Jim Hawkins grinned at him. "I thought you were hot for a bounce in caste, Joe. What the hell—if we can hold them up here for a few hours, the old man'll come up and trim their pants. Then we'll both make lieutenant, and maybe Middle caste."

Joe swore as a round whistled past his ear and splintered an ornate pillar behind him. "Right now, Jim, I'll settle for Lower, if it means staying alive." Gritting his teeth, he fired another burst into the square.

Above him, Jim Hawkins laughed as he squeezed off more shots. "We'll make it, Joe. We have to."

Another bullet whizzed by Joe's head, and he swore again. "Yeah, Jim—we have to . . . nobody's gonna do it for us!"

CHAPTER SEVEN

Joe Mauser woke in a sweat at that point, thankful that he had been saved the worst of it.

Neither he nor Jim Hawkins had made lieutenant that time. Sergeants they remained.

The Pemex mercenaries had brought up some mountain guns on pack mules and shelled the church until it was unrecognizable as a house of God. When their reinforcements finally came, the only men left in any shape to continue the fight were Joe Mauser and Jim Hawkins, and both of them had minor wounds. All but two of the rest were dead. A total of nine men had been shot out of the tower before it collapsed. The old church stank of death.

When they counted the dead the Pemex people had left behind, they found thirty-four in the *Zocalo* and the streets surrounding. How many more there might have been in the half-ruined buildings surrounding the plaza they never knew, since they only held the town for another hour or so.

Colonel Bomoseen didn't come through then, when all the chips were down. He was too caught up in planning brilliant strategy to worry about a small patrol, and had in fact left with the major part of his forces on a futile march to the west, following up on old intelligence regarding the position of the enemy.

It was only by chance that Perkins met up with another Texas Oil patrol. They attacked the Pemex army from behind. The enemy, apparently fooled into thinking that they had met with the main Texas Oil forces by the surprise attack and by Jim's tactics, was routed.

In the end, though, the situation had completely pickled, and the Texas Oil forces took a beating.

The part that Jim Hawkins and Joe Mauser had played was forgotten. Certain it was that none of it had gotten on lens. It had been one of the most gory, meaningless frays Joe Mauser was ever to experience, and it came back almost as often as the worst one of all, the one that dominated his nightmares—the time Jim had copped his last one.

Awake now, he shook his head, stared up at the ceiling, wide-eyed. Dawn washed in on him.

He had been through this before. He knew it was possible to have it in his mind the rest of the day, to have it come back over and over again. He knew what he had to do. He had to concentrate on something else.

It wasn't hard.

He put his hands under his head and rehashed his session with Nadine Haer. It hadn't taken him five minutes to come to the conclusion that he was in love with the girl, and he had been forced to keep himself under rein the rest of the evening and not let the fact get through to her by his attitude or his actions. This was no Lower or Middle girl, easily flattered by an old pro's stories of glory.

He wanted to talk about the way her mouth tucked in at the corners, but she was hot on the evolution of society. He would have liked to have kissed that impossibly perfect ear of hers, but she was all for exploring the reasons why man had reached his present impasse. Joe was for holding hands and staring into her eyes, she was for delving into the differences between the West-world and the Sov-world and the possibility of resolving them.

To keep her company at all it had been necessary to suppress his own desires and go along with the conversation. It obviously had never occurred to her that a Middle might have romantic ideas involving Nadine Haer—no matter the radical teachings she advocated.

Most of their world was predictable from what had gone before, Nadine Haer maintained. In spite of popular fable to the contrary, the division between classes had become increasingly clear since the beginning of the 20th century. Among other things, tax systems were reorganized so that it became all but impossible for a citizen born poor to accumulate a fortune. Through ability he might rise to the point of earning fabulous sums, but the tax collector would devastate such earnings. Only the already-wealthy were in a position to retain the bulk of what they owned.

With these conditions maintaining, one had little chance of breaking into the domain of what finally became the small percentage now known as Uppers. The rising cost of a really good education became such that few other than those born into the Middle or Upper castes could afford the best of schools. Castes tended to perpetuate themselves.

Not sparing her own caste, she pointed out that one born into the wealthiest levels of society was hard put not to remain there. Even if an incompetent inherited one of the larger fortunes, there was no way, in the systems of trusts and estates established by the upper class, that he could squander his own piece of it and then tap into the family fortune.

At the beginning of the 21st century, the nation had fallen increasingly deeper into a situation where both political parties were tightly controlled by the same group of Uppers. Elections became a farce, a great national holiday in which stereotyped patriotic speeches, pretenses, beer busts, and trank binges were the order of the day.

For it was all very well and good that the electorate decided by majority vote who was to lead the nation, but the *nominations* were made by a handful of professional politicians who represented the upper classes and their corporations—in short, the real powers that were.

Economically, too, the precursors of their world had existed for over a century, claimed Nadine. Thanks to automation, production of the basics had become so profuse that poverty in the old sense of the word had become nonsensical. There was an abundance of the necessities of life for all. Social security, socialized medicine, unending unemployment insurance, old age pensions, pensions for veterans and the unfit, pensions and doles for this, that and the other . . . all had doubled and doubled again, until everyone had security for life. The Uppers, true enough, had opulence far beyond that known by the Middles and lived like gods compared to the Lowers. But all had security.

They had agreed, up to that point. But then had come debate.

"Then why," Joe had asked her, "haven't we achieved Utopia, as your brother called it? Isn't it what man has been yearning for, down through the ages? Where did the wheel come off? What happened to the dream?"

Nadine had frowned at him—beautifully, he thought. "It's not the first time man has found abundance in a society, though never to this degree. The Incas had it, for instance."

"I don't know much about them," Joe admitted. "An early form of communism with a sort of military priesthood at the top."

She nodded, her face serious, as always. "Not exactly communists, although they did have a socialist organization. It isn't largely known, but at the time of the Spanish conquest, the so-called Incas—they didn't call themselves that, you know—had a higher standard of living than did contemporary Europeans. They enjoyed better food, in wider variety; they probably lived in homes at least as good as those of the average European and dressed at least as well. And certainly their medicine was as good as or better than what the Europeans had. But above all, they enjoyed a security unheard of in Spain or the rest of Europe at the time. There was no such thing as poverty. From the cradle to the grave, the Incan people had all the requirements of life.

"But they were stifled in their development. They had reached a self-acknowledged zenith, and stayed there. After that, they simply disappeared."

She paused to think, forehead wrinkling delightfully.

"And for themselves, the Romans more or less had it—at the expense of the nations they conquered, of course."

"And . . ." Joe prodded.

"And in each of these examples the same thing happened—society ossified. Joe," she said, using his first name for the first time, and in a manner that kicked his pulse rate up a few points, "a ruling caste and a socio-economic system perpetrates itself as long as it can. No matter what damage it may do to society as a whole, it perpetuates itself—even to the point of the complete destruction of everything around it.

"Remember Hitler? Adolf the Aryan and his Thousand-Year Reich? When it became obvious that he had failed, and the only thing that could result from continued resistance would be destruction of Germany's cities and millions of her people, did he and his clique resign or surrender? Certainly not. They attempted to bring down the whole German structure in a *Gotterdammerung*."

Nadine Haer was deep into her theme, eyes flashing her conviction. "The Roman politico-economic system continued for centuries after it should have been replaced. Such reformers as the Gracchus brothers were assassinated or thrust aside so that the entrenched elements could perpetuate themselves. When Rome finally fell, darkness descended for a thousand years on Western progress."

Joe had never gone this far in his thoughts. He said now, somewhat uncomfortably, "Well, what would replace what we have now? If you took power from you Uppers, who could direct the country? The Lowers? That's not even funny. Take away their fracases and their dope, and they'd go berserk. They don't *want* anything else."

Her mouth worked. "Admittedly, we've allowed things to deteriorate much too far; we should have done something long ago. I'm not sure I know the answer. All I know is that we're not utilizing the efforts of more than a fraction of our people. Nine out of ten of us spend our lives high on trank and watching fracases. Meanwhile, the motivation for continued progress seems to have withered away, with the aid of our Upper political circles. They are afraid that some seemingly minor change might avalanche."

Joe put up a mild argument then. "I've heard the case made that the Lowers are fools and the reason our present socio-economic system makes it so difficult to rise from Lower to Upper is that you cannot make a fool understand he is one. You can only make him angry. If some, who are not fools, are allowed to easily advance from Lower to Upper, the vast mass who are fools will be angry because they are not allowed to. That's why the Military Category is made a channel of advance. Fools don't make it—they die."

Nadine was scornful. "These days we are born within our castes. If an Upper is inadequate, he nevertheless remains an Upper. An accident of birth makes him an aristocrat. His environment, family, training, education, friends, traditions, and laws maintain him in that position. But a Lower who might have the greatest potential value to society is born handicapped and he's hard put not to wind up sitting stoned in front of a telly all day. Sure he's a fool, he's never been *allowed* to develop himself."

Yes, Joe reflected now, it had been quite an evening. In a life of more than thirty years devoted to quiet rebellion, he had never met anyone so outspoken as Nadine Haer, nor one who had thought it through as far as she had.

He grunted. His own revolt was against the level at which he had found himself in society, not the structure of society itself. His whole *raison d'etre* was to lift himself to Upper status. It came as a shock to him to find a person who had been born into

Upper caste desirous of tearing the whole system down.

What purpose had his own battle to reach the status of Upper, then?

His thoughts were interrupted by the door opening and the face of Max Mainz grinning in at him. The little man blurted, "Come on, Joe. Let's go out on the town!"

"*Joe?*" Joe Mauser raised himself to one elbow and stared at the other. "Leaving aside the merits of your suggestion for the moment, do you think you should address an officer by his first name?"

Max Mainz came fully into the bedroom, his grin still wider. "You forgot! It's election day!"

"Oh," Joe Mauser relaxed into his pillow. "So it is. No duty for today, eh?"

"No duty for anybody," Max crowed. "What do you say we go into town and have a few drinks in one of the Upper bars?"

Joe grunted, but got up. "What'll that accomplish? On election day most of the Uppers around here get done up in their oldest clothes and go slumming among the Lowers. It's the one day of the year they figure they're not demeaning themselves by picking up some trank-happy Lower kid and giving her the thrill of a quick roll in the hay with an aristocrat."

Max wasn't to be put off so easily. "Well, wherever we go, let's get going. I'll bet this town is full of fracas buffs. And on election day, to boot. Wouldn't it be something if I found me a real fracas fan, some Upper-Upper dame?"

Joe laughed at him, even as he headed for the bathroom. "Max," he said over his shoulder, "you're in for a big disappointment. They're all the same— Upper, Lower, or Middle."

As a matter of fact, though, he rather liked the

idea of going into town for the show. It had been a long time since Joe Mauser had done much in the way of relaxing. In fact, as he thought back, he couldn't recall getting drenched since Jim Hawkins had copped the big one. And how long had it been since he had relaxed with a woman?

"Yeah?" Max grinned back at him. "Well, I'd like the pleasure of finding out if that's true by personal experience."

Lieutenant Colonel Michael Fodor looked speculatively at the man standing before him.

"So you're Smith," he said dryly. "John, I assume."

"Are there any others?"

"Sit down," Fodor said, not amused. He came to his own feet and walked over to the small bar built into the wall of his office.

Smith took the straight chair that sat to one side of the intelligence officer's desk and fished in his jerkin pocket for a small plastic container. He opened it and extracted a white pill. He was a man of averages, quite undistinctive. In his early middle years, medium of height and weight, colorless in costume and in facial expression. There was an empty something about him, especially in his eyes.

Michael Fodor said sharply, "Is that trank? This assignment doesn't lend itself to drugs."

The other shook his head very slightly and popped the pill into his mouth. The effect seemed almost instantaneous, as though psychological rather than physiological. His eyes came alive, his skin took on a new life.

Fodor splashed an inch of liquid from a bottle into a tall glass, reached for a carafe of water, but then decided against it and returned with the glass to the swivel chair behind his desk.

He said, "You were recommended to me."

Smith said nothing to that. He crossed his legs and sat there looking at Fodor.

Michael Fodor was unhappy. He didn't like this Smith. However, time was running out; he wouldn't be able to locate another operative of this type. He took a pull at his drink and launched into the meat of the thing.

"You won't have to have much background."

"The less the better," Smith said. "Just tell me what you want. I get paid for . . . for the operation, not for knowing the reason for it."

Fodor finished his drink, put the glass down on his desk and leaned back in his chair.

"All right, this is it. Very shortly now, there's going to be a fracas on the Catskill Reservation here. Suffice to say, I represent one of the contestants."

Smith took in Fodor's uniform, that of Baron Zwerdling's permanent staff, but said nothing.

An edge of irritation in his voice, Lieutenant Colonel Fodor said, "It is of no interest to you to even know which side."

"All right."

Michael Fodor looked at Smith impatiently. The man inspired exactly nothing, neither confidence, respect, nor a modicum of liking. Fodor began to have qualms about this. However . . .

"Suffice to say that there is a certain Captain Joseph Mauser, who has become a—say a sore thumb. It has become necessary to eliminate him from the fracas to come."

"All right."

"This Captain Mauser is tough. He's seen a great deal of combat."

"Nobody's tough," Smith said emptily. "Some think they are, but nobody's tough. You'd be surprised, Colonel."

Fodor got up and went back to the bar for another drink. As before, he didn't offer one to the other man. One didn't drink with one's inferiors; certainly an Upper didn't drink with hired hoodlums.

He didn't like this. Besides that, he was surprised and somewhat disgusted with Field Marshal Stonewall Cogswell. It simply wasn't playing the game, eliminating even a junior officer from the fracas, for whatever reason. He suppressed the fact that he, himself, hated the mercenary in question, hated his guts as much as he had hated anyone since reaching adulthood.

He snapped, "You don't seem to have the build to take on an old combat man such as Joe Mauser."

Smith had a distant amusement in him. "Size doesn't count, Colonel. You'd be surprised."

The intelligence officer was miffed by Smith's condescending attitude, no matter how distant the air.

"You have assistance?"

Smith shifted very slightly in his chair and shook his head. "Wouldn't you rather this be done with as few knowing about it as possible?"

"Of course."

"All right. Nobody will know about it except you and me."

Fodor resumed his seat. He told himself that he liked this less and less. He said, "There's one share of Common Basic stock in it for you."

"Two," Smith said, without inflection at all. "Two shares of Convertible Common Basic. Untraceable."

Fodor was irritated again. The marshal hadn't mentioned how much he could spend. Fodor had thought he had understood his commanding officer's reticence. The marshal didn't *want* to know the details. Supposedly, such matters were beneath the famed Stonewall Cogswell. He hadn't told Fodor why it was that he wanted Mauser eliminated from the fracas, had left all the details to his intelligence aide. However, intelligence had a certain leeway when it came to funds; it was universally expected that certain opportunities might come up in any fracas which would involve undercover expenditures.

"Very well," he snapped. "Two shares of Convertible Common Basic, payable upon report of your success."

Smith recrossed his legs, shook his head. "Payable now," he said softly. "You'll never even have to see me again."

Fodor stared at him. "Do you think me drivel-happy? How do I know you'll perform successfully?"

Smith's smile was distant again. "Who recommended me, Colonel?"

That stopped him. Michael Fodor didn't have to answer that; of course the recommendation had been from one who had used this man's services many times in maintaining a high political position. Fodor looked at him testily. It seemed a confounded large amount for beating one man up to the point where he would be hospitalized for, say, a week or two.

However, once again, time was running out.

Fodor snapped, "Very well." He came to his feet once again and crossed the room to a wall safe.

Smith stood also, fishing in his pocket again for his white pills.

After Smith had received his wages of violence and left, Michael Fodor stared after him at the door which had closed on the colorless man. He spent several minutes wondering over the fact that the small man thought he could take on Joe Mauser so easily.

It never occurred to him that Smith, and the man who had referred Smith to him, might have misunderstood the intent expressed in his desire to "take Joe Mauser out of action."

CHAPTER EIGHT

In the faraway past, Kingston had once been the capital of the United States. For a short time, when Washington's men were in flight after being routed from New York City, the government of the fledgling United Colonies had held session in the Hudson River town. That had been Kingston's one moment of historic glory, and afterward the town had slipped back into being a minor city on the edge of the Catskills.

In recent years it had become one of the two recruiting centers which bordered the Catskill Military Reservation, which in turn was one of the score or so cleared areas on the continent where rival corporations or unions could meet and settle their differences in combat—given permission of the Category Military Department of the government. And permission was becoming ever easier to acquire.

It had slowly evolved, the resorting to trial by combat to settle disputes between competing corporations, disputes between corporations and unions, disputes between unions over jurisdiction. Slowly, but predictably. Since the earliest days of the first industrial revolution conflict between these elements had often broken into violence—sometimes into minor warfare. One early example occurred in Colorado, when armed elements of the Western Federation of Miners shot it out with similarly armed "detectives" hired by the mine owners, and later with the troops of an unsympathetic State government.

By the middle of the 20th century, unions had become one of the biggest businesses in the country, and a considerable portion of the industrial conflict had shifted to fights between them for jurisdiction over dues-paying members. Battles on the waterfront, assassination and counter-assassination by gun-toting goon squads dominated by gangsters, industrial sabotage, frays between pickets and scabs—all were common occurrences.

Those events set the stage for the fracases of the 21st century, but one of the first inklings of what was to come could be seen in the early cinema. The taste for violence was planted and nutured while that industry was still making silent pictures. That first great feature-length classic, *The Birth of a Nation*, thrilled the country with its Civil War battle scenes and race conflict. Then followed the great war movies, such as *The Big Push* and *All Quiet on the Western Front*, the films on the opening of the American west, and the gangster movies.

The movie moguls found a prime demand for films depicting violence and death, indeed found themselves forced to deliver such fare or face bankruptcy. The populace had had its taste of death, and demanded more. Even while sex was a taboo topic— and the demand for it served by its own special underground—violence went public.

The pattern continued throughout the rest of the century, with television providing daily doses of vio-

lence to the faithful and cinema countering with a
spate of poorly-plotted horror films which depicted
blood and gore on a new level of realism. Dismem-
berment, beheading, and a whole gamut of graphic
violence was introduced. Television soon followed
suit.

But increasing realism was demanded, and the
coming of live telly news finally brought the public
what it wanted—real violence, no simulations. Zealous reporters made ever greater efforts to bring the
actual mayhem before the eyes of their viewers, and
their efforts were highly rewarded.

The telly reporter fortunate enough to be on the
scene of a police arrest, a rumble between rival
gangs of juvenile delinquents, or a longshoreman's
fray in which scores of workers were hospitalized
could rocket to the top in his field. When attempts
were made to suppress such broadcasts, the howl of
freedom of speech and the press went up, financed
by tycoons clever enough to realize the value of the
subjects they covered so adequately.

The *need* was there. Bread the populace had. Trank
was available to all. But the need was there for the
circus, the vicious, sadistic circus; and bit by bit,
over the years and decades, the way was found to
circumvent the country's laws and traditions to supply the need.

A way is always found. Despite the final Universal
Disarmament Pact, which banned all weapons invented since the year 1900 and provided for complete mutual inspection, the fear of war had still not
been excised from the West-world psyche. And thus
there existed an excuse to give the would-be soldier,
the potential defender of the country in some future
international conflict, practical experience.

Slowly tolerance grew to allow union and corporation to fight it out, hiring the services of mercenaries who in turn constituted the forces of the West-world in perpetual training. Rules grew up to govern such fracases, and a special department of government evolved. The Military Category became as acceptable as any other, and the mercenary a valued—even idolized—member of society. And the field became practically the only one in which a status quo-oriented socio-economic system allowed for advancement in caste.

And the public had their circuses, government-sanctioned and controlled.

Mauser had restrained Max's enthusiasm long enough for the two to stow a hearty meal beneath their belts. It was his experience that things didn't really get underway until noon or after.

They ate their breakfasts, which Max had whipped up after a quick trip to the Haer supply depot, and then headed into town in Mauser's hovercar.

Max, wearing the vividly colored beret which was the headgear of the Rank Private of the Haer forces, was impressed all over again by the vehicle.

He said, "Damn, Captain, you must've had to pay plenty to get a private license for this job!"

"As a matter of fact," Mauser replied, "the license didn't cost me anything."

Max shot him a look of disbelief. "I know better than that, sir. Getting a private license is almost like impossible. In fact," he looked sidewise at Joe, "I heard that private licenses haven't been available to anyone for years—the parking and pollution problems, they have to keep them under control, and all that. You *have* a license for this, sir? I mean, I ain't saying it's wrong or nothing, but I have heard you can operate one without a license, long as you don't get caught . . ."

Mauser swerved to avoid a horse-drawn army ambulance heading back toward the reservation. The hovercraft slowed to one side, then fishtailed before the vertical gyros took over and stabilized it. "Max, you have a lot to learn about People's Capitalism as a social system. Sure, I have a license—I don't need any flak from Category Security."

"Then how'd you get it?"

"Max, you're right—no new licenses have been issued in years. But one came with this baby. Sort of a built-in license."

"I don't get it."

"Let's just put it this way, Max. If you could afford to buy this hovercraft, you would have a license. The manufacturers make sure of that."

Max was still confused. "But you just said that the license didn't cost you anything—sure it did! You had to buy this rig."

"Wrong again, Max." Mauser chuckled. "It was given to me by a rather zealous fan. Remind me to tell you about it someday."

Joe guided the vehicle into an underground parking garage owned by Vacuum Tube Transport, considering as he did this the irony of his owning a vehicle manufactured by one of Vacuum Tube's competitors.

It was also an irony that mechanized transportation was exempted from the rule that forbade any technology post-dating 1900 to be used in the vicinity of a military reservation. Practical it was, but still ironic. And it was going to work to his advantage, in the coming fracas.

The vehicle safely parked, Mauser and Max lost no time in making their way up to ground level, passing along the way a Rank Private in the Haer kilts who patrolled the depths of the garage. He looked unhappy, having had the bad luck to draw guard duty on election day. Mauser flicked him a quick salute; Max looked smug.

They emerged from the entrance tunnel into bright sunlight. On foot, the city presented a facade of riotous color—special decorations brought out for the occasion.

Joe Mauser and Max Mainz strolled the streets of Kingston in an extreme of atmosphere seldom to be enjoyed. Not only was the advent of a divisional-magnitude fracas only a short period away, but the freedom of an election day pervaded, as well. The carnival, the Mardi Gras, the fete, the fiesta—all rolled into one. Election day, when each aristocrat became only a man and every man an aristocrat, free of all of society's artificially conceived, caste-perpetuating rituals and taboos.

Carnival! The day was young, but already the streets were thick with revelers, with dancers, with drunks. A score of bands played, youngsters ran about attired in costume, usually military. Food and liquor of all varieties were to be found at every corner and in booths lining the streets. The cost—free, on election day, ostensibly borne by the ubiquitous government, but shared in fact by the Uppers whose products were represented. On the outskirts of town were mechanized amusements—rides for the thrill-seeking, and houses of fun and sensuous pleasure. And, for those who could not bear to be away from their favorite telly shows for even a day, giant screens were set up every few blocks.

Carnival!

Max said happily, taking it all in, "You drink, Joe?

Or maybe you like trank better." He rolled Mauser's first name over his tongue with obvious relish.

Mauser wondered in amusement how often the little man had found occasion to call a Mid-Middle by his first name. For that matter, how often did Max have occasion even to talk with someone as far above his caste as Joe? Except in Category Military, where lines were of necessity not quite so strictly drawn, one could easily go through life without coming into close contact with fellow citizens more than one or two ranks above or below the class into which he had been born.

"No trank," he said. "I've tried it a couple times, and I find that I have enough delusions and illusions without resorting to hallucinogens. Same with weed. Alcohol for me—mankind's old faithful."

"Yeah, but," Max debated, "get high on alcohol and you end up with a hangover in the morning. But trank? You wake up with a smile."

"And a desire for more trank to keep the mood going," Joe said wryly. "Get smashed on alcohol and you suffer for it eventually. That makes you think twice about giving too much of your time—and of yourself—to it."

"Well, that's one way of looking at it," Max argued happily. They were passing into a street of eateries and hotels. "So, let's start off with a couple of quick ones in this Upper joint."

Joe looked the place over. He didn't know Kingston overly well, but by the appearance of the building and its entryway, it was probably the swankiest hotel in town. Fine. This place would doubtless be an improvement over what either of them was used to; and he had always appreciated the greater comfort and the better service of his Middle-caste bars,

restaurants and hotels over the ones he had patron-
ized when a Lower.

Unlike Max, however, he didn't have an immediate desire to push into the preserves of the Uppers;
not until he had won their status rightfully. He was
not a ragged child, peering wistfully through the
window of a toy shop; he wanted to march in the
front door of the shop and take to himself those
playthings that appealed.

But on this occasion the little fellow wanted to
drink at an Upper bar. Very well, it was election
day. "Let's go," he said.

The uniform of a Rank Captain of the Military
Category offered little to indicate caste level, and given
the correct air of nonchalance Joe Mauser ordinarily
would have been able to go anywhere, without so much
as raising an eyebrow—until he presented his credit
card, which indicated his caste. But Max was another
thing. He was obviously a Lower, and probably a
Low-Lower at that.

But space was made for them at a bar packed with
election-day celebrants, politicians involved in the
day's speeches and voting, higher-ranking officers of
the Haer forces having a day off, and various Uppers
of both sexes in town for the excitement of the fracas.

One or two representatives of Middle and Lower
castes were also defiantly present. Mauser knew that
thousands more Middles and Lowers would have
liked to walk into a place like this today, but couldn't
raise themselves above their ingrained, cultivated
sense of what was *right*. They did not, as Max would
put it, have the guts to intrude.

"Beer," Mauser said to the bartender, specifying
his favorite brand.

"Not me," Max crowed. "Champagne. Only the
best for Max Mainz. Give me some of that champagne liquor I always hear about."

Mauser had the bill credited to his card, and they took their bottles and glasses to a newly abandoned table. The place was too packed for them to have awaited the services of a waiter, although Max probably would have loved such attention. Lower, and even Middle bars and restaurants, were universally automated.

Max looked about the room in awe, taking in the opulent decor, the flashy costumes of the Uppers. "This is living," he announced. "I wonder what they'd say if I went to the desk and ordered a room."

Mauser wasn't as highly impressed as his batman. He'd often stayed in hostelries as sumptuous as this, though only of Middle status. Kingston's best was on the mediocre side. He said, "They'd probably tell you they were filled up."

Max was indignant. "Because I'm a Lower? It's *election* day."

Mauser said mildly, "No, because they probably *are* filled up. But for that matter, they might brush you off. It's not as though an Upper went to a Middle or Lower hotel and asked for accommodations. But what do you want—justice?" He sipped his beer. "There ain't none, not in this world. Not unless you've got the power to *make* it, or buy it."

Max dropped the subject. He poured a glass, put it to his lips. "Hey!" he complained, "what'd they give me? This stuff tastes like weak hard cider!"

Joe laughed. "What did you think it was going to taste like?"

Max took another unhappy sip. "I thought it was supposed to be the best drink you could buy. You know, really strong. It's just bubbly wine."

Before Joe could reply, a voice said dryly, "Your companion doesn't seem to be a connoisseur of the French vintages, Captain."

Mauser turned. Balt Haer and two others occupied the table next to them.

Mauser chuckled amiably and said, "Truthfully, it was my own reaction, the first time I drank sparkling wine, sir."

"Indeed," Haer said. "I can imagine." He fluttered a hand. "Lieutenant Colonel Paul Warren of Marshal Cogswell's staff, and Captain Lajos Arpad, of Budapest—Captain Joseph Mauser."

Joe came to his feet and clicked his heels, bowing from the waist in approved military protocol. The other two didn't bother to come to their feet, but did shake hands.

The Sov officer said, disinterestedly, "Ah yes, this is one of your fabulous customs, isn't it? On an election day, everyone is quite entitled to go anywhere. Anywhere at all. And to, ah"—he made a sound somewhat like a giggle—"associate with anyone at all."

Mauser resumed his seat, then looked at him. "That is correct. A custom going back to the early history of the country, when all men were considered equal in such matters as law and civil rights. Gentlemen, may I present Rank Private Max Mainz, my orderly."

Balt Haer, who had obviously had a few, looked at him dourly. "You can carry these things to the point of being ludicrous, Captain. For a man with your ambitions, I'm surprised."

The infantry officer—Lieutenant Colonel Warren, of Stonewall Cogswell's staff—said idly, "Ambitions? Does the captain have ambitions? How in Zen can a Middle have ambitions, Balt?" He stared at Mauser superciliously, then scowled. "Haven't I seen you somewhere before?"

Mauser said evenly, "Yes, sir. Five years ago we

were both with the marshal in a fracas on the Little Big Horn reservation. Your company was pinned down on a knoll by a battery of field artillery. The marshal sent me to your relief. We sneaked in, up an arroyo, and were able to get most of you out."

A strange look came over Warren's face. "Yes, I was wounded . . ." he said. His superior air had evaporated.

Mauser said nothing. He knew what was going through Warren's mind now, and felt a certain embarrassment for the man. Only he and Joe knew it, but Warren had just put himself on the spot with his silly Upper posturing.

Max, meanwhile, was more than a little unhappy by now. These officers were talking above his head, even as they ignored him. He had a vague feeling that he was being defended by Captain Mauser, but he didn't know how, or why.

Balt Haer had been occupied in shouting for fresh drinks. Now he turned back to the table. "Well, Colonel, it's all very secret, these ambitions of Captain Mauser. I understand he's been an aide de camp to Marshal Cogswell in the past, but the marshal will be distressed to learn that on this occasion Captain Mauser has a secret by which he expects to rout your forces."

Mauser suppressed, just barely, the urge to smash the young Haer's mocking face. Someone else should have done that long ago—and often.

"Indeed, yes, the captain is quite the strategist," Balt Haer continued, then laughed abruptly. "And what good will this do the captain? Why, on my father's word, if he succeeds, all efforts will be made to make the captain a caste equal of ours. Not just on election day, mind you, but all three hundred sixty-five days of the year."

Mauser was on his feet, face expressionless. He said, "Shall we go, Max? Gentlemen, it's been a pleasure. Colonel Arpad, a privilege to meet you. Colonel Warren, a pleasure to renew acquaintance." He turned and, trailed by his orderly, left.

Lieutenant Colonel Warren, pale, was on his feet, too.

Balt Haer was chuckling. "Sit down, Paul. Sit down. Not important enough to be angry about. The man's a clod."

Warren looked at him bleakly. "I wasn't angry, Balt. The last time I saw Captain Mauser, I was slung over his shoulder. He carried, tugged, and dragged me some two miles through enemy fire."

Balt Haer carried it off with a shrug. "Well, that's his profession. Category Military. A mercenary for hire. I assume he received his pay."

"He could have left me," Warren persisted. "In that particular situation, common sense dictated that he leave me."

Balt Haer was unmoved, even annoyed. "Well, then we see what I've contended all along. The ambitious captain doesn't have common sense."

Colonel Paul Warren shook his head. "You're wrong there. Common sense Joseph Mauser has. Considerably ability, he has. He's one of the best combat men in the field. But I'd hate to serve under him."

The Hungarian was interested. "But why?"

"Because he doesn't have luck, and in the dill you need luck." Warren grunted in sour memory. "Had the telly cameras been focused on Joe Mauser, there at the Little Big Horn, he would have been a month-long sensation with the telly buffs, with all that means." He grunted again. "There wasn't a telly team within a mile."

"The captain probably didn't realize that," Balt Haer snorted. "Otherwise his heroics would have been modified. The captain is an ambitious man, Paul. Like most of his ilk, he does nothing out of altruism."

Warren clenched his fists, leaned toward Haer. Abruptly he relaxed and sat down. Haer, apparently unaware that death had brushed his elbow, guzzled his drink and turned to call for more.

When Haer's attention had returned to the table, Warren said, "Possibly we should discuss the business before us. If your father is in agreement, the fracas can begin in three days." He turned to the representative of the Sov-world. "You have satisfied yourselves that neither force is violating the Disarmament Pact?"

Lajos Arpad nodded. "We will wish to have observers on the field itself, of course. But preliminary observation has been satisfied." He had been interested in the play between these two and the Lower-caste officer. He said now, "Pardon me. As you know, this is my first visit to the, uh, *West.* I am fascinated. If I understand what just transpired, your Captain Mauser is a capable junior officer ambitious to rise in rank and status in your society." He looked at Balt Haer. "Why are you opposed to his so rising?"

Young Haer was suddenly testy. "Of what purpose is an Upper caste if every Tom, Dick, and Harry enters it at will? In theory, I am not opposed to genuinely suitable Middles being bounced in caste, but this man is an obvious clod, as you undoubtedly could see. Imagine entering a respectable public room in the presence of his batman!"

Warren looked at the door through which Mauser and Max had exited from the cocktail lounge. He opened his mouth to say something, closed it again, and held his peace.

The Hungarian said, looking from one of them to the other, "In the Sov-world we seek out such ambitious persons and utilize their abilities."

Lieutenant Colonel Warren laughed abruptly. "So do we here, *theoretically*. We are *free*, whatever that means. However," he added sarcastically, "it does help to have good connections, relatives in positions of prominence, abundant shares of good stocks, that sort of thing. And these things one is born with, Colonel Arpad; such are not given."

The Sov military observer clucked his tongue. "An indication of a declining society."

Balt Haer turned on him. "And is it any different in your world?" he said, without bothering to suppress the sneer in his voice. "Is it merely coincidence that the best positions in the Sov-world are held by Party members, and that it is all but impossible for anyone not born of Party-member parents to become one? Are not the best schools filled with the children of Party members? Are not only Party members allowed to keep servants? And isn't it so that—"

Lieutenant Colonel Warren said, "Gentlemen, let us not start World War Three at this spot, at this late occasion."

It was at that moment a harried hotel employee approached and said, "Colonel Arpad? Is one of you gentlemen Colonel Lajos Arpad?"

Warren said, "This is Colonel Arpad."

"You are wanted on the phone, sir."

The Hungarian seemed somewhat surprised. However, he shrugged slight shoulders in his tight uniform tunic and came to his feet. "If you gentlemen will excuse me . . ." He bowed from the waist, turned, and followed the bellhop.

He was taken into a small room leading off the reception offices and containing little save a terminal, a small desk, and several chairs.

The bellhop said, "It should be fairly quiet in here, sir," and left, closing the door behind him.

The terminal's screen was blank, but the connect indicator was on. The Hungarian took the chair before it, frowning now. He said, "Colonel Arpad."

A mechanical voice issued from the screen. "Scrambled."

The colonel's eyebrows, so thin as to be suspect of having been plucked, went up. He looked about the room, came back to his feet, and checked the door. He then returned to the phone and, taking a device from an inner tunic pocket, attached it to the terminal.

The screen lit up and the man who had introduced himself to Lieutenant Colonel Fodor as Smith said, "Comrade Arpad, please excuse this intrusion."

Arpad was scowling puzzlement now. "Very well, Troll. How in the world did you know where I was? And what are you doing away from Greater Washington?"

"I spotted you, Comrade Colonel, quite by accident. You've been in the company of a man I was . . . assigned to."

"I see. Well?"

"There are some uncommon angles, Comrade Colonel. In view of your being on the scene, I thought I had better check with you."

"So?" Arpad prompted.

"The man who just left—this Captain Mauser. I have been given the assignment of eliminating him."

"Eliminating him!" Arpad fairly shouted in surprise. "Eliminating him from what? That is, for what reason?"

"Evidently, the orders came indirectly from Field Marshal Cogswell, in command of Continental Hovercraft."

Arpad stared at Smith's image in the screen. "Marshal Cogswell doesn't order the assassination of junior officers of the forces opposing him."

He who had named himself Smith said nothing.

Lajos Arpad thought about it, scowling his disbelief. He ran a manicured thumbnail along a moustache so trim as to be all but pretty. "Why?" he asked. "Why does Cogswell wish this Captain Mauser killed?"

Smith shook his head. "I don't know, Comrade Colonel."

"Obviously something to do with the fracas coming up, eh? There could be no other reason."

"I do not know, Comrade Colonel. I was hired by their chief of intelligence. It is obviously very hush-hush. The pay was excellent."

Colonel Lajos Arpad was unhappy. His little moustache twitched. "When are you to accomplish this, Troll?"

"Just so it is before the fracas, Comrade Colonel."

"I do not like it. It may not be advisable to proceed."

"Comrade Colonel, if I fail in the assignment, I am afraid it may affect my cover. As it is, my reputation is such that I am beginning to make the inner contacts we wished. I am infiltrating with considerable success and being used by the highest of their power elite in their more desperate confrontations with one another. This is a relatively mild assignment, but I cannot afford to drop it. It would destroy the image I have so carefully built."

"I understand all that," Arpad said impatiently. "But I want to know why it is deemed necessary to eliminate this junior officer."

Now it was Smith-Troll who was unhappy. "That won't be easy, Comrade Colonel." He frowned. "Do you . . . think possibly it has something to do with violating the Disarmament Pact?"

"Very possibly," the Hungarian mused. "Don't read more into the Pact than is to be found here, Troll. For instance, are you aware that many elements of military technology are not used in these fracases simply because there is not substantial difference between their ancient and modern implementations? Solid-fuel rockets, for instance."

Smith-Troll said, puzzlement in his voice, "Yes, Comrade Colonel."

Arpad said impatiently, "The point I was making is that Budapest would not like to discover that the West-world was 'experimenting' with rockets to the extent of turning them out in factories supposedly devoted to the fracases. I am not saying that *is* what Mauser is up to, and is what Cogswell fears; I am simply pointing out that we must keep constant track of such mysterious matters as these, in case they lead to matters more sinister.

"Find out why it is that the captain has been ordered destroyed, Troll."

"Yes, Comrade Colonel. I will try."

The colonel's face was suddenly both empty and cold. "You will do better than simply try, Comrade Troll."

CHAPTER NINE

Joe Mauser and Max Mainz made their way down the street, pushing and wedging themselves through the flocks of revelers, many of whom were already either stoned or drunk. Mauser was inwardly fuming, but Max had already forgotten the hassle in the hotel, in view of the fun at hand.

"Hey, Joe," he chortled, "lookit those two mopsies over there giving us the eye! What do you say— should we give 'em a fling?"

Mauser didn't even look at the girls in question. "No, there's plenty more where they came from," he grumbled. "Pick up a couple of curves now, and you'll be stuck with them for the rest of the day."

"Well, maybe that wouldn't be so bad. That little short one's got a lot of sparkle."

"Yeah, and you'd like to make her sparkle even more, I know." His mind wasn't on the conversation. He was fuming over Balt Haer's attempt to humiliate him. Thank whatever gods applied that he hadn't told that asshole his plans. The little jerk would have spread it all over town, thereby blowing his chances— or, worse yet, fired Mauser on some pretext and taken Joe's plan for his own.

Would he have done that? A sudden thought

brought Joe up short. What if Balt Haer actually *wanted* his side to lose? His actions had certainly given plenty of indication that it wouldn't bother him if Vacuum Tube Transport lost the fracas, and he *had* seemed to be doing his best to steer Joe Mauser away from employment with his father's concern. And hadn't he scorned Mauser's advice?

And there was something else . . . Joe shook his head. He couldn't quite put his finger on it. On the face of it, though, Balt Haer was hoping that Vacuum Tube would lose the fracas with Continental Hovercraft.

But why? Surely not just to spite his father, for whom he apparently had no little hatred. Balt Haer's fortunes were tied up with those of Vacuum Tube—or were they? Now it came to Joe; Balt Haer had called him a fool for investing everything he owned in Vacuum Tube Transport. If the younger Haer knew something that Joe didn't and was, in fact, working for a defeat for Vacuum Tube, then he would have good reason to react that way.

Joe nodded again, then returned to his surroundings. He had stopped and the crowds were flowing around him like the rushing waters of a river around a boulder.

He looked around, spotted a bar that was more suited to his tastes. "Come on," he snapped to Max. "Let's go in here and get a man's drink."

With some reluctance Max tore his eyes away from the girls, who were by now waving. "What's this, a Middle bar? I never been in a Middle bar before. Let's go!"

Inside it was cool and dark—and crowded. It was easily as crowded as it had been in the hotel, but here were to be found a wider variety of castes among the celebrants. Evidently, those of Lower status found it easier to intrude on a Middle-caste establishment than on an Upper one. A few Uppers on a slumming expedition were also present. The fact that they were wearing their older clothing couldn't disguise their mannerisms, that aristocratic air. Moreover, Scottish and Irish tweeds, no matter what their age, were a far cry from the synthetic, disposable textiles that most Middles and all Lowers wore.

The traffic into and out of the place was brisk; Joe and Max had to wait only a moment before finding an empty booth. Without waiting to ask Max his choice, Joe punched in an order for two double rums. The center of the table sank, then rose with the double shot glasses a few seconds later.

Mauser held his drink up. "Here's to the Upper caste," he toasted, sarcasm heavy in his voice.

"Yeah, OK," Max said, uncomprehending. "We gotta have somebody smart to run the country. You won't hear me saying anything against the government or the old-time ways. What was good enough for—"

"Screw the government!" Mauser spat. He knocked back the large drink.

Max blinked at him, took down half of his own rum. Then he blinked at the glass. "Wow!" he gasped. "That packs a helluva punch!"

"Want another?"

"Well, not 'til I finish this. I don't want to get drenched this early in the day, and that champagne was stronger than I thought."

Mauser punched another double for himself. As he reached for the drink, he recalled where he had picked up his taste for dark rum: down in the islands, that time with Jim Hawkins when they'd fought on the Jamaica Military Reservation. The whole fracas had been a farce, a continuing comedy with both sides hard put to come together in the inland tropical jungle. At least there'd been few casualties—hangovers, yes, and quite a few AWOLs thanks to the local prostitutes who'd infiltrated the reservation—but neither side lost more than a dozen men. Jim, as Mauser recalled, had been disgusted with the whole mess, having looked forward to the experience of jungle fighting.

Max was looking at him. "You taking another one, Joe? You sure can put 'em down!"

Mauser had put his credit card in the slot and left it there, when he ordered the first round. Now he pulled it out abruptly. He quickly finished the drink in front of him and stood. "Let's get out of here."

"Well, all right," Max said. "I wonder if those curves found anyone yet?"

As they pushed their way through the crowd to the door, Mauser remarked, "Max, never run after a girl or a trolley—there's always another one coming along."

Max laughed unnecessarily long and loud at that one, and was still chuckling as they emerged on the sidewalk. There they found the press even more dense than it had been when they'd entered the bar.

"Looks like it's cranking up to full bore," Mauser remarked, moving to a relatively quiet spot near a wall.

"Yeah!" Max replied. "This is living. I should have crossed over to Military years ago!"

"In which case, chances are you'd be dead by now," Joe told him.

"Well, you're not, and you've been at it a long time."

"Borrowed time, Max," Mauser said soberly. "Time

borrowed from a lot of good men over the years, men who aren't around to talk about it now."

A bevy of girls, at least a dozen all attired in an imitation of the Haer uniform, suddenly swarmed around them. One threw a handful of confetti in Joe's face, and laughed at his grumbles of protest. Her eyes were bright with trank.

"Surrender! Surrender!" they were yelling. "You've copped one, and we've got the cure!"

The small mob ebbed, flowed, ebbed again, chanting, yelling, laughing. Mauser looked around, seeking a way to lose himself in the greater crowd. When he looked back, Max was gone. That wasn't exactly a surprise. He had most likely taken off with one of the girls, impatient with Joe's poor humor. Possibly Mauser would run into him again later in the day or evening. In the meantime, he wasn't particularly sorry to be left to his own devices. He wasn't in the frame of mind to keep pace with the smaller man's partying.

Mauser pushed and wedged his way down the street, going nowhere in particular but feeling a need to move. From time to time he stood in doorways, watching the musicians and drunks and low-lifes shamble by. Eventually he came to another bar—there seemed to be an inordinate number of them in Kingston—and entered, grateful to get out of the riot.

There were no empty tables, nor would he have taken one. He was alone and had no wish to monopolize that amount of room, or to share the space, since that would inevitably lead to conversation with strangers. Instead, he found a corner at the bar and fished out his credit card, looking about as he did so.

It was another Middle establishment, which suited him fine. He wanted neither the plush atmosphere of an Upper bar nor the noise, confusion, and unkempt qualities of a Lower dive.

He put the card in the slot at the edge of the bar and started to punch his order.

A man in civilian dress moved toward his end of the bar. "Buy you a drink, soldier?" he said.

Irritated, Mauser said, "I don't swing that way, thanks." He pointedly focused his attention on ordering his drink.

"Uh, nothing like that, friend. Just being hospitable."

"No, thanks."

"Why not?"

Mauser felt a flash of anger; the whole world irritated him at the moment. He looked up and said, "Because I don't particularly like buffs."

"I don't blame you," the other said. "Neither do I."

Joe regarded him. "Neither do you what?"

"Look," the stranger said, "I'm in town on business. I don't follow the fracases. I haven't seen one in ten years or more. There's enough violence out on the street without having to organize it."

Joe looked him over. He saw a rather wiry type, conservatively dressed, not particularly outstanding in any respect. He seemed to mean what he was saying, and Joe felt some slight remorse at having been so short with him. "What're you drinking?" he asked.

"Barack," the man replied. "Try one. Name's Smith."

"Mine's Mauser." They shook hands. "What's barack?"

"A brandy made from apricots. Very good."

Joe made a face. "Sounds too sweet. I've been drinking rum."

"Have a rum, then. But barack's not sweet. It's

distilled, and re-distilled, until there's no sweetness to it. It has a very distant flavor of apricots, but no sweetness."

"All right," Mauser said. "I'll have a barack."

The drink was delivered by the auto-bar, and Mauser motioned toward Smith with the glass, as though in toast, and knocked it back. He was somewhat surprised. The stuff was as strong as any liquor he could remember drinking, stronger than the potent rum he'd had earlier. It was dry too, dry enough to curl his tongue.

Smith said, "Zen! You're not supposed to toss it off like that. Barack is sipping liquor."

"It is at that," Mauser agreed. "The next one's on me. I'm in no mood for slow drinking, though."

"Something wrong?"

"Why don't you like the fracases?" Joe countered, ignoring the question.

"I told you. There's enough violence in the world without asking for it."

"There is at that." He was beginning to feel his drinks. After all, he'd had nothing to eat since breakfast, and it was well into the afternoon now. He added, "I don't like them either," and was mildly surprised to find that he had a slight slur in his voice.

"Oh?" Smith said, an inflection of understanding in his tone. "But you're scheduled for this one coming up?"

Joe finished the new barack and blinked as he spotted a fresh one in front of him. He took it up. "Yeah, but this is the last one. The final fracas for Mauser."

"That's interesting," Smith said. "Have enough savings to call it quits, eh?"

"Not yet." Joe chortled, more to himself than aloud. "But after this one, after this one, old pro Mauser calls it quits." He tossed back the new drink and looked at the order board owlishly. He had really been knocking them back these past few minutes. But what the hell? Why not? He seldom overindulged, and this was an election day. There was no duty. Tomorrow he'd be elbow-deep in work, whipping those inexperienced, trank-happy yokels into some semblance of Rank Privates. Tomorrow was another day.

His newfound friend put his credit card in the payment slot and ordered up yet another round.

"Figure on making your bundle on this one, eh?" Smith said, pushing the new drink in Joe's direction.

"Yeah," Mauser confided. "I got a new gimmick that'll really set them back." He scowled, trying to bring something to mind that he knew he should recall, but failing. Something was wrong.

"Hey, you're not drinking!" he accused Smith.

Smith held up his own glass, which was half full. "Yes, I am. What kind of gimmick? I'm afraid I'm not knowledgeable about the ins and outs of the fracas."

Joe said, "What'd you say the name of this drink was?"

"Barack."

"Where's it from? I never heard of it."

Smith hesitated only momentarily. "I think it originally came from Hungary. But they must make it over here now; I don't imagine they import it from the Sov-world."

"Hungary?" Mauser said. Then it snapped into focus; it came to him why he had thought that something was wrong. He had glimpsed, fleetingly, Smith's credit card.

The name on the card hadn't been Smith.

Some part of his mind had apparently been working for him, immune to the alcoholic fog he was in.

He said, "Your name isn't Smith."

Smith looked at him and took a small plastic case from his jerkin pocket. He opened it and extracted a white pill, which he popped into his mouth. "What difference does it make? We'll never see each other again after today. What was it you were saying about a special gimmick that was going to pay off so well in this fracas?"

Mauser's eyes narrowed. He picked up his glass, to finish it off, then set it down. "Screw off, funker," he snarled.

"What's the matter, Joe?"

Joe Mauser looked at him. He shook his head to clear away some of the brandy fumes. "How'd you know my name was Joe?"

"Uh, you told me."

"Like hell I did! I told you my name was Mauser, that was all." He turned abruptly and made his way toward the door to the street.

Smith looked after him and swore beneath his breath.

CHAPTER TEN

Out on the street, the change in temperature hit Joe Mauser hard. It had been cool and comfortable in the bar, but the afternoon heat was oppressive out here. Nor did the milling, perspiring mob make it any more comfortable.

The fog rolled in on him.

When it rolled out, he was several blocks away from the bar where he had met the civilian who called himself Smith. Save for a slight irritation, Mauser had all but forgotten the man. He was concentrating now on clearing the haze from his mind.

Somebody was saying to him. "Hi, Major. You look a bit worse for the wear."

She was strictly in current style, with a pile of flaming red curls on her head, a small, alert face, and skin like cream. Her bright blue eyes were crinkled in amusement. And she was wearing a takeoff on the Haer uniform, as so many of the female contingent of the celebrating crowds were today. On her, Joe decided, the Vacuum-Tube Transport colors looked fetching, particularly since the material and the tailoring were not mass-produced.

"I *feel* a bit the worst for wear," Joe told her ruefully. "Take it from an old hand—don't mix rum and barack!"

She stood there before him, hands on hips, legs spread slightly. "I could ask you what barack is," she grinned, "but to hell with it. I can guess. Major, I feel a good deed coming on. How would you like a sandwich, or maybe two, and a cold beer to sober up on?"

The situation was not exactly new to him, only a slight variation on a theme. He shook his head to achieve a modicum of clarity. She was as attractive an item as he had seen today. Her voice denoted education, she was most certainly neither drunk nor stoned, and she seemed to have a sense of humor. And if there was more in the offing, he certainly wouldn't run from it.

Joe Mauser took her in again. Yes, there was a glint of amusement, and something more, in her eye.

Joe took a deep breath. "A sandwich, I could use. Where can we buy one?"

She laughed and took his arm, pulling him along with her. "Major, I wouldn't wish a restaurant-bought snack on you in this town today, even if I were a secret agent for old Baron Zwerdling."

He was mildly surprised. "You mean you'll make it yourself?" He didn't know where she was taking him and didn't particularly care.

"Zen forbid! Here we are."

She had led him up a side street to where a natty, low-slung hoverlimo was parked. He recognized it vaguely as a model produced in Common Europe.

She opened the door for him in a mock gesture, helped him in as though he were elderly, then went around the car and slid in behind the driver's controls.

He tried to rally. "Where away?" he said.

"I'll never tell," she told him, dropping the lift lever. Air-cushion borne, the vehicle slipped slowly ahead, gathering speed.

She touched a button. His window opened and he breathed in the cool air gratefully. "That's better," he said.

She looked over at him from the side of her eyes. "Anything'd be better. You should have seen yourself coming up the street, tacking to starboard."

They were quickly out of town and up the road that bordered the Hudson River, passing endless apple orchards. After a few miles, she turned to the left, over an air cushion strip that seemed to be private.

"Where're we going?" he asked again.

"To my place," she said easily.

"Oh?" He looked over at her. She was a bit older than he had at first thought. Probably in her early thirties, rather than her mid-twenties. There were the very slight lines at the sides of her eyes, very slight wrinkles at her throat. She was probably a fairly well-to-do Upper Middle, Joe guessed. All of which was for the good. He had certain masculine qualms about the young girls on the make who often turned up in the fracas staging cities.

He said, "You live here in the Catskills?"

"Sometimes." She brushed it off. "Say, you don't appear to be the bottle-baby type, Major. Some special event?"

He was mildly irritated by her prying. "Not really. Just got going too early on the festival."

They turned up another side road, then rushed by a sizable estate, getting a fast view of gardens, lawns, tennis courts, an extensive swimming pool, before they were at the door of the house. It was on the ultra-modern side, and Joe Mauser wasn't particularly taken by the trends in architecture this past decade or two. However, who was he to complain?

Offhand, he couldn't remember ever having been in quite this opulent an establishment.

"You live *here?*" he said.

"As much as anywhere," she said, popping her door open. She was out and around and going through the mocking motions of helping him again. However, Mauser moved quickly, and was up almost before she reached him.

She ran her eyes up and down him. "Recovering already, eh?" she said. "Without my ministrations, even. You're a fake, Major. I don't think you were really in distress at all."

She turned and skipped up the steps of the entry, and he plodded along behind. He wasn't feeling as recovered as all that. Somewhat to his surprise, he noted that the day was well along. He couldn't remember what had happened to it all. Possibly he had been out of it longer than he thought. Or possibly he had been in some of the bars longer than he had thought. Or in more of them. This wasn't his usual style, and he regretted now having started on the binge.

As it turned out, the house was plush, but only moderately large. Mauser looked about as he followed the girl down a hall. There was a library to one side, a dining room to the other. Somehow, it all had an unlived-in quality. He had run into the same thing before in the homes of the very rich, a sterile something that gave you the feeling that nobody, even the proud owner of the overly swank house or apartment, was really comfortable there.

He wondered vaguely what type of home man would gravitate toward if nothing but his real desire, his real idea of comfort, was involved. No status symbolism, no keeping up with the neighbors, no artificial stimulus to own or control more rooms than needed. He grunted in amusement. He had known Uppers, in the Category Military, whose idea of the best of all possible times was to retreat to Alaska and spend a few weeks in a one-room log cabin.

"What's funny?" she said. "By the way, I'm Ann."

"I'm Joe. This is a pretty luxurious layout you've got here."

"Like it?" She led him into a sunken living room, complete with a monstrous fireplace and other anachronisms from yesteryear.

"No."

He had decided by now that she wasn't an Upper-Middle. Not with this kind of wealth to throw around. She was probably at least a Low-Upper.

While he sank into a comfort-couch, she put her hands on her hips again, in the stance in which he had first seen her, and regarded him, a small frown creasing her brow.

"Hmm," she said, "at least you've sobered up enough to make cracks. You want some food first, or a drink?" She made a motion with her hand. "The bar's over there. Do you know how to mix your own, or have you used auto-bars all your life?"

There had been a slight tone of deprecation in that last. Joe looked at her. "I can mix my own," he said gently. "However, I think I'd prefer the sandwich right now."

She made a mock salute, did an about-face, and marched from the room, the Haer kilts swaying bewitchingly about her full hips.

She was gone long enough for Joe to have second thoughts about that drink she had offered. He was either going to have to get some food on his stomach, or take up the blast where he had left off.

When she did return, his eyebrows rose.

She carried a tray; on it were three smaller platters, each piled high with sandwiches. They were elaborate productions, and he doubted that she had made them. There were also smaller dishes with nuts, crackers, small cakes, and such. All in all, it seemed the kind of food to settle an alcoholic stomach on the quick—if it wasn't *too* far gone.

She placed the tray before him and gestured for him to dig in.

But it hadn't been the food he was staring at.

Ann had gotten into something thin and slick and . . . just enough that she could still be considered clothed.

He selected a ham and Swiss cheese sandwich, and glanced at her as he took his first bite. He wasn't completely unknowledgeable about food, although he made no pretense of being a gourmet. The cheese was undoubtedly from Switzerland and the ham had never seen a government processor.

She said brightly, "Beer? I have some real *pivo* from Belgrade."

"What's *pivo*?"

"The best beer in the world. Serbian. Very strong, very dark, very heavy."

He took up another sandwich. "From the Sovworld, eh? You do have expensive tastes. There doesn't seem to be anybody else around . . . do you own this place?"

"I rent it, Joe," she said, her face expressionless. "I let the servants off for the day."

Joe said slowly, around the sandwich, "You rent it just for a few weeks, immediately before and during a fracas?"

The shine he had noticed in her eyes earlier, and hadn't quite understood, was there again. She leaned forward, showed the tip of her tongue, and licked her full lower lip. She had slid slightly closer to him, and her new position was even more revealing. She was an unbelievingly attractive woman.

"How did you guess?" she said. "I'm a real gone fracas buff, Joe. I . . . I *love* it. The telly's all right, but—you know what? This house is built very advantageously. From the tower, with the telescope, you can see an amazing amount of the reservation. If you have the good luck for the fighting to swing down this way, you can often pick it up live."

"I see."

She moved slightly, edging closer. Joe started to move toward her, then stopped; he would let her make the moves. After all, she was the instigator here.

She said, "Joe. Captain Joe Mauser. The old pro of them all. Joe, I've followed the fracases since I was a kid. I simply can't get enough. I *love* it. I love everything about it. Joe, you know why I brought you here? I know what you like before a fracas."

He sighed. "How'd you know my name? All I told you was Joe." There was a weariness in his voice now.

She smiled slowly at him, her mouth slack.

"I've known your face, your figure, your walk, the tone of your voice even, for more than ten years, Joe Mauser. Since you were no more than a lance corporal. I can remember that time on the Big Sur Reservation in California, when you copped three mini balls and they left you for dead for several hours. And then you spent almost six weeks in the hospital. I can remember that. It was the first time you were ever written up in the buff magazine."

Yes, Joe could remember it, too.

"The articles weren't really about you, though. They dealt mostly with the man in the bed next to yours, Jim Hawkins. You got in on the stories because you became his friend. I remember it all."

And Joe could too. Yes, that's where he had met Jim. Off and on for the next six years or so they had remained buddies, participating in a dozen fracases together. Jim. Come to think of it, Jim wasn't only the best friend he had ever had, he had probably been the only real one he had ever had.

She was saying, "Yes, I know what you boys like, before a fracas, Joe Mauser . . . but first, let's talk about combat a little. Do you remember the first man you ever killed, Joe?"

He remembered, all right. But it wasn't exactly a man. The kid couldn't have been more than seventeen, and it was obviously his first fracas. He had jumped into a shell hole, trying to find cover, but had found Joe there instead. Joe had finished him with a trench knife, but it had taken several hours for the boy to die. Several hours during which Joe couldn't leave, since the whole area was pinned down by a barrage.

Joe said, "No, I can't remember that."

She laughed throatily. "That's the way it is with you mercenaries. It's just a job to you; a good buff can remember better than you can."

She leaned forward again, her eyes hot now, smoldering. "Joe Mauser, I can remember the biggest one you were ever in. I'll tell you about it. Then . . . then you can do whatever you want to me . . . Joe."

He looked at her emptily.

She said, "It was those two big aircraft concerns. Lockheed-Cessna and McDonnell-Boeing. Do you remember what they were fighting about?"

"No," Joe said. "I seldom know what they're fighting about, even at the time."

"Stonewall Cogswell—they were already beginning to call him that—was commanding your flank of the

Lockheed-Cessna forces, but he was only a general then."

Joe said nothing. She licked her lower lip again and went on. "You were a second lieutenant."

So had Jim Hawkins been.

She was saying, "You people were doing all right until Langenscheidt—he was commanding Douglas-Boeing—brought in those portable French machine guns—what do they call them?"

"*Mitrailleuse*."

"Yes. Up until then, in the fracases, machine guns were the heavy type, as was usual pre-20th century. Gatling guns, and Maxims with water-cooled jackets, which have their shortcomings in the field. You can't always find water."

What was with this curve? She was talking shop, like a pro. "No you can't always find water when your gun has a water-cooled jacket," Joe replied, in a weak attempt at conversation. He suddenly found himself dredging up memories—the time on the Chihuahua Reservation when his battalion was completely surrounded and they hadn't even water to drink and were down to one Maxim gun. They had to keep it going or the enemy, largely cavalry, would have overrun them. They had passed a helmet around, and each man had urinated in it. That kept the gun going, and postponed their surrender for a full forty-eight hours. The smell had nearly driven them out of the trenches, though.

And there were other memories, more painful ones.

"But," she continued, "somebody on General Langenscheidt's staff had done some research and came up with the fact that the French had used a light machine gun back in the Franco-Prussian War of 1871, the *mitrailleuse*. And they had them all ready for you."

Mauser said nothing.

Her eyes were wide and shining.

"Cogswell made his mistake when he ordered that charge up the hill. He couldn't have known that a dozen rapid firers were up there. He thought the fracas was in the hat, that one determined charge would end it."

Joe shook his head, as though refuting what was to come. Jim, coming up that hill for him, after the situation had pickled and Joe had been hit. He'd almost made it when the machine guns found him. Joe remembered the bullets ripping into Jim's body, and the . . .

Suddenly, he came to his feet.

"I'll be going now," he said. It had come to him what her game was; she was one of the worst types of buffs, one who was really turned on by violence, by death. She *wanted* him to remember—but no. He moved across the room, toward the door.

"Thanks," he said, "thanks for the lift, the food."

Ann crossed the room, stood before him. She did something that Joe missed, and the thin something that she was wearing dropped to the floor. Joe eyed her, taking in the luscious curves of her body, the sensuous cast of her face.

She moaned. "Joe, take me now. Anything you want, any way you want!"

Even as she reached for him, Mauser was out the door.

He could have taken her limo. It was still parked in front of the house. But he didn't. He walked down the air-cushion strip toward the highway. It would be completely dark in another half hour or so, but he didn't care. He could use the walk.

Very briefly, he wondered if he had made a mistake. Certainly, he had known that she was setting him up, that she was a buff on the make. But the way she was psyched up—she got off on death, and Joe just couldn't bring himself to that. He was more than a little disgusted by it, especially in his present frame of mind.

He was cold sober now. He would have expected his thoughts to be bitter, but they weren't. He was turned off completely, thinking of nothing whatsoever.

The highway wasn't quite so far as he had remembered. He swung out onto the edge of it and turned right and began to walk toward Kingston.

He heard the sound of a car coming up behind him and moved further to the side to avoid it. But it pulled to a stop and a male voice called out, "Want a ride, soldier?"

Mauser shook his head and went on walking. It was a rented car, one of the standard models. "No thanks," he said.

"You better get in, Joe," the voice said.

Joe Mauser came to a halt and peered into the vehicle. For a moment he didn't recognize the man, but then it came back to him. The fellow next to him in the bar, the one who had introduced him to that Hungarian drink, barack. Mauser had been pretty well drenched at the time, but he knew that there was something about the guy that he hadn't liked. He couldn't quite remember what it was . . .

"No, thanks," he said again.

"Come on, come on," the man said impatiently. "I have something I want to talk to you about."

What the hell, Joe thought. He'd changed his mind about that walk. He shrugged, half angrily, and climbed into the car through the door the driver had opened for him.

"I've forgotten your name," he said ungraciously. He was in no mood for amenities.

"Smith," the driver said. "And you're Major Joe Mauser."

He remembered then. Earlier in the day, the man had used Joe's first name, in spite of the fact that Joe had introduced himself only as "Mauser." He felt an edge of caution. It was one thing the girl knowing him, since she was a fracas buff, but this fellow claimed that he didn't follow the fracases, didn't like them.

Smith was saying, "You know, it's lucky I ran into you like this. I have been thinking of something you were saying, back there in the bar."

A small part of Mauser's mind informed him that it wasn't luck that this fellow had run into him again; it was planned. He had heard the car start up behind him after he had come down the side road from Ann's rented house. Smith had obviously trailed him.

There was more to this bird than showed, for sure. Almost instinctively Mauser fell into an act. He slumped back into the corner of his side of the car and muttered, "Mmm . . . am I drenched! You haven't got anything to drink, have you?"

"No," Smith said, even as they surged ahead. "I'm afraid not, but I'll buy you one in Kingston. But meanwhile, Joe, this idea I've had—there's a way we can both accumulate some Basic shares off it."

"How?" Mauser slurred. He was thinking furiously. If this so-called Smith had actually followed him since Mauser had left the bar where they had been drinking together, then the last time Smith had seen Joe—just before he had entered the house with Ann—he had indeed been under the weather. Smith probably believed that Joe had had still more to drink inside the house. In short, Smith thought that he was completely drunk. Well, let him. This was getting interesting.

Smith said earnestly, "I don't suppose you know that the odds against Vacuum Tube Transport are something like ten to one?"

"That bad?" Mauser mumbled.

"Yes, at least that bad. Now, it so happens I have a bit of Variable Basic Common that I could immediately convert for wagering. At ten to one, even if we split fifty-fifty, that would mean that each of us would have five times the amount I would bet."

"Watcha gonna bet on?" Mauser muttered. Then, for effect, "I feel awful."

"Why, you implied, back there at the bar, that you knew of something that was going to make you rich. That this was to be your last fracas. You were going to be able to retire after it. Now, obviously, the only thing that could make you rich so quickly would be some inside information about this fracas, probably something that will enable Baron Haer to win. You've probably got everything you can get hold of wagered on the outcome. All I'm suggesting is that you let me in on it, and I'll split my earnings with you, fifty-fifty."

Mauser suppressed a chuckle; this fellow thought him very drunk indeed. The scheme he presented was so simplistic that even a child would have been suspicious. Now he knew where the man was coming from; all too many people had been interested in his scheme lately. It remained only to find out who had put this Smith on him—Balt Haer or Marshal Cogswell.

He said finally, "Suppose I don't have any . . . any inside dope?"

"But you do have, Joe Mauser."

"What makes you think that?"

"I just know. And I think it would be wisest if you told me."

"Well, *I* don't."

"You refuse?"

"I haven't anything to tell you. So let's just forget about it."

A gun materialized in Smith's grip. It wasn't the kind of weapon that Joe was used to seeing in the fracases; Smith's gun was small, sleek, and apparently of foreign manufacture. So; the man drank barack from Hungary and carried a gun made outside the West-world. Very interesting.

Smith maneuvered the car to the side of the road and stopped. "Don't move, Mauser," he said, fumbling beneath the seat with his free hand. "I'm going to inject you with a hypo."

"Hypo?" Joe protested, continuing the sham. "I don't want to take nothing, except another drink."

"It's Scop." Smith's voice was smooth but dangerous. "Truth serum. And I'll put this to you very clearly—you either take it, or I'll shoot you square in the stomach and dump you—"

Smith had just made his first serious mistake in a long career of avoiding mistakes. He had no way of knowing that his victim was cold sober. Nor was he aware of the abnormally quick reflexes of old pro Joe Mauser, reflexes that had seen him through a score of times and more in the past two decades.

Mauser's left hand blurred into motion, chopped Smith's gun hand. Smith grunted in surprise, lurched after the weapon. Mauser caught it with his right hand before it hit the floor.

He ground the gun into the agent's ribs. "Now, talk!" he snarled. "Who sent you?"

But Smith was no coward, and no fool. He knew that he couldn't afford to be taken by West-world authorities. They too had Scop, or its equivalent. His whole career would be out in the open. His life would be less than worthless then; if the West-world authorities didn't execute him as a spy, his own organization would extract the price of failure. . . .

He lunged . . .

. . . and Mauser pressed the gun's trigger—a soldier's reflex action.

The man who had called himself Smith was suddenly very dead. Mauser got out, walked around to the driver's side, opened the door, and pulled the agent free. He wasted little time regretting that he'd killed the man, although it would have been far better to take him alive.

It was all luck now, all in whether or not another car came along while he was disposing of the body. He had killed in self-defense, but that wasn't his worry. He had no doubt that ultimately he would be exonerated by the authorities, especially after he'd had a look in the man's wallet. The only thing was, it might take time, and he didn't have time. He *had* to be in the action when the forces of Barons Haer and Zwerdling clashed.

CHAPTER ELEVEN

Baron Malcolm Haer's field headquarters were in the ruins of a farm house in a town once known as Bearsville. His forces, and those of Marshal Stonewall Cogswell, were on the march but as yet their main bodies had not come in contact. Save for skirmishes between cavalry units, there had been no action. The ruined farm house had been the victim of an earlier fracas. This reservation had seen in its comparatively brief history more combat than Belgium, that cockpit of Europe.

A sheen of oily moisture could be seen on the baron's bulletlike head, and his officers weren't particularly happy about his mood, his attitude. Malcolm Haer characteristically went into a fracas with confidence, an aggressive confidence so strong that it often carried the day. In battles past, it had become a tradition that Haer's morale was worth a thousand men; at the same time, the energy he expended was the despair of his doctors who had been warning him for a decade. But this time something was missing.

A foreigner traced the military chart before them. "So far as we know, Marshal Cogswell has established his command here, to the north. Anybody have any suggestions as to why?"

A major grumbled, "It doesn't make much sense, sir. You know the marshal. It's probably a fake. If we have any superiority at all, it's our artillery."

"So the old fox wouldn't want to join the issue on the plains, down near the river," a colonel added. "It's his game to stay up in the mountains with his cavalry and light infantry. He's got Jack Altshuler's cavalry. Most experienced veterans in the field."

"I know who he's got," Haer growled in irritation. "Stop reminding me. Where in the devil is Balt?"

"Coming up, sir," Balt Haer said. He had entered only moments ago, a sheaf of signals in his hands. "Why didn't they make that date 1910, instead of 1900? With radio, we could speed up communications—"

His father interrupted testily. "Better still, why not make it 1945? Then we could speed up to the point where we could polish ourselves off. What have you got?"

Balt Haer said, his face in a sulk, "Some of my lads based in West Hurley report concentrations of Cogswell's infantry and artillery near Ashokan reservoir."

"Nonsense," somebody snapped. "We'd have him."

The younger Haer slapped his swagger stick against his bare leg and kilt. "Possibly it's a feint," he admitted.

"How much were they able to observe?" his father demanded.

"Not much. They were driven off by a superior squadron. The Hovercraft forces are screening everything they do with heavy cavalry units. I told you we needed more—"

"I don't need your advice at this point," his father snapped. He went back to the map, scowling still. "I don't see what he expects to do, working out of there."

A voice behind them said, "Sir, may I have your permission—"

Half of the assembled officers turned to look at the newcomer.

Balt Haer snapped, "Captain Mauser. Why aren't you with your lads?"

"Turned them over to my second in command, sir," Mauser said. He was standing to attention, looking down at Baron Haer.

The baron glowered at him. "What is the meaning of this cavalier intrusion, Captain? You must have your orders. Are you under the illusion that you are part of my staff?"

"No, sir," Mauser clipped. "I came to report that I am ready to put into execution—"

"The great plan!" Balt Haer laughed bitterly. "The second day of the fracas and nobody really knows where old Cogswell is or what he plans to do. And here comes the captain with his secret plan."

Mauser looked at him. He said, evenly, "Yes, sir."

The baron's face had gone dark, as much in anger at his son as with the upstart cavalry captain. He began to growl ominously, "Captain Mauser, rejoin your command and obey your orders."

Joe's facial expression indicated that he had expected this. He kept his voice level however, even under the chuckling scorn of his immediate superior, Balt Haer.

He said, "Sir, I will be able to tell you where Marshal Cogswell is, and every troop at his command."

For a moment there was silence, all but a stunned silence. Then the major who had suggested that the location of Cogswell's field command headquarters were a fake laughed derisively.

"This is no time for levity, Captain," Balt Haer clipped. "Get to your command."

A colonel said, "Just a moment, sir. I've fought with Joe Mauser before. He's a good man."

Joe said flatly, "Have a semaphore man posted here this afternoon. I'll be back at that time." He spun on his heel and left them.

Balt Haer rushed to the door after him, shouting, "Captain! That's an order! Return—"

But the other was obviously gone. Enraged, the younger Haer began to shrill commands to a noncom in the way of organizing a pursuit.

His father called wearily, "That's enough, Balt. Mauser has evidently taken leave of his senses. We made the initial mistake of encouraging this idea he had—or thought he had."

"*We?*" his son snapped in return. "I had nothing to do with it."

"All right, all right. Let's tighten up here. Now, what other information have your scouts come up with? Above all, we've got to locate Marshal Cogswell's main force."

Twenty minutes later, Mauser joined Max Mainz in the hanger area of the Kingston airport.

"Everything go all right?" the little man said anxiously.

"No," Mauser said. "They almost stopped me. I still couldn't tell them the story—I'm not sure who on that staff can be trusted, and old Cogswell is as quick as a coyote. We pull this little caper this afternoon, and he'll be ready to meet it tomorrow, which is fine; I just don't want him to know about it today!"

He looked at the two-place sailplane which sat on the tarmac. "Everything all set? Have you got everything into it?"

"Far as I know," Max said. He looked at the sailplane, doubt plain on his face. He had only been informed of Mauser's plan a few hours earlier. "You sure you been checked out on these things, Captain?"

Mauser chuckled grimly. "Yes," he said. "Don't worry about that angle. I bought this glider more than a year ago, and I've put almost a thousand hours in it. That's a lot of soaring, Max. Now, where's the pilot of that little plane?"

A single-engined sports plane was attached to the glider by a fifty-foot nylon rope. Even as Mauser spoke, a youngster poked his head from the plane's window and grinned back at him. "Ready?" he yelled. "Let's get this show on the road."

"Come on, Max," Mauser said. "Let's pull the canopy off this thing. We don't want it in the way when you're doing your semaphoring."

A figure was approaching them, without haste, from the airport's Administration Building.

"A moment, Captain Mauser!"

Mauser placed him now: the Sov-world representative he had met at Balt Haer's table in the Upper bar at the hotel a couple of days ago. What was the man's name? Colonel Arpad. Lajos Arpad from Budapest, capital of the Sov-world.

The Hungarian approached and looked at the sailplane in interest. "As a representative of my government, a military attaché checking upon possible violations of the Universal Disarmament Pact, may I ask what you are about to do, Captain Mauser?"

Joe looked at him emptily. "How did you know I was here, and what I was doing?"

The Sov-world colonel smiled gently. "I received the hint from Marshal Cogswell—second-hand. He is a great man for detail, isn't it so? It disturbed him that an . . . what did he call it? . . . an *old pro* like yourself should join with Vacuum Tube Transport rather than Continental Hovercraft. He didn't think it made sense and suggested that possibly you had in mind some scheme that would utilize weapons of a post-1900 period in your efforts to bring success to Baron Malcolm Haer's forces. So I have gone to the bother of investigating."

"And the marshal knows about this sailplane?" Joe Mauser's face was blank. Surely it couldn't all go to pot now, not after all the planning, all the time and expense.

"I didn't say that, did I?" The Hungarian was shaking his head, even as he continued to stare at the glider, flicking a manicured thumbnail over his dainty moustache. "So far as I know, he doesn't."

"Then, Colonel Arpad, with your permission, I'll be taking off."

The Hungarian's eyes narrowed. "With what end in mind, Captain Mauser?"

"Using this glider as a reconnaissance aircraft, obviously."

The Sov-world officer shook his head. "Captain, I warn you! Aircraft were not used in warfare until well past the turn of the century. They were first utilized by the Italians in the Balkan Wars—"

But Joe Mauser cut him off. "As a matter of fact, Colonel, they were used even earlier than that by Pancho Villa's forces in Mexico, during the revolution that started in 1910. But those were powered craft, as were the Italian planes used against the Turks. This is a glider, invented and in use before the year 1910 and hence open to utilization."

The Hungarian began to protest, "But the Wright brothers didn't fly even gliders until the year . . . ."

Mauser looked at him full in the face. "But we weren't talking about the Wright brothers. You of the Sov-world do not admit that the Wrights were the first to fly, do you?"

The Hungarian closed his mouth abruptly. He stared at Joe Mauser, blinking, suppressing a smile.

Mauser said evenly, "But even if Ivan Ivanovich, or whatever you claim his name was, didn't invent flight with heavier-than-air-craft, the glider was flown by a number of people before 1900, including Otto Lilienthal in the 1890s. For that matter, a glider was designed by Leonardo da Vinci, although admittedly that model was never flown."

The Sov-world colonel continued to stare at him for a long moment, then chuckled. He stepped back and flicked Joe Mauser a salute.

"Very well, Captain. As a matter of routine, I shall report this use of an aircraft for reconnaissance purposes, and undoubtedly a commission will meet to investigate the propriety of the departure. Meanwhile, good luck!"

Joe returned the salute and swung a leg over the cockpit's side. Max was already in the front seat, his semaphore flags, maps, and binoculars on his lap. He had been staring in dismay at the Sov officer, now was relieved that Joe had evidently pulled it off.

Mauser waved to the plane ahead. Two mechanics had come up to steady the wings of the glider for the initial ten or fifteen feet of the motorless craft's passage over the ground behind the towing craft.

Mauser said to Max, "Did you explain to the pilot that under no circumstances is he to pass over the line of the military reservation, that we'd cut before we reached that point?"

"Yes, sir," Max said nervously.

Mauser signaled the pilot of the tow plane. There was a jerk, and they lurched across the field, slowly at first, then gathering speed. And as the sailplane took speed, it took grace. After it had been pulled a hundred feet or so, Mauser expertly eased back the stick and the plane slipped gently into the air, four or five feet off the ground. The tow plane was still taxiing, but with its tow airborne, it picked up speed quickly. Another two hundred feet and it, too, was in the air and beginning to climb. The glider behind held it to a speed of sixty miles or so.

A few minutes later, the plane leveled off. Ten thousand feet. The pilot's head swiveled to look back at them. Joe Mauser waved to him and dropped the release lever which ejected the nylon rope from the glider's nose. The plane dove away, trailing the rope behind it. The pilot would later drop it over the airport where it could easily be retrieved.

Joe scanned the horizon. In the direction of Mount Overlook, he could see cumulus clouds and dark turbulence. That meant strong updrafts. He headed in that direction.

Except for the whistling of wind, there was complete silence in the soaring glider. Max Mainz began to call to his superior, but was taken aback by the volume, and dropped his voice. He said, "Look, Captain. What keeps it up?"

Mauser grinned. He loved the exhilaration of soaring, and thus far everything was going well. He told Max, "An airplane plows through the air currents; a glider rides on top of them."

"Yeah, but suppose the current is going down?"

"Then we avoid it. This sailplane has a gliding angle ratio of only one to twenty-five, but it's a real workhorse, with a payload of four hundred pounds. A really high-performance glider can have a ratio of as much as one to forty."

Mauser had found a strong updraft where a wind ran up the side of a mountain. He banked, went into a circling turn. The gauge indicated they were climbing at the rate of eight meters per second, nearly fifteen hundred feet a minute.

"Uh, what's a gliding ratio?" Max had no background in aerodynamics. That was obvious in his expression.

"A glide ratio is the rate at which a plane will drop without an updraft. A twenty-five to one ratio means that the plane will drop one mile for every twenty-five miles it travels horizontally."

Joe Mauser, even while searching the ground below keenly, went into it further. "A wind up against a mountain will give an updraft, storm clouds will, even a newly plowed field in a bright sun. So you go from one of these to the next." Mauser suddenly leaned forward in his seat. "Look—what's that down there? Get your glasses on it." He pointed at the ground.

Max caught his excitement. His binoculars were tight to his eyes. "Soldiers. Cavalry. They sure ain't ours, Sir. They must be Hovercraft lads. And look—over there—field artillery."

Joe Mauser was piloting with his left hand, his right smoothing out a military chart on his lap. He growled, "What are they doing there? That's at least a full brigade of cavalry. Here, let me have those glasses."

With his knees gripping the stick, he went into a slow circle as he stared down at the column of men.

"Jack Altshuler," he whistled through his teeth in

surprise. "The marshal's crack heavy cavalry. And several batteries of artillery." He swung the glasses in a wider scope and the whistle turned into a hiss of comprehension. "They're going to hit Baron Haer from the rear, from the direction of Phoenicia."

He reached forward and patted Max on the shoulder. "Now we earn our pay!"

The glider banked sharply, dropped, and circled.

Marshal Stonewall Cogswell directed his old-fashioned telescope in the direction his chief of staff had indicated a moment earlier.

"What is it?" he grunted.

"It's an airplane, sir," the other said, shock in his voice.

"Airplane? Don't be ridiculous. Over a military reservation with a fracas in progress?"

"Yes, sir," the chief of staff said unhappily, as though unconvinced. He put his own glasses back to his eyes, and directed his view back to the circling object. "Then what is it, sir? Certainly not a free balloon."

"Balloons," the marshal snorted, as though to himself. "Legal to use. The Union forces had them at the siege of Richmond toward the end of the Civil War. But they're practically useless in a fracas of movement. Can't get them up and down quickly enough."

They were standing before the former resort hotel which housed the field marshal's headquarters. Other staff members were streaming from the building, and one of the ever-present telly reporting crews, headed by Freddy Soligen, was hurriedly setting up its cameras.

The marshal turned and barked, "Does anybody

know what in Zen that damn thing is, circling up there?"

Baron Zwerdling, head of Continental Hovercraft, hobbled onto the wooden veranda and stared with the others. "An airplane," he croaked. "Haer's gone too far this time. Too far, too far. This will strip him. Strip him, understand?" Then he added, "Why doesn't it make any noise?"

Lieutenant Colonel Paul Warren stood next to his commanding officer. "It looks like a glider, sir."

"A what?" Cogswell glowered at him.

"A glider, sir. A powerless aircraft."

"What keeps the damn thing up?"

Paul Warren looked at him. "The same thing that keeps a hawk up, or an albatross, a gull—"

"A vulture, you mean," Cogswell snarled. He put his glass back to his eye and watched it for another long moment, his face working. He whirled on his chief of artillery. "Jed, can you bring that thing down?"

The other had been viewing the craft through his field binoculars, his face as shocked as the rest of them. Now he faced his chief and lowered the glasses, shaking his head. "Not with this artillery. No, sir."

"What *can* you do?" Cogswell barked.

The artillery man was shaking his head. "We could mount some Maxim guns on wagon wheels, or something. So we can move them around quickly, keep him from coming low."

"He doesn't have to come low," Cogswell growled in disgust. He spun on Lieutenant Colonel Warren again. "Is this legal? When were they invented?" He jerked his thumb upward. "Those things."

Warren was twisting his face in memory. "Some time about the turn of the century."

"How long can they stay up?"

Warren looked at the surrounding mountainous countryside. "In these conditions, indefinitely, sir. A single pilot, as long as he is physically able to operate. If there are two pilots up there to relieve each other, they could stay until food and water ran out."

"How much weight do they carry?"

"I'm not sure. One that size, certainly enough for two men and any equipment they'd need. Say, five hundred pounds."

Cogswell had his telescope glued to his eye again. He muttered under his breath. "Five hundred pounds! They could even unload dynamite over our horses. Stampede them all over the reservation."

"What's going on?" Baron Zwerdling shrilled. "What's going on, Marshal Cogswell?"

Cogswell ignored him. He watched the circling, soaring aircraft for a full five minutes, knuckles white on the telescope. Then he lowered his glass and swept the assembled officers on his staff with an indignant glare. "Fodor!" he snapped.

The intelligence officer came to attention, "Yes, sir."

Cogswell said heavily, deliberately, "Under a white flag, a dispatch to Baron Haer. My compliments and request for terms. While you're at it, my compliments also to Captain Joseph Mauser—unless I am strongly mistaken!"

Zwerdling was aghast. "Terms?" he rasped.

The marshal turned to him. "Yes, sir. Face reality. We're in the dill. I suggest you sue for terms as short of complete capitulation as you can make them."

"You call yourself a soldier?"

"Yes, sir," Cogswell snapped. "A soldier, not a butcher of the lads under me." He called to the telly reporter, who was hovering nearby. "Mr. Soligen, isn't it?"

Soligen scurried forward, flicking signals to his cameramen for proper coverage. "Yes, sir, Freddy Soligen, Marshal. Could you tell the telly fans what this is all about, Marshal Cogswell? Folks, you all know the famous Marshal Stonewall Cogswell, who hasn't lost a fracas in nearly ten years, now commanding the forces of Continental Hovercraft."

"I'm losing one now," Cogswell said grimly. "Vacuum Tube Transport has pulled a gimmick out of the hat and things have pickled for us. It will be debated before the Category Military Department, of course, and undoubtedly the Sov-world military attachés will have things to say. But as it appears now, the fracas is going to be markedly changed—revolutionized."

"Revolutionized?" The telly reporter was flabbergasted. "You mean by that thing?" He pointed upward, and the lenses of the cameras followed his finger. "By Major Mauser?"

"Yes," Cogswell growled unhappily. "Do all of you need a blueprint? Do you think I can fight a fracas with that thing dangling above me throughout the day hours? Do you understand the importance of reconnaissance in warfare?" His eyes glowered. "Do you think Napoleon would have lost Waterloo if he'd had the advantage of perfect reconnaissance such as that thing can deliver? Do you think Lee would have lost Gettysburg? Don't be ridiculous."

He spun on Baron Zwerdling, who was stuttering in confusion.

"As it stands, Baron Haer knows every troop dispensation I make. All I know of his movements are from my cavalry scouts. We have the upper hand in defending our position—but not on the offensive, not now. Haer can wait us out and be right on the spot when we come out in the open, no matter what we do. It would be a massacre!

"I repeat, I am no butcher, sir. I will gladly cross swords with Baron Haer another day, when I, too, have . . . what did you call the confounded things, Paul?"

"Gliders," Lieutenant Colonel Warren said.

CHAPTER TWELVE

It had been a long week—a very long week. The coup had worked. The Category Military investigation of his tactics was still pending, but Joe Mauser had won the major battle of his private war.

He was the toast of the town, and more. They'd had to post extra guards around the Haer staging area to keep the fracas buffs away, and wherever Mauser went he was all but mobbed, both by the fracas buffs and by his fellow officers, whose admiration he found to be the most gratifying aspect of this new fame. Telly interviews were forced on him. Major Joseph Mauser was at the top, as far as fame went, in the Category Military.

Expensive gifts and congratulary messages poured in. Max Mainz was hard-pressed to keep up with it all. Max supervised the distribution of the gifts from the fracas buffs, unable to understand why Joe didn't want the expensive clothes, the fine foods and liqueurs, the gadgets of all descriptions that poured in. Most of this booty he was directed to donate to charities; some of it he shared with his comrades-in-arms.

Yes, Mauser had won the big battle, but there remained one small matter: the icing on the cake, so to speak, to be provided by old Baron Haer. The matter of the jump in caste.

Haer had been conspicuously absent during the week following Cogswell's surrender. Mauser had written it off to business; the fracas over, the baron was undoubtedly back hard at work, picking up the pieces and delighting in the new power and status that Mauser's victory had won for his company.

Yes, the baron was going to be grateful.

Now attired in his best off-duty Category Military uniform, Major Joe Mauser spoke his credentials to the receptionist in the New York offices of Vacuum Tube Transport. "I have no definite appointment, but I am sure that the baron will see me," he said.

"Yes, sir." The receptionist did the things that receptionists do, then looked up at him again. "Right through that door, Major."

He crossed the room and gave the indicated door a quick double rap, then entered without waiting for an answer.

Balt Haer, in mufti, was standing at a far window, holding a drink rather than his familiar swagger stick. Nadine sat in an easy chair, across from a massive desk at which no one sat.

Mauser made the usual amenities.

Balt Haer finished his drink without answering and stared at him. The same old stare, the aloof stare of an aristocrat looking at an underling as if wondering what made him tick. He said, finally, "I see that you have been raised to the permanent rank of Major."

"Yes, sir," Mauser said.

"We are obviously occupied, Major. What can either my sister or I possibly do for you?"

Mauser kept his voice even. He said, "I wish to see the baron."

"Indeed," Balt Haer replied, eyebrows arched. "You are talking to the baron, Major Mauser."

Joe looked at Balt Haer, then at his sister, red-eyed and obviously upset.

It all fell into place.

He wanted to say something, even "Oh, no," but he could not speak.

Balt Haer's tone was bitter, bitter and self-righteous. He was very obviously enjoying this, lording over the man who had embarrassed him. "I assume that you are here, Major Mauser, to extract your pound of flesh. And look at you—even in our time of grief . . ."

"I . . . didn't know. Please believe . . ."

". . . you are so constituted that your ambition has no decency. Well, Major Mauser, I can only say that your arrangement was with my late father. Even if I thought it a reasonable one—and I certainly do not—I doubt if I would want to sponsor *your* ambitions."

Nadine looked wearily. "Oh, Balt, cut it out," she said. "The fact is, the Haer family fortunes have contracted a debt to you, Major Mauser, a debt that we cannot pay . . ." She looked into his face.

Mauser stared back, blankly.

". . . for two reasons. First, my father's governmental connections do not apply to us, so we cannot sponsor your rise in caste in any event." She glared at her brother. "Second, my father, worried about his failing health, transferred all of the family stocks into Balt's name six months ago—an attempt to avoid certain taxes.

"Balt saw fit, immediately before the fracas, to sell all of the family's Vacuum Tube Transport stocks—"

"That's enough, Nadine!" her brother snapped.

"—and re-invest in Hovercraft."

"I said, that's enough, Nadine!" There was a nasty tone to Balt Haer's voice now.

"You're damn well right that's enough," she bit back.

"I see," Mauser said. So he *had* been right about the younger Haer. He came to attention. "Doctor Haer, my apologies for intruding upon you in your time of bereavement." He then turned to the new baron. "Baron Haer, my apologies for *your* bereavement."

Balt Haer glowered at him.

Barely, just barely, Mauser stifled the urge to laugh in his face. He spun smartly on one heel and marched for the door.

Out on the street, he turned and looked up at the splendor of the building housing the Haer offices.

Common shares of Vacuum Tube Transport had skyrocketed following the victory, leaving Joe with liquid assets equal to those of many Low-Uppers. He had that, and more. His permanent rank had been upped to Major, and old Stonewall Cogswell had offered him the staff position of commander of aerial operations—no small matter of prestige. The problem was, the money wasn't what he was after, nor the higher rank—nor the prestige, for that matter. The one thing he had been after, his major goal in life, had eluded him once again.

He shook his head and turned to go to his hotel. It was time to move on.

"Joe?"

He turned. An unbelievably beautiful girl came down the steps of the building.

"Yes?"

She put a hand on his sleeve. "We have to talk, Joe."

"About what?" He was infinitely weary now.

"About goals," Nadine Haer replied. "As long as they exist, whether for individuals or nations, or a whole species, life is still worth living. Things are a bit bogged down right now, but at the risk of sounding trite, there is tomorrow."

He didn't know how to take Nadine Haer; she was certainly no drivel-happy fracas buff, but she didn't act quite like an Upper, either—at least, not all the time. He shrugged. At the moment, it didn't matter to him why she was interested in him. To have her attention was enough.

"Sure," he said at last. "When? Now?"

"No," she said, descending the steps. "I'll be in touch. Things are too . . . too unsettled just now, but I wanted you to know that things aren't as bleak as they seem."

In other eras, he might have been described as swacked, stewed, stoned, smashed, crocked, cock-eyed, soused, shellacked, polluted, tanked, lit, stinko, pie-eyed, three sheets to the wind, wasted, or simply drunk.

In his own time, Joe Mauser, Category Military, Rank Major, caste Mid-Middle, was drenched.

Or getting there rapidly, at least.

He wasn't happy about it. It wasn't that kind of a binge.

He lowered one eyelid and concentrated on the list of potables offered by the auto-bar. He'd decided earlier that it was physically impossible to get through the whole list, but he was making a strong attempt at having a representative of each category of drink. He'd already had a cocktail, a highball, a sour, a flip, a punch, and a julep. Now he wagged a finger forth to punch in an order for a fizz.

Mauser occupied a small table in a corner of the Middle Caste Category Military Club in Greater Washington. His current fame would have made him welcome as a guest in the Upper Military Club, located in the swank Baltimore section of town; old pros in Category Military had comparatively little sufference for caste lines among themselves.

But Joe didn't want it that way. You don't devote the greater part of your life to fighting your way up the ladder of status to be content to associate with your social superiors on the basis of being a nine-day wonder, an oddity to be met at cocktail parties. No, Joe would stick to his own position in the scheme of things until he won through to that rarefied altitude in society which was his ambition. He'd almost made it—so close—only to have his prize snatched away by cruel fate. But though he was bitter, Joe was no cynic; the fact that he'd come this close proved that he could do so again, and he would.

Besides, he was known here. The regulars left him alone when he wanted.

A voice said, "Celebrating, Captain—opps, Major? So you did get something out of the Hovercraft fracas. I'm surprised."

A scowl, Mauser decided, would be best. Various others, during the course of the evening, had attempted to join him. Three or four fellow mercenaries, one journalist, and some women he didn't know. A growl had driven some away. This one, he decided, called for an angered scowl, particularly in view of the tone of voice he used, a tone which seemed a taunt at the fact that he'd not gained the one thing he was after.

He looked up. "Go to—" he began, then stopped. It was Freddy Soligen.

The other slid into the seat opposite him. "Mind if I join you?"

"Why?"

"Major," Soligen said, "from the looks of things, you're going to have a hell of a hangover in the morning. Why don't you stick to trank?"

" 'Cause I'm not a slob," Mauser sneered. "Why?"

"Why what? Listen, you want me to help you on home?"

"I have no home—I live in hotels and military clubs and barracks. I have nothing but my rank and caste." He grimaced. "Such as they are."

"Mid-Middle, right? And a major. Most would say that you have nothing to complain about, and I heard that you cleaned up with Vacuum Tube stock."

Mauser grunted his contempt. He was well into his thirties, and his life's goal was still out of reach. And he was living on borrowed time, time borrowed from men who had used theirs up on the battlefield.

But he didn't want to get started on *that*. He looked at Soligen. "Tell me why, will you? Why are you an exception? What makes you get right in the middle of it, running coverage of battles, when you could sit back in a pillbox safe and sound, out of the fire? Like when we were in the dill together, or that time at the Panhandle Reservation? You could've copped one. You don't have to risk yourself, you know."

Soligen frowned. "Don't you read the publicity, follow the telly?"

Mauser shook his head. "No. It's a bunch of garbage. I don't have time for it; hardly keep up with the real news."

"Well," Soligen chuckled. "I *did* cop one—was in the hospital for a few days. Got me bounced a rank *and* raised to a Low-Middle." There was the faintest surly tone to his voice as he added, "I was born a Lower, Major."

Mauser snorted. "So was I. But you didn't answer my question—why do you stick your neck out?"

Soligen looked surprised. "Stick my neck out? Possibly for the same reason as you. In fact, it's more or less the reason I looked you up. Trouble is, you're probably too drenched to listen to my fling."

Mauser regarded the man. Now here was someone interesting, someone who wanted to *do* something with himself, in a world where there was no need to do anything. Oh, some few were drafted to work in their categories, no matter what their rank, but the vast majority could sit back and enjoy life, such as it was. He'd long suspected that Freddy Soligen was after something more in life, though he'd never brought up the topic. Still . . .

He allowed a cold dignity to creep into his voice. "In the Category Military, Soligen, you never get so drenched that you can't operate."

"OK," Soligen growled. "But a sober-up for you, and an ale for me, anyway. I want to talk serious business."

"I don't want to sober up. I'm being bitter and enjoying it."

"Yes, you do," the little man replied. "I think I have the answer to your bitterness." Soligen pulled out his credit card, scanned the menu on the autobar, and ordered a sober-up. A few seconds later the bar produced a small glass containing a clear liquid.

Mauser made an ugly face as Soligen handed it to him. "I make my own way, Soligen. What are you talking about?"

"That's obvious, but look where it's gotten you—at a dead end, I'd say. Drink up!"

Joe frowned. "Whatever it is you have to say had

better be good." He tossed back the contents of the glass.

Freddy watched in obvious compassion while the sober-up worked its miracle. The drugs worked, but there were unpleasant side effects. Mauser bore them stoically.

Finally, Freddy spoke. "You know one of the big reasons you're only a major?"

Mauser stared at him blankly.

"You don't have a mustache."

Mauser laughed. "Sure, and maybe a beard would make me a general?"

"You think I'm drivel-happy, don't you? Well, maybe a long scar down the cheek would do even better. Or possibly you ought to wear a saber, even in action."

"Come on, Freddy! It's what you do that counts, not what you look like! You said it yourself before— I've just been unlucky enough to miss being on camera when I do something right."

"Right! But I also said that you need a gimmick— and I don't mean the kind of gimmick you pulled with the glider, though that's worth a lot. But people forget you as soon as someone more interesting comes along, unless there's something about you to *make* them remember you, and keep on remembering you.

"Like I told you before, you have that air about you that the buffs like, but you need to enhance it. You've got a lot to learn!"

Mauser held his peace, if only in pure amazement. He ranked the little man opposite him, both in caste and professional attainment. And he was a combat officer and unused to being addressed with anything less than full respect; unlucky Joe Mauser might be in his chosen field, but respected he was.

Freddy Soligen pointed a finger at him, almost

mockingly. "You're on the make, Mauser. In a world where few bother, you're on the way up. The trouble is, you're not exactly on the right path.

"I realize that the military's the only quick way of getting a bounce in caste. I wish I'd figured that one out years ago, before I made a trade out of the category I was born into. It's too late now—I'm in my forties with a busted marriage, but the proud father of a son." He frowned, as if in memory. "By the way, the boy's a novitiate in Category Religion."

Mauser's mind was clearing. "So . . . we're both ambitious."

"That's right, Major. Now, let's get back to fundamentals. The reason you're on the wrong path is because your basic approach to working your way up to the elite is all wrong. You've got to become a celebrated hero on a regular basis, Major; you can't rely on one big fling doing it for you. And it's the telly fan, the fracas buff, who decides who the Category Military heroes are. Those are the slobs you have to toady to; in the long run, nobody else counts."

Mauser started to protest, but Soligen ignored him. "All the old pros, even the big ones like Stonewall Cogswell and Jack Altshuler, think you're a top man. That's fine, but until recently how many buff clubs did you have to your name? How often did the magazines run articles about you? Has anyone ever done 'The Joe Mauser Story'?"

Mauser twisted uncomfortably. Surely the other knew how little love the pro had for buffs. "All that stuff takes time. I've been busy . . ."

"Right! Busy getting shot at."

"I'm a mercenary. That's my trade."

Freddy spread his hands. "OK. If that's all you're interested in, shooting and getting shot at, that's fine. But you know, Major—" he cocked his head to one side, peering knowingly at Joe—"I've got a sneaking suspicion that you don't particularly like combat. Some do, I know. Some love it, but I don't think you do."

Mauser shrugged.

"You're in it because of the chance for promotion. Nothing else counts."

Mauser remained silent. Freddy pushed him. "What're the names every fracas buff knows? Robert Maynard, captain at the age of twenty-one, and damned sharp in those fancy uniforms he wears. And how many times, since he made the upper ranks, have you heard of him really being in the dill? He knows better! He spends his time prancing around on that famous palomino of his in front of telly lenses, not dodging bullets. Or Colonel Tom Clark, the dashing Clark with his six-shooters slung low on his hips and that romantic limp and craggy face. Yeah, the female buffs go for Colonel Clark, but I wonder how many of them know he wears a special pair of boots to give him that limp? Old Tom's a drinking buddy of mine—he's never copped one in his life. What's more, another year or so and he'll be a general and you know what that means. An almost automatic jump to Upper Caste."

Mauser's face was working. This was not really news to him. Like his peers, he was fully aware of the glory-grabbers. They had always been around, from the mythical Achilles, who sulked in his tent while his best friend died before the walls of Troy, to Alexander, who conquered the world with an army conceived and precision-trained by another man whose name is all but forgotten, to the swashbuckling Custer, who sacrificed self and squadron rather than wait for assistance.

Freddy Soligen was rolling now. "How come you're

never on lens when you're in there going good,
Major? Ever thought about that? When you're commanding a rear-guard action, maybe, trying to get
your men out alive, who's on lens where all the
stupid buffs are watching? One of the manufactured
heroes, that's who."

Mauser scowled. "The who?"

"Come off it, Major. You've been around long
enough to know that heroes are made, not born.
Used to be a man could do something really spectacular: climb a mountain, cross an ocean alone, whatever, and be remembered the rest of his life. Then,
before we knew it, everyone was trying to be a hero,
thanks to telly making it easy to show the world what
you were doing. But we got away from the real
heroes, because real heroes ain't all that exciting
most of the time. Real heroes are men who *do* things,
rather than being showmen, and most of their time is
spent doing mundane things. Actors can do it better,
be exciting *all* of the time."

Mauser's mind was working now.

"Your typical fracas buff," Freddy went on, "wants
two things. First, lots of gore, lots of blood. The
Low-Lowers with nothing on the ball, who are silly
enough to get into Category Military, they provide
the blood and gore. Second, your average buff wants
some Good Guys whose first requirement is that
they can be easily recognized. Anybody can tell a
telly hero when he sees one: handsome, dashing,
distinctively uniformed, preferably tall, blond, and
blue-eyed. We'll eliminate those last requirements
in your case, though, if you'll grow a mustache." He
cocked his head to one side. "Yes, sir. A very dashing mustache."

"You think that's all I need to hit the big time?"
Mauser asked sourly. "A dashing mustache?"

"No," Freddy replied, "but it's a start. We're also going to need every bit of stock you've accumulated. We're going to have to buy your way into the fracas buff magazines. We're going to have to bribe other telly reporters and camera crews to keep you on lens when you're looking good and, more important still, *off* it when you're not. It's going to take every credit you can lay your hands on."

Mauser was beginning to see the logic of it; it had been done before. "I see," he said. "And when it's all done, what do you get out of this, Freddy?"

"When it's all done, you'll be an Upper. But I'm ambitious, too, as much as you are. I need an *in*. You'll be it. I'll make you; I have the know-how and the contacts in the business. I can still do it. And when you're made, you'll make me."

CHAPTER THIRTEEN

Less than a month after Joe Mauser returned to home base in Greater Washington, Freddy Soligen started to implement his plan. As promised, he had been able to buy mentions for Mauser in some of the fracas buff magazines, and more were on the way. Some of Soligen's more subtle schemes were also put into effect, pending another fracas.

And Mauser had his mustache, and his fancy uniform. He had to admit that, after he got used to it, the uniform *was* rather eye-catching. He wasn't sure that he wanted to wear it into battle, however. The mustache he had not gotten used to; that would take a while, if ever.

True to her word, Nadine Haer got in touch with him. A late-night telephone call arranged a rendezvous for the following evening. Mauser was left wondering, not for the first time, just what Nadine Haer did with her time. One of the idle rich? Perhaps, but he sensed that there was much more to Nadine than was visible.

When he met her at the tube terminal, she was, if possible, more stunningly attractive than he remembered.

"Shall we take a hovercab uptown?" she asked, once they were out of the terminal building.

"Let's walk." He offered his arm. She took it and fell into step alongside him.

They ended up in a rather exclusive Upper club on the east side of the city. Nadine Haer was known there, but even without her influence, Major Joe Mauser would have been granted immediate entrance; for now, at least, his uniform and face, known to everyone who had even heard of a fracas, buff or not, was enough to gain him entrance into any establishment in the West-world.

As they entered the fashionable Gentry Room of the Ultra Hotel, the orchestra—composed of musicians, no canned music here—ceased the upbeat tune it had been playing and struck up the lilting "The Girl I Left Behind Me."

They followed the maitre d'hotel to their table, Nadine frowning in puzzled memory. After they were seated, she said, "That piece: where have I heard it before?"

Mauser cleared his throat uncomfortably. "An old marching song come down from the American Civil War—revived, actually. General Custer's Seventh Cavalry rode forth to that tune on the way to their rendezvous with the Amerindians at a place called the Little Big Horn."

He glanced around, then said, "By the way, would you care to go soaring sometime soon? It's an experience you won't soon forget." It was a clumsy attempt at changing the topic, but Mauser didn't want to dwell on his bid for fame.

"Sure." Then she frowned at him, puzzled still. "You seem to know more than a little about antique tunes, Joe, especially that one." She smiled. "Ah—now I remember where I've heard that before! Right after the fracas, the clubs in town started playing it—something about it on the telly, I heard, something to do with your cavalry background." Mauser flushed with embarrassment. "Why, Joe, that's your song!"

Mauser picked up the menu and scanned it, hoping that Nadine would not continue in *that* vein. "What'll you have, Nadine?" He wasn't quite at ease with her first name, but she'd insisted he use it. Offhand, he couldn't remember ever having been on a first-name basis with a Mid-Upper of either gender.

Nadine laughed. "Yes, the Joe Mauser theme song! I knew that the fracas buffs were hot for you, but—a theme song? They must worship the ground you walk on. No doubt, there are Major Joe Mauser Fan Clubs galore by now."

"As a matter of fact," Mauser said unhappily, "there are three. One in Mexico City, one in Bogotá, and one in Portland. I've forgotten if it's Oregon or Maine."

Nadine smiled at him, ignoring the waiter who stood at their table. It made Mauser nervous; establishments that boasted live waiters were rare enough in his experience that he could easily remember the number of occasions he'd attended them. Nadine Haer, to the contrary, was totally unaware of the flunky's presence, and would remain so until she required him.

She looked at Mauser from the side of her eyes. "Joe, the mustache and the new uniform are so very gallant—you look like one of those old Imperial Hussars or something. And your telly interviews . . . by a stretch of chance I saw one of them the other day. The interviewer seemed to think that you were the most dashing soldier since Jeb Stuart."

Mauser said to the waiter, "Champagne, please."

"May I see your credit card, Major?" the waiter said apologetically. "The Gentry Room is limited to Upper—"

"Perhaps you don't recognize Major Joe Mauser,"

Nadine said coldly. "And I am Doctor Nadine Haer."
Her voice held the patina of those to the manor
born, and was not to be gainsaid. The waiter bowed
hurriedly, murmured something placating, and was
gone.

A tic had started at the side of Mauser's mouth
which normally manifested itself only in combat. He
said stiffly, "I am afraid we should have gone to a
Middle Club."

"Nonsense! What difference does it make? Besides, don't change the subject, Joe Mauser. You
can't fool me—you're up to something!"

The tic had intensified. Mauser looked at her,
realizing suddenly that there was more than a physical attraction between them. His voice went very
even, very flat. "When we first met, Nadine, I told
you that I had been born a Mid-Lower. Why, I don't
know, but from the earliest I revolted against the
situation I had been born into. But history tells me
that there have been few socio-economic systems
under which the strong, intelligent, aggressive, cunning, or ruthless couldn't work their way up to the
top. Very well, I intend to do it, in our People's
Capitalism."

"Industrial Feudalism," she murmured.

"Call it what you will, it doesn't matter. But I
won't be happy until I'm at the top, with the Uppers."

"And are you sure you'll be happy then?"

"I don't know," he said angrily. "But I won't know
until I get there, will I?"

Nadine Haer's voice held angry overtones, too.
"All right," she snapped. "But I'll tell you this, Joe
Mauser—the world is out of gear, but the answer
isn't for individuals to work their way up using the
existing system. That's selfish!"

The waiter brought their wine. They both held
their peace until he had left.

"And what *is* the answer?" Mauser demanded, mocking her. "It's easy for you to tell me that the answer isn't in making my way to your level. You don't know what it's like down here."

Nadine's reply was drowned out by the ceiling speakers. The emcee, or perhaps the club manager, stood in the middle of the stage, his amplified voice overwhelming the room.

He went into a long routine about the celebrities present. This politician, that actress, this baron of industry. Joe and Nadine ignored most of his chatter, and the applause, until . . .

"And those among us who are fracas buffs," the booming voice announced, "will be thrilled to know that they are spending the evening in the company of the intrepid Major Joseph Mauser . . ."

Behind him, the orchestra broke into the quick strains of "The Girl I Left Behind Me." Mauser wondered in passing just how much that had cost him.

". . . whose most recent act of sheer military genius resulted in his all but single-handedly winning the fracas between Continental Hovercraft and Vacuum Tube Transport, and thus inflicting defeat upon none other than Marshal Stonewall Cogswell for the first time in more than a decade!"

Thunderous applause rose up, and a spotlight danced briefly about Mauser and Nadine, then moved on as the emcee babbled on about another celebrity present, a retired boxer once a champion.

Finally, the emcee was finished, and there was only the music against which to compete.

Nadine looked into his eyes. "I think I understand now. You mentioned that those who can will work their way to the top in any society. Well, you've tried strength, intelligence, and aggression, haven't you, Joe? They didn't work. At least, not fast enough. So now you're giving cunning a try. What will happen when this fails? There's not much left. . . ."

Mauser was saved an answer by the arrival of a hulking body in evening wear. He looked up into a face glazed over by either drugs or alcohol. He didn't know the man and for a moment failed to realize his purpose. The other was mumbling something.

Irritated, Mauser said, "What the hell do you want?"

The stranger shook his head, as though to clear it. Then he sneered, "The famous Joe Mauser, eh? The brave soldier-boy. Well, lemme tell you something, soldier-boy. You don't look so tough with your cute little mustache and your fancy uniform. You look like a mopsey to me!" He glared belligerently.

"That's too bad," Mauser said, feeling hot anger rising in him. "If you'll just excuse us . . ." he turned away from the other.

"Joe!"

Nadine's warning shout caused him to half turn, and he caught the unsuspected cuff full on his jaw. Mauser barely caught himself on the table edge, then jumped up, kicking his chair to one side.

His attacker shuffled backward, and Mauser recognized the trained step of the professional boxer. The other's idea was plain now, although Mauser was no follower of pugilism. The sport was largely out of favor since the growth of televised fracases. Boxing at its top had never been more than an inadequate replacement for blood and guts.

"How'd you like that, soldier-boy?" the other taunted. His left fist flicked forward, and Mauser barely ducked in time.

Mauser threw aside, for the time, his questions about the other's uncalled-for behavior. Unless he did something, and quick, he was going to be a laughingstock rather than the hero Freddy Soligen was trying to build.

Nadine said something urgently, but Mauser didn't hear her. The room and the people in it seemed to move away, to cloud over, as the trained fighting man took over. His senses were applied solely to the task at hand.

Cool, fast, and ruthless, Mauser moved in, his shoulders hunched slightly forward, hands forward and to the sides, choppers rather than sledges. While the boxer might have fisticuffs in mind, Mauser was using a more effective mode of fighting, proven by the Japanese long centuries ago.

He stepped closer, as quick as a jungle cat. His left hand darted forward, hacked at the other's neck, came back in a blurring swing, hacked again.

His opponent grunted in pain. But a man does not become a champion fighter without being able to take punishment as well as give it. The big man tucked his chin into his shoulder, fighter-style, and moved to the attack, throwing off the effects of the karate blows. Somehow, he seemed considerably less drunk or doped than he had moments earlier, and his face held rage, rather than glaze.

One of his blows caught Mauser on the shoulder and sent him reeling back. At the same time three other men moved into Mauser's field of vision, behind the boxer. He was going to have to do something and do it quickly, or be branded a boorish Middle who had intruded into the domain of Uppers, only to be expelled.

The former champ, his eyes narrowed in confidence, came boring in, quick for all of his bulk. His movements lithe, Mauser turned sideways. He lashed out with his right foot, at this angle getting double the leverage he would have otherwise, and caught the other on the kneecap. The pugilist bent forward in agony, his mouth opening as though in protest.

Mauser stepped forward. His hands were now knitted in a huge double fist. He brought them up and into his opponent's face with crushing force. Without even waiting for the other to fall, he turned, righted his chair, and resumed his seat facing Nadine, his breathing only slightly faster than before. The fight had taken all of five seconds.

Nadine's eyes were wide. The maitre d' was at their table. "Sir—" he began.

"This brawler attacked me," Mauser said curtly. "I'm surprised that you allow your patrons to get into the shape he is. Please bring our bill."

The head waiter stuttered, his eyes casting about in despair, even as his assistants were lifting the fallen champion to his feet and hustling him away.

A diner at a nearby table spoke up then, collaborating Mauser's story. Somebody else called out a similar comment and was echoed by several more voices. It suddenly occurred to Mauser that a brawl in an Upper establishment was no different than one in a Middle—or even a Lower-caste bar.

But it was impossible for them to remain. Even if it was not in poor taste Mauser would have been uncomfortable. Probably he would be pressed by most of the patrons there to discuss the incident, even to sign autographs.

He fumed inwardly as he waited for Nadine to settle the account. He had looked forward to a quiet evening alone with her, discussing something more than politics.

As they walked from the room, Nadine said coldly, "I suppose that you realize you broke that man's nose and injured his eye?"

He rolled his eyes upward in mute protest. "What was I supposed to do? Hand him a rose?"

"Violence is the last resort of the incompetent," she retorted.

"You must tell that, some time, to a jungle animal being attacked by a lion." He regretted the words even as they left his mouth.

Nadine was unusually quiet during the hovercab ride to the tube terminal. Mauser did manage to get her to commit to a date in his sailplane, however. They tentatively set the soaring session for two weeks later, Nadine ostensibly tied up with other matters in the interim.

Whatever her reason for putting him off, Mauser told himself that it was just as well that they didn't see each other for a while. Her preaching was wearing rather thin, and their views on fighting clashed rather more than he liked. Or maybe it was that her badgering had gotten him to thinking and questioning a little too much that bothered him.

CHAPTER FOURTEEN

A servant took Joe Mauser's cap at the door of Nadine Haer's New York home and requested that the mercenary follow him. Mauser trailed behind on the way to the living room, somewhat taken aback by the ostentatious display of the luxuries of yesteryear, including a butler. Servants, other than military batmen, simply did not exist in Joe Mauser's world.

Only Uppers were in a position to demand—and get—the luxury of individual servants. Anyone called upon to work in the category into which he was born—and for which he had received the obligatory training—had to work, or face severe penalities. However, none but an Upper could afford the cost of employing a servant of any caste. Uppers themselves worked, but only in what had been known in the past as professions, and only if they wished to.

The servant announced him, then disappeared during the brief moment that Mauser was bowing formally over Nadine Haer's hand. He briefly wondered how one acquired the ability to seemingly vanish once one's services were no longer needed. Each man to his own trade, he decided.

He was there for the soaring date with Nadine, but it turned out that his favorite Upper was not alone. In fact, it was obvious that she had not as yet gotten around to dressing for her appointment with Mauser. She was attired, as always, as a woman dresses who has never considered the cost. And again Mauser was taken with her intensity, and with her almost brittle beauty. What was it that aristocrats seemed to be able to acquire after a generation or two of what they were pleased to call "breeding"? That aloof quality, the highness of nose, the exquisite gentility.

"Joe," Nadine said, after their initial greetings, "you'll be pleased to meet Philip Holland, Category Government, Rank Secretary. Phil, Major Joseph Mauser."

The other, possibly forty, shook hands firmly and looked into Mauser's face, as if trying to remember something. "Good heavens, yes," he finally said. "That remarkable innovation of using an engineless aircraft for reconnaissance. My old friend, Marshal Cogswell, was speaking of it just the other day. I assume that you purchased stock in the firms that manufacture such craft, Major? They must be booming."

Mauser grinned wryly. "No, sir. I wasn't smart enough to think of that, I guess. Professional soldiers are traditionally stupid, you know. What was the old expression? They can take their shirts off without unbuttoning their collars."

Philip Holland cocked his head. "I detect a note of bitterness, Major," he chuckled.

"Joe is ambitious," Nadine said airily. "He thinks that the answer to all of his problems lies in jumping his caste to Upper."

Mauser looked at her impatiently.

"Possibly he's right, my dear," Holland replied. "Each of us has his own requirements for happiness."

To Mauser, Holland sounded a little on the stuffy

side, even in his crisp tone of voice. Holland seemed to try to project an air of calm that didn't quite come off in a man apparently nervous and quick-moving by nature. Mauser wondered what his relationship with Nadine could be, and felt a twinge of jealousy there. But that was ridiculous. Nadine must be at least ten years younger than Holland. Obviously she knew, and had known, many men as attracted to her as Mauser was, and men of her own caste, at that. Somehow, he felt that Holland was no Upper; the other simply didn't have the air.

Mauser said to him, "Nadine simply doesn't get my point. I contend that in a status-divided society, it's hard to realize yourself fully until you're a member of that society's elite, its upper class. Admittedly, you may not realize your ambitions even then, but at least you haven't the obstacles with which the lower classes are faced."

"Interestingly stated," Holland replied. He returned to the chair from which he had risen and looked at Nadine. "You said, earlier, that Joe would be glad to meet me, my dear. Why, especially?"

Nadine laughed. "Because I have been practicing your arguments on him."

Both men frowned at her.

Nadine looked at Mauser. "Phil Holland's the most interesting man I know. He's secretary to Harlow Mannerheim, the Minister of Foreign Affairs, and almost no one is more privy to the inner workings of government. It was Phil who convinced me that something is wrong with our system."

"Oh?" Mauser looked about for a chair, then sat. He wasn't really interested, having already had his fill of the topic from Nadine. Let society solve its own problems; he had his own. However, conversation had to be kept moving. "I've heard it said that any type of government is good, given capable, intelligent personnel, and bad if not so managed. What was the example I read somewhere? Both heaven and hell are despotisms."

Holland shrugged. "And interesting observation. However, institutions, including socio-political ones, can become outdated, or they can evolve in directions that make them something other than what they were intended. When this happens, if capable, honest, and intelligent persons are available, changes will be made to set the system back on track."

Nadine had come to her feet. "That's my favorite subject, but I must change. Joe is taking me soaring in his sailplane, and I'm sure that this frock isn't *de rigueur*." She was off before they had time to respond.

Mauser settled himself again, crossing his legs. "So," he said idly, "you think our basic institutions have reached the stage of needing change?"

"Perhaps, although as a member of the government it should hardly be my position to advocate such." He seemed to change the topic then. "Are you familiar with the Roman *ludi*, the games as we call them?"

"The gladiators and such?" Mauser shrugged. "I've read a bit about them. It's been pointed out, in fact, that our fracases serve the same purpose as those games. That instead of the bread and circuses provided by the Roman patricians to keep the unemployed Roman mob from becoming restive, we have trank pills and telly violence."

"Uh-huh," Holland nodded. "But that isn't the point I'm after right now. What I was thinking was how the Roman games began as athletic affairs without bloodshed, patterned after those of the Etruscans. It wasn't until 264 B.C. that things turned ugly— three pairs of slaves were sent into an arena to fight with swords. By 183 B.C. the number had risen to sixty pairs. Less than thirty years later they were up to ninety pairs, fighting for three days.

"But that was just the beginning. The killing went big-time under the dictators. Sulla put a hundred lions into the arena, but Julius Caeser topped that with four hundred and Pompey with six hundred, plus over four hundred leopards and twenty elephants. Augustus beat them all with thirty-five hundred elephants—and he had ten thousand men killed in a series of games. But it was the emperors who really changed the *ludi* into wholesale slaughter. Trajan, for instance, had ten thousand animals killed in the arena for a public celebration of his victory over the Dacians, not to mention eleven thousand people."

The other smiled at the intent look on Mauser's face, then continued. "Are you surprised at my memory, Major? The subject has always fascinated me; for one thing, I'm a great believer in the theory that history repeats itself. But back to the Roman games. As time went on, arenas were built all over the empire—the emperors knew they had a good thing going. Even small towns had their arenas. In Rome itself there were so many games that an avid follower could attend one every day.

"As the games increased in number, they also had to grow more extreme to hold the public's attention. The Emperor Philip, in celebrating the thousandth anniversary of Rome's founding, sponsored a game in which were killed a thousand pair of gladiators, a rhinoceros, six hippopotami, ten hyenas, ten giraffes, twenty wild asses, ten tigers, ten zebras, thirty leopards, sixty lions, thirty-two elephants, forty wild horses. I'm afraid I forgot the rest, but you can count on the fact that the mob loved it."

Mauser stirred in his chair. The other's personality

had grown on him; his tone of voice had a certain quality that made what he said seem important. However, Mauser's interest in Roman history wasn't exactly paramount.

"You wonder what I'm driving at, don't you?" Holland said. "Do you realize the expense involved in getting, say, a rhino to Rome in those days? Not to speak of the other exotic animals. Few people realize the extent to which the Romans went to acquire exotic animals for slaughter to appease the mob. They penetrated as far south as Kenya—there are still ruins of a Roman fort there—as far east as Indonesia and as far north as the Baltic. There is even evidence that they brought polar bears from Iceland."

Holland was obviously caught up in his topic; Mauser held his peace as the other continued. "But the mob wearied of this type of spectacle. What they really wanted was human sacrifice. Thus what began as fights between skilled swordsmen, observed by knowledgeable combat soldiers of a warrior people, degenerated into a circus. As the majority of Roman citizens lost their warlike ardor and became a worthless mob performing no useful function for themselves or the state, they no longer appreciated a drawn-out duel between equals.

"They wanted blood and lots of it, and they turned to the mass slaughter of Christians, runaway slaves, criminals, and whoever else they could find to throw to the lions, crocodiles, or whatever. Even this became increasingly old hat. Humans were hung by their heels and animals turned loose to pull them down. Men were tied face to face with rotting corpses and so remained until death. Certain types of animals were taught to abuse humans in a particular manner."

Mauser stirred again, unhappy with the turn this

had taken. Certainly such had occurred in the past, but there was no need to wax so eloquently over it. What the hell was this long monologue leading to?

"The games officially ended with the closing of the arenas in 404 A.D., following decades of gradual decline as Christianity grew in power. By then, the Roman empire was a mockery. All in all it lasted half a millennium, but things move faster these days."

The other's tone of voice changed abruptly. "Judging by your age, I would imagine that you've spent no more than fifteen years in the fracases. How have they changed in that time?"

Mauser was taken aback. "Why . . ." he said, hesitating as he got Holland's point. Then he went on, nodding. "Yes, they used to be company-size, a few hundred mercenaries in all. After a while, a battalion-size fracas became fairly commonplace, and then about ten years ago a corporation of any size had to be able to field at least a regiment. The biggies had brigades."

"And now?" Holland prompted.

"Now a divisional-size fracas is the thing."

"Yes, and if a corporation isn't among the top dozen or so, a single defeat can mean bankruptcy."

Mauser nodded. He knew of such cases.

Holland leaned back in his chair, as though all his points had been made. "Our so-called Welfare State took the same road. It sponsors the equivalent of the Roman *ludi* as a part of their plan to keep the masses in a state of stupefied acceptance of the status quo. And, as in the case of Rome, our games are bankrupting us. Our present-day patrician class, our Uppers, have a tiger by the tail, and can't let go. Simply put, if the mob isn't doped, fed, and entertained, they'll start thinking for themselves, and the Uppers will fall. It's not really a full-blown conspiracy. Most Uppers aren't conscious of this but act in accordance with it anyway; it's natural self-defense.

"We need those capable and intelligent people, of whom we spoke earlier, to make some basic changes. Where are they? Nadine said that your great driving ambition is to be bounced to Upper caste. But even if you do make it, what will you have on your hands but these problems that the Uppers seem unable to solve?"

"Possibly you're right," Mauser said impatiently. "What you say about the fracases becoming bigger and more expensive is true. They're also becoming more bloody. In the old days, one force or the other would surrender before too many were killed and wounded. They were conscious of the high cost of replacing trained soldiers, as well as of insurance, indemnities, pensions, all the rest of it. Not any more, though. These days they fight to the bitter end. The fans want lots of blood, and they want the cameras right in the middle of it."

Mauser shook his head. "But it's not my problem to solve. I've got my goal. I'll worry about the world's problems when I've solved mine."

A voice behind them spoke superciliously. "I do believe it's the status-hungry captain—ah, that is, major. To what do I owe the unexpected visit, Major?"

Mauser came to his feet and faced the newcomer.

Baron Balt Haer stood in the doorway, wearing a colonel's uniform and flicking his swagger stick along his booted leg, just as the first time Mauser had met him months before. His voice was lazily arrogant. "And Mr. Holland. I must say, the Middle caste seems to have taken over the house. Well, Major Mauser? I hope that you do not labor under the illusion that you are welcome here."

In Category Military, rank is observed whilst in uniform. As the old saying went, "You salute the uniform, not the man." Thus, Mauser had automatically come to attention. Now he said stiffly, "Sir, I am calling on your sister, Dr. Haer."

"Indeed," Baron Haer said, his nostrils high in that attitude once perfected and affected by grandees of medieval Spain, landed gentry of England, Prussian Junkers. "I find that my sister, in her capacity as a medical scientist, seems to go to extremes in her, ah, 'research.' What aspect of the lower classes is she studying in your case, Major?"

Mauser flushed. "Baron Haer," he said, "we seem to have gotten off on the wrong foot in the recent fracas. I would appreciate the opportunity to start over again."

"Would you indeed?" Balt Haer said loftily. He turned his eyes to Philip Holland, who had leisurely come to his feet, mouth bearing the slightest suggestion of surpressed humor. "Unless I am mistaken," he continued, "the conversation at the time of my entry seemed to have a distinctly subversive element. I find this somewhat surprising in the secretary of the administration's foreign minister."

"Not at all," Holland replied. "You evidently sneaked—er, that is, entered—at the end of a sentence, Baron Haer. We were merely discussing past and current events in a speculative vein. The various methods, down through the ages, that ruling classes have utilized to perpetuate their power."

"Yes?" Haer obviously didn't like Holland's comeback. "For example?"

"There are many examples," Holland said, reseating himself. "For instance, the medieval feudalistic class who dominated the ignorant and highly superstitious serfdom in Europe found it expedient to add to their titles *by grace of God,* as though it was by divine right that they be count or baron, prince or king. What serf would dare attempt the overthrow of his lord in the face of God's wishes?"

"I see," Haer said. "And other examples?"

Holland shrugged. "The Chinese Mandarins utilized possibly the most unique method, certainly one of the most gentle."

Haer was scowling at him, obviously out of his depth. So was Mauser, for that matter.

Holland said crisply, "The mandarins devised a written language so complicated that it took at least ten years to master, thus assuring that only the very well-to-do could afford to educate their sons. When invaded, as China has so often been, only the mandarins were in a position to serve the conquerors by carrying on the paperwork so vital to any advanced society. So, still in control of the machinery of government after an invasion, they perpetuated themselves until shortly—as history is reckoned—the conquerors were assimilated and the mandarins back in power."

Balt Haer said impatiently, "I seemed to be under the impression that you were speaking of more recent times, perhaps current times, when I entered, Mr. Holland."

Nadine was at the door. "Balt! Are you badgering my guests again?"

The three men turned to face her.

Balt said nastily, "I am astonished that you persist in bringing members of the lower orders into my home, Nadine."

"*Our* home, Balt." Nadine Haer's voice, and her eyes, were suddenly cold and hard. "In fact, if you must bring up such matters before outsiders, you will recall that you converted your portion of the estate—the majority of the estate, I might add—to our competitor's stock. This, I feel, is the root of your problem with Major Mauser, since he was the cause of the victory that ruined you!"

Her brother was obviously enraged, just barely holding his anger. "Are you suggesting that I am not welcome to stay in this, our family home, simply because the property is in your name?"

Mauser stood alert, ready to move if the situation got ugly, which appeared possible.

The brother and sister locked eyes for a long moment. Then Nadine Haer seemed to relax. "Not at all," she sighed. "You are always at home here, Balt. I simply demand that you exercise common courtesy to my guests."

Balt Haer turned and walked from the room.

Mauser relaxed a bit, too. "Sorry," he said to Nadine.

"Why? The fact of the matter is that he and I are continually fighting. Our ideologies clash, for one thing. He is quite an active member of the Nathan Hale Society."

"What's that?"

Holland chuckled. "An oddball organization devoted to what used to be called witch hunting in its efforts to maintain the status quo, Major. Not appropriately named, I fear, since Nathan Hale, the American patriot, would have abhorred the society we find ourselves a part of! But some people enjoy hiding behind symbols." He looked at Nadine. "I must be going, my dear. My, how charming you look. If this is the customary garb for soaring, I shall have to take up the sport."

"Why, Phil! Inane words of flattery from serious you?"

Mauser squirmed inwardly, wondering again about the basis for their friendship.

Just then, the butler entered and said, "A call for Major Mauser, if you please."

Mauser was more than a little surprised. Who,

other than those present, knew that he was here? He said to Nadine, "Would you pardon me a moment? I assume that it's something important, or I wouldn't be disturbed."

"Undoubtedly one of the feminine members of a Joe Mauser fan club," Nadine said demurely.

Mauser chuckled and followed the butler down a short hall to an alcove containing a terminal. On the viewscreen he could see the head and shoulders of a man in a sergeant's uniform.

"Mauser here."

"Marshal Cogswell's compliments, sir. He requests that you report to his headquarters at your earliest convenience."

Mauser pursed his lips. That was formal military for "Get your carcass in here now." He nodded. "All right, Sergeant. My compliments to the marshal, and will you tell me where the headquarters are located?"

The sergeant rattled off an address just outside Greater Washington. Mauser flicked the set off and sighed. His date with Nadine was off, of course; you don't ignore a summons from Marshal Cogswell. Not if you have any ambitions in Category Military.

CHAPTER FIFTEEN

It was common practice among high-ranking Category Military men to maintain skeleton staffs between fracases. That of Marshal Stonewall Cogswell was one of the most complete in existence, Cogswell habitually keeping upward of a hundred officers in his private uniform. It paid off. With such a skeleton force of highly skilled professionals the marshal could easily attract veterans for his rank and file and whip together a trained fighting force in a reasonably short period.

And nothing was more of the essence as time, in Category Military. For when two corporations sued for permission to meet on a military reservation for trial by combat to settle their commercial differences, the sums involved were staggering. Joe Mauser had been correct in saying that the fracas had grown, even in his memory, from skirmishes involving a company or two to full-fledged battles with a division or even more on either side—forty thousand men at one another's throats.

Thus a commanding officer became noted not only for his abilities in the field but for his skills in cutting financial corners, recruiting his force of mercenaries, whipping them into a unit, and getting them into the action quickly. In fact, corporations invariably stated the period of preparation time when they petitioned Category Military for a fracas permit. It was usually a month, three weeks of which would be used for recruiting and drill and the final week for the fracas itself. And nobody could excel Marshal Cogswell in using those three weeks to best advantage.

Major Joe Mauser came to attention before the desk of the lieutenant colonel who was acting as receptionist before the sanctum sanctorum of the field genius. The man looked vaguely familiar. He saluted and snapped, "Joseph Mauser, sir. Category Military, Rank Major. On request to see the marshal."

Lieutenant Colonel Paul Warren returned the salute, then stood, grinning, and extended his hand. "Good to see you again, Mauser. Hope you're in this one with us." His grin turned rueful. "That trick of yours with the glider cost me a pretty penny. I'd made the mistake of wagering heavily on Hovercraft. But the marshal is waiting. Right through that door, Major. See you later."

Evidently, Mauser decided, the marshal was recruiting for another fracas. He had been polite in his offer of a position on his staff, but not urgent; Mauser didn't think this summons had to do with anything so general.

Mauser rapped three times on the indicated door, then entered. Marshal Cogswell looked up from his desk, where he had been scowling at a military chart. The scowl disappeared and his strong face lit up with pleasure.

Mauser snapped a salute which the marshal acknowledged with a flick of his baton, then stood to shake hands. "Ah, Major Mauser. Bit of trouble locating you." His eyes narrowed momentarily. "I trust you are not at present affiliated with any company colors?" He took in Mauser's uniform, not placing it.

Mauser said in self-deprecation, "This is of my own devising, sir. I figured, if I was going to have to present myself to be killed for a living, I might as well show as good a face to the public as possible. I've been told that ultimately the fans make or break you, in our profession."

The marshal frowned, as though unhappy and possibly surprised at Mauser's words. However, he sat down again and repeated his question by simply looking at the other.

"No, sir, I'm free," Mauser hastened to add. "But frankly, I wasn't looking for a commission just now."

"Why not?" Cogswell barked. "Are you convalescing, Major? Surely you didn't manage to cop a wound in that last farce?"

"Personal reasons, sir."

"Very well." Cogswell looked unhappy. "However, I'm going to attempt to sway you, Major. It would seem that I am up against the wall if I don't. In a manner of speaking, it's your fault."

Mauser was bewildered. "My fault, sir?"

The older man was brisk. "This is the situation. I have been approached by United Miners to command their forces in their trial by combat with Carbonaceous Fuel. Same old issues, of course. The contract between the union and the corporation is usually for two years. Each time it comes up for negotiation the union officials try to get a larger cut of the pie for the workers and for themselves, and management resists. Category Military automatically issues a permit; the fracases they've been fighting are so popular that there would be a riot if the permit was refused. Frankly, I'm no great admirer of the group in control of United Miners, but—"

Mauser was surprised enough to say, "Why not, sir?" Old pro mercenaries seldom concerned themselves with the issues or principles involved in a fracas. They chose their side by more mundane considerations, such as money.

Cogswell looked at him testily. "Sit down, Joe. You're not on my staff, as yet. Forget the formality." When Mauser had accepted the chair, Cogswell continued. "I suppose you didn't know that I was born into Category Mining?"

"No, sir."

"Well, I was. But even as a boy I could see automation cutting the number of employees involved in the category—a category that did not lend itself well to automation in many respects."

"That's happened in every field, sir. Including my original one." Mauser was thinking, *so what?*

"Of course," Cogswell rapped. "My objection is with what happened to the union. With the number of employed miners down to a few thousand, the union officials—and there are nearly as many of them today as there were fifty years ago—have forgotten their original goals and purposes. They wax fat, existing merely to perpetuate themselves and their positions."

He looked at Mauser, obviously conscious that he was being inordinately candid. He cleared his throat and went on, "Not that it's my affair. I switched categories in my youth, to escape the futility of life in a lower caste." He cleared his throat again. "Now, let's get to the point, Mauser. I've been caught napping."

Now *that* was an unexpected confession, considering the source. Mauser said nothing, waiting for more.

The marshal shook his baton at the younger officer. "By using that damned glider of yours as a recon aircraft, you've revolutionized the state of the art in available military technology. That was an act of genius, and I admire it. Unfortunately, I failed to realize the speed with which every commanding officer would jump on the bandwagon and secure gliders for himself."

Mauser began to see what the other was getting at.

"I've been caught short," the other rapped. "Short of gliders—don't have even one. And within a few weeks I'm to command a divisional-size fracas. General Hollingsworth is in command of the Carbonaceous Fuel forces. Met him before, and always brought up victory only by the skin of my teeth. But this time he has two gliders. I have none."

"But sir, surely you can obtain several craft on the market."

"It's not the damned machines that are unavailable, but the trained pilots. The sport hasn't been that popular, certainly not among military men, for a century."

"But training a pilot—"

"Training a pilot, nonsense! A *pilot* won't do. He must also be a trained reconnaissance man. Must be able to follow the terrain from the air, identify military forces in both nature and number. But I needn't tell you this, Major. You, more than anyone else, should know the problems involved."

It hadn't occurred to Mauser, but the other was right. There couldn't be more than a few dozen men in Category Military who could handle the dual assignment of pilot and recon officer. In another six months the situation would have changed. Officers would be trained. But now? As Cogswell said, he was caught short.

Mauser came to his feet. "Sir, I'll consider the commission. But my plans were otherwise."

Cogswell stared at him grimly. "Joe, you've always been one of the best. An old pro in every sense of the word. However, there have been some rumors going around about your ambitions."

"Sir," Mauser said stiffly, "my ambitions are my own business, whatever these rumors."

"Didn't say I believed them, Major. We've been in the dill together too many times for me to judge you on mere gossip alone. What I was leading up to is this. There's nothing wrong with ambition. If you'll see me through in this, I'll do what I can toward your promotion in the Category Military."

Mauser saluted. "Thank you, sir. I'll consider the commission and let you know by tomorrow."

Cogswell flicked the baton nonchalantly. "That will be all, then, Major."

Joe turned and left. Left with the feeling that, somehow, he was letting someone down. Someone besides Marshal Cogswell. It was time for a talk with Freddy Soligen.

He arrived at Soligen's apartment in a rather ill humor. He hated having to stall Cogswell; a couple of months ago he might have jumped at the opportunity the marshal had presented. But now . . . there were too many things to think about. Nadine, the campaign that Soligen had started, Cogswell's offer, the Disarmament Commission meeting.

He shook hands with the telly reporter in an abrupt, impatient manner. Soligen waved him in.

Mauser sank into a chair and looked up at the reporter accusingly. "This fancy uniform I stood still for. That idea of picking a song to identify with me, and bribing the orchestra leaders to swing into it whenever I showed up, might have its advantages. Getting me all sorts of telly interviews and all those write-ups in the fracas buff magazines I can see the need for, in spite of what it's costing. But what in hell," his voice went dangerous, "was the idea of putting that punch-drunk prize fighter on me in the most respectable nightclub in Greater Washington?"

Soligen grinned ruefully. "Oh, you figured that out, eh?"

"Did you think I was stupid?"

Soligen rubbed his hands together happily. "He used to be the world heavyweight champion, and you flattened him! It was in every gossip column in the country, and every news reporter on telly was talking about it, playing it up. And hell, all it cost was five shares of your Vacuum Tube Transport stock."

"Five shares!"

"Why not? He used to be the champ, didn't he? Too dumb to rate a bounce in caste, and now he's so broke he's got to live on Basic. He was willing to take a dive cheap, if you ask me."

Mauser looked unhappy. "I've got news for you, Freddy. Your hired brawler started off as per instructions, but after a couple of blows he forgot whatever you told him and tried to take me. We're lucky he didn't splatter me all over the dance floor. He didn't take a dive, Freddy; I had to scuttle him!"

Soligen blinked.

"Sure, sure, sure," Mauser growled. "Look: next time you decide to spend five shares of my stock on some deal like this, let me know, eh?"

Soligen suddenly moved across the room to a sideboard, opened it, and pulled out two glasses. "Whiskey?" he asked.

"Tequila, if you've got it," Mauser replied. "Look, I'm beginning to have second thoughts about this campaign."

Soligen poured the fiery Mexican drink for Mauser, followed by one for himself. After handing Mauser his drink he took a place in the chair opposite. "It's going fine." His voice was persuasive. "Your name is on everyone's lips. First thing you know, some of the armaments firms'll be having you endorse their guns, swords, cannon, whatever."

"Oh, great. But what's that going to do for my status? My friends are already ribbing me about this uniform and all the plugs I've been getting. Glory-grabbers aren't popular among pros, you know."

"Who gives a damn? We're not in this to please your mercenary pals. We're in this for Number One, Joe Mauser, and Number Two, Freddy Soligen."

Mauser downed the greater part of his drink. "Sure, but where are we now? Your campaign has been in full swing for almost two months. What's it accomplished?"

Soligen was indignant. "What's it accomplished? Have some patience, Joe! We've got three Major Joe Mauser fan clubs and five more starting up. And next month you're going to be on the cover of the *Fracas Times!*"

"And I'm still a major and still a Mid-Middle. And my stock shares are getting low."

Soligen twisted his mouth and looked worriedly down into his glass. "I know. We need a gimmick to climax all of this. Some kind of gimmick to bring you absolutely to the top."

"A gimmick?" Mauser demanded. "What do you mean, a gimmick? I thought we'd been through that. That's what the uniform and mustache and the rest are for. And I've already pulled my biggest gimmick—the sailplane."

"No, you're going to have to do something really spectacular. We'll have to get you into a fracas and pull something dramatic. Make you the biggest telly hero of them all. I don't know what, I haven't come up with the angle yet. But when I do, I'll guarantee that every telly camera covering the fracas will be zeroed in on Joe Mauser."

"Great," Mauser rumbled. "And I've got just the gimmick. It'll blow them away . . ."

Soligen looked up, hopefully.

"I'll get killed in a burst of glory," Mauser finished. He chuckled grimly. "Look, the sailplane was only good for one fling. Everyone's going to have one now. But I'm all for getting back into a fracas."

"Right. We'll have to come up with a *new* gimmick. Something that will make everyone notice you, get you mobbed every time you step out on the street. The glider was good for a start, but . . ."

"You keep talking about a gimmick," Mauser said impatiently. "Look, I'm a mercenary. A fighting man can't waste all of his time on gimmicks. I've got to *do* something to maintain my reputation, and that means fighting in fracases."

"That's what I'm talking about," Soligen came back. "Look, you tried to handle all this by yourself last time. You dreamed up the glider gimmick, and put it over. But did it do you any good? Like hell! All you did, as far as some of the fracas buffs are concerned, was louse up a perfectly good fight—hardly a drop of blood shed. Sure, you surprised a few people, but the effects are wearing off. The only reason you've been getting all this attention is because I've been buying it . . . with your money, of course.

"But," Soligen continued, "now *that's* gone as far as it's going to take us. Now we need some real action to back up the publicity, something to grab the buffs by their—"

He stopped in mid-sentence and snapped his fingers. "I've got it, Joe! Blood-and-guts combat, up in the sky—it's great! Combine your gimmick with what the buffs want, and we can't lose."

Mauser scowled questioningly.

The little man was on his feet and pacing back and forth now. "Dogfights! I don't know why I didn't think of that before."

Mauser was puzzled. "You mean pit dogs, like in the old days?"

"No, no. In the First World War. All those early fighters—Baron von Richtofen, the German; Albert Ball, the Englishman; Rene Fonck, the Frenchman. And all the rest—Hermann Goering, Ernst Udet, and Werner Voss, and Rickenbacker, and Luke Short. Flying those rickety Fokkers and Albatrosses, Spads and Nieuports."

Mauser nodded, slightly embarrassed at his lapse in memory. He'd spent most of his time studying 19th-Century warfare, but he had not neglected the following century entirely. "I remember now. They'd mount a Vickers or a Spandau to fire between the propeller blades. As I remember, that German, Richtofen, was top in the genre with some eighty victories to his credit."

"OK. They called them dogfights. One aircraft against another. You're going to revive the whole thing, Joe."

Mauser was staring at him. Once again the telly reporter sounded completely around the bend.

Soligen was impatiently patient. "We'll mount a gun on your sailplane and you'll attack those two gliders Cogswell says General Hollingsworth has."

"Right," Mauser said, recalling the interview with Cogswell, at the same time wondering how Soligen had come by that bit of information. "But the Sovworld observers would never stand still for it. In fact, there's a good chance that using gliders at all will be forbidden when the International Disarmament Commission convenes next month. And if the Sov-world delegates vote against use of gliders as reconnaissance craft, the Neut world will vote with them, as will Common Europe."

Mauser frowned, then continued, "It's true enough that gliders were flown before 1900, but they were flimsy fabric and wood constructions—nothing like the advanced technology we have today, spun-fiber materials and all. I knew that I was taking a chance bringing mine in, because of that, but by the same token, some of the alloys and powder mixes used in today's rifles were also unknown before 1900. Certainly, there were no gliders flown in the 19th century that were capable of carrying a machine gun and ammo in addition to a man. That's one reason I'm not too hot on flying one for Cogswell." There were other reasons, reasons involving Nadine Haer and her stand on violence and fracases, but those were none of Soligen's business.

"Look," Soligen demanded, "what was the smallest machine gun in use in the 1800s?"

Mauser considered the question. "Probably the little French *Chaut-Chaut* gun. It was small enough to be carried by one man, and the rounds were packed into a flat, circular pan. I think it goes back that far, anyway. I know they used them in the first World War, and they were around for some time before that."

"Right! OK, you had gliders. You had portable machine guns. All we're doing is combining the existing technology, but it'll be spectacular! You'll be the most famous mercenary in Category Military, and it'll be impossible for the Department not to bounce you to Colonel and Low-Upper. Especially with me and every telly reporter and fracas-buff magazine we've bribed yelling for it."

Mauser's characteristic tic was manifesting itself. It was all so logical—and tempting. But he shook his head. "It wouldn't go, Freddy. Suppose I caught one or both of those gliders, busy at their recon, and shot their tails off, so to speak? So what? The fans still wouldn't have their blood and guts—not close-up. And we'd probably be so high that they wouldn't see the action. All you would be able to see would be the losing glider falling—and maybe a close-up of the crash itself, if you were lucky. The special effects in some of the adventure shows are better—"

Soligen stopped pacing and dramatically pointed a finger at Mauser. "That's where you're wrong! This will be the real thing, and I'll be in the back seat of your sailplane with a portable camera. And every reporter in the West-world will have his most powerful telescopic lens on us. It'll be the most televised bit of fracas this century!"

CHAPTER SIXTEEN

When Joe Mauser entered the swank Agora Bar, the little afternoon dance band broke into a few bars of the tune which was beginning to pall on him.

"... I knew her heart was breaking.
And to my heart in anguish pressed,
The girl I left behind me."

Nadine Haer looked up from the little table she occupied, caught the wry expression on his face, and smiled. "What price glory?" she laughed.

He took the chair across from her and chuckled ruefully. "All right," he came back, "I surrender. However, if you think having a theme song is bad, you'll be relieved that I turned down some of the other ideas that my, uh, publicity agent had."

"Oh, did he want you to dash into a burning building and save an oldster's cat?"

"Not exactly. But he had a singer with a list of nine or ten victories to her credit—"

"Victories?"

"Previous husbands—and two current ones. And I was to be seen escorting her around town."

"A fate worse than death, I'm sure. But, really— why did you turn that down?"

"I wanted to spend the time with you."

Her lips pouted. "So we can continue our never-ending argument over status?"

"No."

She frowned at the sharpness of his reply. He grunted. "At least the tune is appropriate tonight."

She looked up quickly. "Oh, Joe, you haven't taken another commission?"

Mauser found her tone irritating. "I'm considering one, and why not? I'm a mercenary by trade, Nadine."

"But you admittedly made a small fortune on the last fracas. You were one of the very few investors in the country who expected Vacuum Tube stock to boom. You don't have to risk your life any more, Joe."

He didn't bother to tell her that the greater part of that small fortune had been dedicated to Soligen's campaign. "I've told you before that any stock shares I'll make at this kind of thing aren't particularly important," he said. "But Cogswell has pledged that if I help him in this fracas he'll press for my promotion to colonel—which will go a long way toward getting me bounced to Upper."

"But Joe," her tone was low, "to risk your life, your *life,* for such a silly thing—"

"Such a silly thing," he said softly, "as attaining a position which will enable me to openly, uh, court the woman I love." There. He'd said it, that which had been on his mind for so long. What he'd been unable to say even to himself. He found himself surprised, but at the same time he felt a certain satisfaction that he'd been able to give voice to his thoughts.

She flushed, looked into his face for an instant. Her flush deepened and her eyes went to her folded hands.

He said nothing.

Finally, her voice so low as to be almost inaudible, Nadine said, "Perhaps I would be willing to marry a man of Middle caste."

He was surprised. But even as he was thrilling to the meaning of her words, his head was shaking. "Nadine Haer, Category Medicine, Rank Doctor, Mid-Upper, married to Major Joseph Mauser, Category Military, Mid-Middle. Don't be ridiculous, Nadine. It would be as though you'd married someone of another race back in the 20th century."

"There's no law preventing marriage between castes!"

"Nor was there a law, in most of the old American states, against interracial marriage. But there were few who dared, for obvious reasons. I'm just a guest in here, Nadine, a guest of the people for as long as my fleeting fame holds out, which might not be long. And I don't desire to be your guest for the rest of my life."

Her eyes flared in sudden anger. "And do you think that if you do jump to Upper, I will marry you and then enjoy the fact that—from your viewpoint, at least—our marriage was only possible due to your participation in mass slaughter for the sake of millions of trank-happy slobs?"

"I didn't want to even talk about marriage until I'd made it to Low-Upper."

"Well, sir, the matter is before us." Nadine Haer's lips were thin now, and her eyes cold. "And I reject your kind offer in advance." Her voice, tinged with sarcasm, suddenly took a softer tone. "Oh, Joe, if you have to persist in this ambition, drop Category Military and get into something else. You have enough stock and cash reserve to buy your way into another field."

Again he didn't tell her that his fortune was all but

gone. "Those who have, get. The rich get richer, while the poor get poorer. Things are rigged, these days, so that it's impossible to work your way to the top in any category but Military or Religion. The Uppers take care of their own, and at the same time they make every effort to keep the lower orders from joining their sacred circle." He paused, surprised for the second time that night that his thoughts were speaking of their own accord. "I might make it in Category Military, Nadine, but my chances in another field are so remote as to be laughable."

She stood then, and looked down at him emptily. "No," she said, "don't get up. I'm leaving, Major Mauser." He began to rise in protest, but she stopped him with a hand on his shoulder.

"I have seen only one fracas on telly in my entire life," she continued, her tone sharp. "I was so repelled that I vowed never to watch another. However, I am going to make an exception now. I am going to follow your fracas, and if, as a result of your actions, even a single person meets death, I wish never to see you again!"

Things were moving fast. Perhaps impetuously, perhaps defiantly, perhaps not, Mauser had accepted the commission Cogswell offered. Now, barely a week before the fracas, he found himself in Cogswell's final high-level strategy meeting.

Marshal Stonewall Cogswell looked impudently around at the staff officers gathered at the chart table. "Gentlemen," he said. "I assume you are all familiar with the battle of Chancellorsville?"

No one bothered to answer. He chuckled. "I know what you are thinking. Had any of you refrained from a thorough study of any of the campaigns of Lee and Jackson, you would not be a member of my staff."

The craggy marshal traced with his finger on the large military chart that lay before them. "Then you will have noticed the similarity between the projected troop dispensation and that of Joseph Hooker's Army of the Potomac and Lee's Army of Northern Virginia, on 2 May, 1863." He pointed with his baton. "Our stream, here, would be the Rappahannock; this woods, the Wilderness. Here would be Fredericksburg and here Chancellorsville."

One of his colonels nodded. "My regiment occupies a position similar to that of Jubal Early's."

"Absolutely correct," the marshal said crisply. "Gentlemen, I repeat: our troop dispensations, those of Lieutenant General Hollingsworth and myself, are practically identical. Now then, if Hollingsworth continues to move his forces here, across our modern-day Rappahannock, he makes the initial mistake that finally led to the opening which allowed Jackson's brilliant fifteen-mile flanking march. Any questions, thus far?"

There were some murmurs, but no questions. The accumulated years of military service of this group of veterans would have totaled hundreds.

"Very interesting, eh?" the marshal pursued. "Jed, your artillery is massed here. It's a shame that General Jack Altshuler has taken a commission with Carbonaceous Fuel. We could use his cavalry. He would be our J.E.B. Stuart, eh?"

Lieutenant Colonel Paul Warren cleared his throat. "Sir, Jack Altshuler is the best cavalryman in North America."

"I would be the last to deny it, Paul."

"Yes, sir. And he's fought half his fracases under you, sir."

"Your point?" the marshal prompted.

"He knows your methods, sir. For that matter, so does Lieutenant General Hollingsworth. He's fought you enough."

There was silence in the staff headquarters, broken suddenly by Cogswell's curt chuckle. "Paul, I'm going to recommend your promotion to full colonel on the strength of that. You were the first to see what I have been getting at. Gentlemen, do you realize what General Hollingsworth and his staff are doing this very moment? They're poring over a campaign chart of the battle of Chancellorsville."

The craggy veteran bent back over the map. His voice dropped all humor as he stabbed with his baton. "Here, here, and here. They expect us to duplicate the movements of Lee. Very good, we shall. But the advances of Lee and Jackson, we will make feints. And the feints made by Lee and Jackson will be our attacks in force. Gentlemen, we are going to literally reverse the battle of Chancellorsville." He stood and turned. "Major Mauser!"

Mauser had been in the background as befitted his junior rank. Now he stepped to the table's edge. "Yes, sir."

The marshal indicated a defile. "Were we actually duplicating the Civil War battle, this would have been the right flank of Sedgwick's two army corps. We're not dealing in army corps these days, of course, but regiments. However, the positioning is relatively as important. Jack Altshuler's cavalry is largely concentrated here. When the action is joined, he can move in one of three ways. Through this defile is least likely. But if his heavy cavalry does work its way through here, I must know immediately; hence the value of your recon craft. This is crucial, Joe. Any questions?"

"No, sir."

The marshal turned his attention to his chief of artillery. "Jed, when we need your guns, we're going to need them badly, but I doubt if that will happen until the second or third day of the fracas. Going to want as clever a job of camouflage as possible, to hide your guns where Hollingsworth's gliders won't spot them." He looked at Mauser, who, having his instructions, had fallen back from the table again. "When you reintroduced aerial observation, Major, you set off a whole train of related factors, not the least of which is camouflage." He glanced back at his artillery man. "Which reminds me . . ."

"Yes, sir?"

"Put your mind to work on devising Maxim gun mounts to be used to keep enemy gliders at as high an altitude as possible. Or preferably, of course, to bring them down. We'll need an anti-aircraft squadron, in short. Better put young Fergusson on it."

"Yes, sir."

The airport nearest the Grant Memorial Military Reservation was some ten miles distant from the borders which, upon the initiation of a fracas, were closed to all aircraft and all persons not connected with the fighting forces. The only exceptions were the ubiquitous telly crews and the military observers from the Sov-world and the Neut-world, present to satisfy themselves that weapons of the post-1900 era were not being utilized.

The distance was not of particular importance, however. The powered aircraft that would tow Joe Mauser's glider to a suitable altitude would stop short of flying over the reservation, and the hilly terrain would provide sufficient variation in wind and updrafts for Mauser to fly the sailplane the rest of the way.

On the first day of the fracas, Mauser turned up at the airport accompanied by Freddy Soligen, who, for once, was without a crew to help him with his cameras and other gear. Instead he was aided by Max Mainz, who was being somewhat huffy about this telly reporter taking over his position as observer.

Two other gliders were present on the field, in front of a hanger perhaps a quarter-mile distant, but Mauser and his partners conspicuously ignored them.

While Mauser checked out the sailplane in careful detail, Soligen and Mainz began loading equipment into the graceful craft's second seat. Mainz growled, "How are you going to be able to lift all this weight, Major?"

"We'll make it," Mauser said absently, testing the ailerons. "Freddy isn't any heavier than you are. Besides, this is a real workhorse. I sacrificed glide angle for payload with this one."

As before, that meant absolutely nothing to Max Mainz. He shrugged and went on about the business at hand.

As Mainz handed him the final bit of telly gear, Soligen stood suddenly in the back seat of the craft, where he had been stowing his gear. "Uh, oh, here they come, Joe." He quickly returned to stowing his gear, apparently ignoring the approach of three men in uniform.

"Get that you-know-what out of sight soonest," Mauser said out of the side of his mouth. He turned as the trio neared, came to attention, and saluted Colonel Lajos Arpad.

Arpad, so small at the waist that he might have been wearing a girdle under his tunic, answered the salute by tapping his swagger stick against the visor of his cap. "Major Mauser," he said in acknowledgment. He made no effort to shake hands, turning instead to his companions. "Lieutenant Colonel Krishnalal Majumdur of Bombay, Major Mohamed Kamil of Alexandria, may I introduce the celebrated Major Joseph Mauser, who has possibly reintroduced aircraft to warfare."

Mauser saluted and bowed in proper protocol. "Gentlemen, a pleasure." The two neutrals responded as was appropriate, then stepped forward to exchange handshakes.

"Or possibly he has not," Arpad added gently.

Mauser looked at him sharply. The Hungarian seemed to make a practice of turning up every time Mauser was about to take off. He had seen the Sov-world observer at the field on several occasions since the McDonnell/Boeing fracas.

Arpad said airily, "It will be up to the International Disarmament Commission to decide upon that when it convenes shortly, will it not?"

The Arab major was staring in fascination at the sailplane. "Major Mauser, you are certain that such craft were in existence before 1900? It would seem—"

"Designed as far back as Leonardo da Vinci's time," Mauser said defiantly, "and flown in various countries in the 18th century." He looked at the Hungarian. "Including, so I understand, what was then Czarist Russia."

The Sov-world officer ignored the obvious needling. "It is quite true that the glider was first flown by an obscure inventor in the Ukraine; however, this is not what particularly interests us today. Perhaps the commission will find that the use of the glider is permitted for observation, but it is obvious that it cannot be contended that early gliders were used for, say, *bombing*." He turned quickly and pointed at

Soligen, who, already strapped into his seat, was watching them, his face impassive. "What has this man been hiding away within the aircraft, Major?"

"Gentlemen," Mauser said formally, "may I introduce Frederic Soligen, Category Communications, Subdivision Telly News, Rank Senior Reporter. Mr. Soligen has been assigned to cover the fracas from the air."

Soligen looked at the Sov-World officer. "Hiding? You mean my camera? Or maybe the power-pack, or—"

"All right, all right," Arpad snapped. But the Hungarian was no fool and obviously smelled something wrong. He turned to Mauser. "I would remind you, Major Mauser, that you as an individual are responsible for any deviations from the basic Universal Disarmament Pact. You, and any of your superiors who can be proven to have knowledge of such deviation."

"I am familiar with the articles of war, as detailed in the pact," Mauser said dryly. "And now, gentlemen, I am afraid duty calls." He bowed stiffly, saluted correctly. "A pleasure to make your acquaintance, Colonel Majumdur, Major Kamil. Colonel Arpad, a pleasure to renew acquaintance."

They answered him in kind and stared after him as he climbed into the sailplane and signaled the pilot of the tow plane. Mainz ran to the tip of one wing, lifting it and steadying the glider until forward motion gave it some stability.

As they moved forward, Soligen growled. "Zen! If they'd known I had a machine gun tucked away in one of these cases!"

"The Sovs have obviously decided to protest the use of aircraft in West-world fracases," Mauser said unhappily. He shifted his hand on the stick, and the glider, which had been sliding along on its single wheel, bumped once and lifted gently into the air.

CHAPTER SEVENTEEN

The tow plane cut them loose at just over nine thousand feet, with the altimeter showing a good climb rate.

When they were near ten thousand feet, Mauser leveled off and surveyed the horizon; he could just make out a group of hills that marked the western boundary of the reservation.

Soligen had remained quiet as Mauser set their course. Now he spoke up. "Hey! How come the Hungarians are so important? I thought it was the Russians who started the whole Soviet, the Communist thing."

"That's something that some of the early timers like Stalin didn't figure on when they began moving in on their neighbors," Mauser answered. "They could have learned a lesson from the film business about the Hungarians. The saying in that business was always, 'If you've got a Hungarian for a friend, you don't need any enemies.' "

Soligen laughed, even as he looked apprehensively over the sailplane's side. "Yeah, or that other one. 'The Hungarians are the only people who can enter a revolving door behind you and come out in front.' "

"Well," Mauser chuckled, "that's what happened

213

to the Russians." He pointed. "There's the reservation. Listen, I forgot to ask earlier—were you able to find out who either of General Hollingsworth's glider pilots are?"

"Yeah," Soligen told him. "Both are captains. One named Bob Flaubert and the other Jimmy Hideka."

Mauser swore under his breath. "Bob Flaubert? He's an artillery man. He saved my life once. Five minutes later, I saved his."

Soligen had been staring below, trying to interpret the terrain from this perspective. "Both of them used to fly light planes for sport, but you ought to be able to fly circles around them. They just haven't gotten in the time you have in a glider." Soligen began moving equipment around in the back. "And this is no time to be thinking of the past. You're even with him, and you're both hired mercenaries in a fracas."

"But I've got a gun and he hasn't," Mauser protested.

"Good!" Soligen snapped.

As they crossed the range of hills Mauser had spotted earlier, Mauser banked the glider to head it toward the area that Cogswell had ordered him to scan. Jack Altshuler was a fox. His heavy cavalry had more than once swung the tide of a battle, even an entire fracas.

At the same time, he kept himself alert for the other gliders. One of them had, he'd observed during the conversation with Arpad at the airport, taken off perhaps fifteen minutes before him. He had not seen the second take off, and presumably the enemy forces would use the two gliders in relays. Which meant that it was unlikely that Mauser would find them both in the air at once. In other words, if he attacked the one, possibly shooting it down, then the other would be warned, would mount a gun of its own . . . and it would no longer be a matter of shooting a clay pigeon.

Mauser turned to tell Soligen this just in time to catch the shadow above and behind him.

"Damn!" he spat, kicking right rudder, thrusting the stick to the right and forward.

"What?" Soligen protested weakly, looking up from adjusting a camera lens.

Three or four thirty-caliber slugs tore holes in their left wing, the rest of the burst missing entirely.

Mauser dove sharply, gained speed, winged over and reached desperately for altitude. The other—no, the *others* were above him. He yelled back at the cameraman. "Put that gun together for me. Be ready to hand up pans of ammo. And if you want action on that camera, get moving!"

It still hadn't got through to Soligen. "What the hell's going on?"

Mauser banked again, grabbing for a current rising along a hill slope, then circled, reaching for altitude before they could get over him to make another pass. "Did I say something about poor old Bob Flaubert not having a gun?" he asked bitterly. "Well, poor old Bob's got at least as much firepower as we have."

The other was startled. Mauser pointed to where the other aircraft circled, possibly a hundred meters above and five hundred to the right of them. Each of the gliders bore a single passenger. They were seemingly moving as quietly as Mauser's craft, but gliders in motion are deceptive. Mauser glanced at the rate of climb indicator. He was doing all right at six meters per second, a thousand feet a minute, considering his weight.

Soligen had at last awakened to the fact that they were in combat, that the enemy had drawn first blood. The wound in the wing was not serious, but the holes that the rounds had poked through the lightweight wing material were obvious. Soligen did not let this bother him; true to his reputation, he moved fast to get the small machine gun into Mauser's hands and himself into action as a cameraman.

"What's the situation?" he snapped, shoving the gun up over Mauser's right shoulder.

"We weigh too much," Mauser replied. "Altitude counts. What've you got back there that can be thrown out?" As he talked, he was shrugging out of his leather flying jacket.

"Nothing," Soligen said in anguish. "I cut my equipment down to the bare minimum, like you said."

"You've got extra lenses and stuff. Out with them." Mauser tossed his coat over the side, began unlacing his boots. "And all your clothes—clothes are heavy."

"I need my equipment for long-range shots, like when one of them crashes!" The telly reporter was scanning the others through a viewfinder and slipping off his own jacket.

The updraft suddenly gave out. The rate-of-climb meter began to register a drop. Mauser swore and shot a glance at his opponents. Happily they, too, had lost the currents.

"We're not going to be getting shots of them crashing," Mauser yelled, "unless we lose more weight. Overboard with everything you can possibly afford, Freddy. That's an order."

There was one thing in Mauser's favor: he had a year's flying experience in the sailplane. The stick and rudderbar were appendages of his body. One flies by the seat of his pants in a sailplane, and Mauser flew his as though born in it. The others, obviously, were not yet acclimated to engineless craft.

He banked away from them, trying to conserve altitude, begrudging each foot dropped. He could feel the craft jump lightly each time the cursing telly reporter jettisoned another article of equipment or clothing. He had already lost pants and shoes.

The others evidently had their guns fix-mounted, to fire straight ahead — that was why they hadn't fired on Mauser more than once. He wondered, even as he slid away from them, how they had managed to escape detection by the field observers. Well, that could be worried about later.

One of them fired at him at too great a range. Then both pilots, realizing that they were dropping altitude too quickly and that soon Mauser would be on their level, turned away to seek a new updraft. As they banked, their faces were clearly discernible. One raised a hand in mock salute.

"Look at that curd-loving Bob," Mauser laughed grudgingly. He steadied the small *mitrailleuse* on the edge of the cockpit, holding the stick with his knees, and squeezed off a burst which rattled through the other's fuselage without apparent damage. The enemy slid away quickly, losing precious altitude in the maneuver.

"Ah, ha!" Mauser said wolfishly. "Now they know we've got a stinger, too!"

"I got that," Soligen crowed. "I got it perfectly. Listen, we're too high for the boys down below. Get lower so they can get you on lens, Joe."

Mauser snorted in disgust. "I hope every fracas buff in North America chokes on his trank," he snarled. "We're in the dill, Freddy. Understand? We're too heavy, and there's two of them and one of us. On top of that, those are Maxim guns they've got mounted, not pea-shooters like this *chaut-chaut*."

"That's your side of it," Soligen said, not unhappily. "I take care of the photography. Get closer, Joe. Get closer."

Mauser caught another light updraft. It gained them a few hundred feet—but the others had found it, too. They circled. His experience balanced their weight advantage. Happily, their glide ratios didn't seem to be much better than his own. Had they higher-performance gliders of forty, even thirty-five to one glide ratios, he would have been lost.

"Nothing else you can toss out?" he demanded.

"You want me to jump?" Soligen muttered nastily.

"That's an idea. I should've realized when you were giving me your fling about reviving aerial warfare that it was something that anyone might come up with. It was just as easy for them to mount a gun as it was for us. Now we're both wasting time with fighting, when we should be doing recon—"

Mauser broke off in mid-sentence. His face blanched. He shot a quick look downward. All three gliders had climbed considerably, and the terrain below was indistinct.

"Hand me those glasses!" he snapped.

"What glasses? I threw them out, with everything else—semaphore flags, the sun blinker you had. It all went overboard with my extra lenses."

The craft was so banked as to almost have the wings perpendicular to earth. Mauser shot an agonized look at Soligen, then back to the earth below, trying desperately to narrow his eyes for keener vision.

"What the hell's the matter with you?" Soligen asked. "What difference does it make what they're doing down there? We're occupied up here, thanks."

"This is a frame-up," Mauser growled. "Bob and that other pilot weren't on recon. They were laying for me. They're out to keep me from seeing what's going on down there. And I know what's going on— Jack Altshuler's pulling a fast one. Here we go, Freddy. Hang on!"

He slapped the flap brake lever with his left hand, winged over, and began dropping like a shot as his glide angle fell off from twenty-five to ten. In seconds, the other two gliders were after him, riding his tail.

Freddy Soligen, eyes bugging, shot a look of fear at the two tailing craft, whose noses periodically blazed brilliant cherry-red. Maxim guns, emitting their blessings.

The telly reporter turned to Mauser, pounding him on the shoulder. His voice was desperate. "Joe! You're on lens with the telly teams down there, and you're running!"

"Cut that out," Mauser rapped. "Duck your head. Let me train this gun over you. I've got to keep those bastards from shooting our tail off before I can get to Cogswell."

"The marshal!" Soligen yelled. "You can't get to him anyway. I told you I threw away your semaphore flags, your blinker—everything. Listen, Joe, you've still got time. You can stunt these things better than they can! Loop over and get 'em!"

"Duck!" Joe yelled. He fired a burst at the pursuing gliders over the smaller man's head, just missing his own tail section.

They sped down almost to tree level at a fantastic speed. The two enemy craft were hot after them, their guns firing in continuous excitement, trying to catch Mauser in their sights as he kicked rudder right, left, right, in evasive maneuver.

His guess had been correct, he saw now. The swashbuckling Jack Altshuler had known his many-times commander even better than Cogswell realized. Instead of using one of the three alternative maneuvers available to him, the wily cavalryman had ferreted out a fourth. His full force, hauling mountain guns on muleback, was trailing over a supposedly impassable mountain path which originally could not have been more than a deer track.

Soligen, behind him, was holding his hands high in surrender. He might have focused his camera on the troops below, but the desire wasn't in him. Not one fracas buff in a hundred could comprehend the complications of combat, the need for adequate reconnaissance—the need for Mauser to get through to his commander.

He made one last plea. "Joe, we've put everything into this, every share of stock you've accumulated. All I have, too. Don't you realize what you're doing? All the buffs will see is those two half-trained pilots chasing you away, and you not fighting back."

"And," Mauser growled, "twenty thousand soldiers down there are depending on me to report on Altshuler's horse."

"But you can't win anyway. You can't get your message to Cogswell."

Mauser grinned as the terrain slipped by beneath them. He pulled back on the stick, gaining some altitude, but slowing. "Want to bet? Ever heard of a crash landing, Freddy? Hang on!"

By continuing his evasive maneuver and firing bursts behind him when he could, Mauser managed to keep the enemy gliders back. But they didn't break off the pursuit until he approached the area of Cogswell's field headquarters. As they came within range, the big, carriage-mounted Maxim guns ringing the area spoke. Hollingsworth's gliders banked away.

Now all that was left was for Mauser to bring the craft in—as he said, in a crash landing. The field headquarters were hidden in trees, and Mauser knew that he wasn't going to avoid them all. Instead he swooped down, skimming some of the higher trees, aiming for an area where the tree trunks were spaced at about the right distance.

A sharp jolt and a bang told him that something had caught the stabilizer, and the craft nosed downward. They were perhaps fifty feet above the ground then. The glider took a sickening lurch, nosing toward the ground sooner than he had intended.

Mauser fought the stick and rudder, and the glider leveled out for an instant before hitting the ground with a jolt that snapped his teeth together. Then they were sliding through a small forest, fuselage shredding and wings ripping against tree trunks. Something large flew at him—and everything went black.

Through a mass of pain he heard voices calling and Soligen cursing. He cursed, himself, and began reeling off his report on the enemy cavalry, heedless of whether anyone was listening. Eventually, the darkness closed in completely.

CHAPTER EIGHTEEN

Stretched out on the hospital bed, Mauser grinned up at his visitor and said ruefully, "I'd salute, sir, but my arms seem to be out of commission." With his eyes, he indicated the wrappings that covered most of his upper body. "And come to think of it, I'm out of uniform."

Cogswell looked down at him, unamused. "You've heard the news?"

Mauser's face straightened at the other's tone. "You mean the Disarmament Commission? They've ruled? I've been trying to get word, but—"

"They found against the use of aircraft, other than free balloons, in any military action," Cogswell said bitterly. "They threw the book, Mauser. The court ruled that you, Robert Flaubert, and James Hideka be stripped of rank and barred from Category Military. You have also been fined all stock shares in your possession, other than Basic."

Mauser's face went empty. It was only then that he noticed that the other was attired in the uniform of a brigadier general. The implication was obvious.

Seeing the direction of Mauser's gaze, Cogswell shrugged. "My Upper-caste status helped me. I was able to pull just enough strings that Category Military Department merely reduced me in rank and belted me with a stiff fine. Your friend—your former friend, Freddy Soligen—testified in my behalf, that I had no knowledge of your mounting a gun."

The former marshal cleared his throat. "His testimony was correct. I had no such knowledge and would have issued orders against it, had I known. The fact that you enabled me to rescue the situation into which I'd been suckered helps somewhat my feelings toward you, Mauser, but only somewhat."

Mauser could imagine the other's bitterness. He had fought his way up the hard way. At his age, he wasn't going to regain that marshal's baton.

Brigadier General Stonewall Cogswell hesitated for a moment, then said, "One other thing. United Miners has repudiated your actions, even to the point of refusing to pay your medical expenses. I told the hospital managers to charge your bill to my account."

"That won't be necessary, sir."

"I'm afraid you'll find it is, Mauser." The former marshal frowned. "Besides, I owe you something for that spectacular scene where you came flying in over the treetops, the enemy right behind you, and crashed into those trees not fifty feet from my headquarters. In forty years of fracases I've not seen anything so dramatic."

"Thank you, sir."

The old soldier grunted, turned, and marched from the room.

Freddy Soligen had been miraculously saved from the physical beating Mauser took in the crash. The pilot, so close in front of him, had cushioned Soligen with his own body.

He had been saved financial disaster, as well, save for that amount he had contributed to his campaign to raise Mauser's status. His superiors had not even charged him for the equipment he had jettisoned from the glider during the flight, nor that which had been destroyed in the crash. If anything, his standing with the higher-ups was probably better than ever. He'd been in there pitching, as a telly reporter, right up until the end.

All that he had lost was his dream. It had been so close. He could almost taste the victory. Joe Mauser at the ultimate top of the hero heap. Joe Mauser receiving bounces in both rank and caste. And then, Joe Mauser being properly thankful and helpful to Freddy Soligen.

Mauser began his twentieth day in the hospital much as he'd begun the previous nineteen—lying or sitting in his room, stewing over matters past. Reconstructive therapy had been more painful than the original injuries, but Mauser took that in stride. He was glad that it wasn't like the old days, when a broken bone would have taken months to heal. Sometimes, though, he felt like a piece of machinery, damaged or worn in use, then patched up and sent back out to perform its function. Well, there would be no more of that.

No more of a lot of things. No more of the little luxuries that he'd taken for granted, now that he'd been stripped of his accumulated wealth. No more of life in Category Military and the camaraderie of fellow career officers.

In short, his old life was gone, forever. Especially the one element that he tried to avoid thinking about entirely.

The element of his old life showed up on the morning of his twentieth day of confinement. She walked into his room unannounced and stood before his bed, her face unreadable. "Well, Joe."

He looked up at her, felt a sudden urge to return her coolness. "I didn't break the terms you set for me," he said. "No one was injured by my action, except me. Am I still receivable?"

She frowned.

A bitter tone crept into Mauser's voice. "You told me that you were going to watch the fracas, and if my actions resulted in any casualties, you never wanted to see me again."

She sighed and sat next to him. "I did watch. For a while, the battle below was totally ignored, and you were full on camera for at least twenty minutes. I was never so frightened in all my life."

"The first step toward becoming a buff," Mauser said sarcastically. "First, you're scared. Vicariously. But it's fun to be scared, when nothing can really happen to you. It becomes increasingly exciting to see others threatened with death—and then see them actually die in front of you. After a while, you're hooked."

She studied the sheet on the bed, carefully smoothing an imaginary wrinkle. "That's not exactly what I meant, Joe. I was frightened *for* you. Not thrilled."

He looked at her for a long moment. "Well, you'll never have to worry about that again. I suppose you know that I'm no longer in Category Military?"

"It was in the news, Joe." She laughed, without amusement. "In fact, I knew about it before most, even though the hearings were private. Balt was tried, too."

"Balt?"

She nodded. "You first used your glider in the fracas with Hovercraft. Balt was a senior officer in that fracas, and now head of what remains of Vacuum Tube. He's been fined and barred from Category Military for life." She laughed emptily again. "It hasn't exactly improved his feelings toward you."

Mauser hadn't heard that part of it. As usual, he had used his hospital stay to isolate himself from matters that did not concern him directly. However, he could find little sympathy for Balt Haer. He said, "Why did you take so long to show up here?"

"I was thinking, Joe."

"And you finally decided to come."

"Yes."

He looked away and into unseen distances in time, working at accepting a decision he'd made days ago. Finally he cleared his throat and said, "Nadine, the first time I talked with you to any extent, I mentioned that I wanted to make it to the top in this world. I told you that I felt that I had no other choice but to follow the rules in doing so."

She twisted her lips into a smile. "I remember. And I've been telling you ever since that the rules might be changed."

Mauser nodded, slowly. "OK. Now I'm willing to listen. How do we go about changing the rules?"

CHAPTER NINETEEN

Two more days saw Mauser completely mended, and the doctors released him from the hospital. Save for having lost eight or ten pounds, he felt fine.

Nadine insisted on taking him to meet her "underground" as soon as he left the hospital. Indeed, he barely had time to go home and change into fresh clothing before she was at his door.

She was quite mysterious about their destination. Mauser knew nothing about it, except that it was somewhere in Greater Washington. He rode with her in an expensive hovercar to the center of the city and into an underground garage. When the car was parked, she led the way to an elevator. He still had no clue to their destination; the garage was quite large and could have served any of several buildings.

He had held his curiosity in check during the drive, listening to her hold forth on the absurdity of the fracases and the need for changes—her favorite topics. Now, however, he wanted more information. Certainly he trusted her. He was willing to give this a fling, but he did not want to walk into a situation totally unprepared.

"Well," he cleared his throat. "Where *are* we going? These are government buildings."

"We are going to see about doing something with your abilities. Something other than shooting at people, or being shot at."

Mauser said wryly, "Oh, I love mysteries. When do we find out who killed the victim?"

Nadine looked at him from the side of her eyes. "I killed the victim," she said. "Major Mauser, mercenary by trade, is no more."

There was bitterness in him, and he found that he was unable to respond to what she meant as humor. He followed her silently, and his puzzlement grew. The office building through which they moved was as ornate as any he could remember having seen, even on telly. Surely they couldn't be in the Octagon or the New White House.

Nadine said, "Here we are," and indicated a door which opened at their approach.

There was a receptionist in the small office beyond, a bit of ostentation that Mauser seldom met with in the modern world. What could anyone need other than a terminal and a good staff? Didn't efficiency mean anything here?

The receptionist said, "Good afternoon, Dr. Haer. Mr. Holland is expecting you."

Philip Holland, secretary to Harlow Mannerheim, the Minister of Foreign Affairs. The man he had met at Nadine's home. Why was Nadine bringing him here?

Holland stood briefly at their entrance and shook hands quickly, almost abruptly, then motioned them to chairs as he resumed his own. Then he spoke into the terminal on his desk. "Miss Mikhail, would you ask Frank Hodgson to drop in?"

Then Holland began tapping the terminal's keyboard. After a few seconds he stopped and scanned the display; Mauser couldn't quite see it himself.

"Joseph Mauser." Holland was obviously reading. "Born Mid-Lower, Category Clothing, Sub-division Shoes, Branch Repair." Holland looked up. "A somewhat plebian beginning, let us admit."

Mauser's nervous tic started up, but he said nothing. If long years of military discipline had taught him anything, it was patience. The other man had the initiative; let him use it.

Holland looked up and, without reading further, said, "Crossed categories at the age of seventeen to Military, remaining a Rank Private for three years, after which time he was promoted to Corporal. At the age of twenty-five he was bounced in caste to High-Lower. After distinguishing himself in a fracas between McDonnell-Boeing and Lockheed-Cessna he was further raised to Low-Middle caste. By the age of thirty he had reached Mid-Middle caste, Rank Captain. By thirty-three, the present, had been promoted to Major—and had been under consideration for Upper-Middle Caste."

Mauser had not known about that last. Now he spoke up. "Also at present: expelled from future participation in fracases on any level of rank, and fined his complete resources beyond the Basic common stock issued him as a Mid-Middle." His voice was bitter.

"The risks run by the ambitious," Holland said briskly.

At that moment the office door opened, and a tall man entered. He had a strange gait, one shoulder held considerably lower than the other, to the point that Mauser would have thought it the result of a wound, had the other obviously never been a soldier. The newcomer, office pallor heavily upon him, had an air of languor that was obviously assumed, an affectation. His eyes darted about the room, to Holland, to Nadine, and finally to Joe Mauser, where they rested for a moment.

"Nice to see you again, Dr. Haer," he said, then approached Mauser, who had automatically come to his feet and extended a hand to be shaken. "I'm Frank Hodgson. You're Joe Mauser. I'm no fracas buff, but I know enough about current developments to know who you are. Welcome aboard."

Mauser shook hands, in some surprise.

"Welcome aboard?" he repeated.

Hodgson looked to Philip Holland, eyebrows raised in question.

"You're premature, Frank. Dr. Haer and Major Mauser have just arrived."

"Oh." The newcomer found himself a chair, crossed his legs, and fumbled in his pockets for a pipe, leaving it to the others to resume the conversation he had interrupted.

Holland turned to Mauser. "Frank is assistant to Wallace Pepper." He looked at Hodgson and frowned. "I don't believe you have any other title, do you, Frank?"

"I don't think so," Hodgson yawned. "Can't think of any."

Mauser looked from one to the other, confusion adding to confusion within him. Wallace Pepper was the long-time head of the North American Bureau of Investigation, a position he'd held under at least four administrations.

Nadine said dryly, "Which just goes to show you, Joe, how little titles mean. Commissioner Pepper has been all but senile for the past five years. Frank here is the true head of the Bureau."

Frank Hodgson said mildly, "Why, Nadine, that's a rather strong statement."

"Head of the Bureau of Investigation!" Mauser

blurted. He had gathered the impression that he was being taken to meet some members of an underground, organized for the purpose of changing the present socio-political structure.

He turned to Mauser. "I'll try to take you off the hook as quickly as possible here. Tell me, Joe, when you hear the word revolution, what comes to mind?"

Flustered, Mauser said, "Why, I don't know. Fighting, I guess, riots and people running in the street with banners. That sort of thing."

"Uh-huh," Hodgson nodded. "The common conception. However, a social revolution isn't, by definition, bloody."

Mauser said carefully, "I'm no authority, but it seems to me that if changes take place in a socio-economic system without bloodshed, we call it evolution. Revolution is when they take place with conflict."

Holland shook his head. "No. Poor definitions. Among other things, don't confuse revolts, civil wars, and such with revolution. They aren't the same thing. You can have civil war, military revolts, and various civil disturbances without having a socio-economic revolution. Social revolutions occur sometimes spontaneously, sometimes by design—the one that got us where we are today, that knocked the old American democracy off its wheels, was a combination of both, accomplished with help from the inside. We are, incidentally, dedicated to restoring that."

Mauser shrugged. "What's this got to do with me?"

Nadine leaned forward in her earnestness. "All of your life you've revolted against the status quo, Joe. You've beaten your head against the situation that confronted you, against a society that you felt didn't allow you to develop to your full potential. But now you admit that you've been wrong, that what is needed," —she shot a defiant glance at Hodgson—"is to change the rules, if the human race is to get back on the road to progress.

"Very well. You can't expect it to be done single-handedly. You need an organization, others who feel the same way you do. Here we are."

He was truly amazed now. When he had finally admitted interest in what Nadine had hinted to be a subversive organization, he'd had in mind some secretive group, their headquarters possibly in a hidden cellar complete with printing press and, perhaps, some weapons. He most certainly hadn't expected to be introduced to the secretary of the Foreign Minister and the working head of the North American Bureau of Investigation. To have them introduced as a part of a conspiracy . . .

"But . . ." Mauser was momentarily overwhelmed. "You mean that you Uppers are actually planning to subvert your own government?"

"I'm not an Upper," Holland said. "I'm a Mid-Middle. What're you, Frank?"

"Darned if I know," Hodgson replied. "I forget. I think I was bounced to Upper-Middle about ten years ago, for some reason or other, but I was busy at the time and didn't pay much attention. Every once in a while one of the Uppers I work with gets all excited about it and wants to jump me to Upper, but somehow or other we've never gotten around to it. What difference does it make?"

Mauser was not the type to let his mouth gape open, but he stared at the other unbelievingly.

"What's the matter?" Hodgson asked.

Mauser shook his head.

Holland spoke up. "Let's get on with it. Nadine is one of our most efficient talent scouts, so to speak. It was no mistake that I met you at her home a few weeks back, Joe. She thought you had the potential to be one of us. I admit to having formed the same opinion, during our brief meeting. I now put the question to you direct. Do you wish to join our organization, the purpose of which is to change our present socio-economic system and, as Nadine put it, to get back on the road to progress?"

Mauser regarded him carefully. So this was it. The direction of his future would be determined by one word.

"Yes," he replied. "I do."

"Very well. Welcome aboard, as Frank said. Your first assignment will take you to Budapest."

It was moving too fast for Mauser. Noted among his senior officers as a quick man, good at thinking on his feet, he still wasn't up to this sort of thing. "Budapest!" he yelped. "The capital of the Sov-world? But . . . but why—"

"There are many ramifications to revolution, Joe," Holland said, looking patient. "Particularly involving the relationships between the country in question and other nations. The Frigid Fracas—sometimes called a Cold War—has been going on for generations between the West-world and the Sov-world, with other factions taking one side or another as they saw fit. That war can heat up in no time if the Sovs see a weakness on our part, and massive change can create weaknesses.

"But really successful revolutions come from within, when handled properly. If we're going to handle this one peacefully, we've got to take every possible measure to assure efficiency. One of those measures involves gaining a thorough knowledge of where the Sov-world stands and what it might do if there were any signs of a change in the present state of affairs here in the West-world."

"You've met Colonel Lajos Arpad?" Hodgson interjected.

Puzzled again, Mauser said, "Why, yes. One of their military attachés. An observer, here to enforce the Universal Disarmament Pact."

"Colonel Arpad is also the most competent espionage agent working here. We hope," he added to Holland.

"That idiot?"

"If an old pro like you hasn't spotted him," Hodgson chuckled, "then we have one more indication of Arpad's abilities."

Philip Holland took up the conversation again. "The presence of Colonel Arpad in Greater Washington is no coincidence. He is here for something, we're not sure what. However, rumors have been coming out of the Sov-world—particularly some of the more backward regions, such as Siberia and Sinkiang. Rumors of an underground organized to overthrow the Party."

"And that religious thing," Nadine added.

Hodgson muttered, "Yes, indeed. We received two more reports on it today."

All looked at him. He said to Mauser, "Some fanatic in Siberia. A Tuvinian, one of the Turkic-speaking peoples of the area once known as Tannu-Tuva and now as the Tuvinian Autonomous Oblast. He's attracting quite a following. Destroy the machines, he says, go back to the old ways. Till the soil by hand, let the women spin and weave, make clothing on the hand looms. Ride horses, rather than hovercraft. That sort of thing. And, oh yes, kill those who stand in the way of this holy mission."

"And you mean that this is catching on?"

Hodgson laughed. "That part of the world has always had a tendency toward religious fantacism.

During the last half of the 20th century, for instance, religious dictators controlled most of the Middle East either by direct rule or through terrorism, and their followers were willing to die for their beliefs. More than willing, as a matter of fact; in many instances, the poor bastards carried out suicide terrorist attacks which were quite successful, their motivation being a fervent belief that such would be their gateway to heaven."

Hodgson paused, yawned, then continued. "Right now, Joe, I wouldn't be too surprised if that sort of thing caught on over here. Pressures are building; they're not obvious, but we'll either make changes peaceably, or all hell will break loose. Something inside a man rebels at this ranked society—something to do with a desire for freedom. The Sovs haven't been exposed to religion for several generations. The Party heads have probably forgotten about it as a potential threat. Here, we do better. The Temple provides us with a pressure valve in that particular area, but I wouldn't like to see our drugged morons subjected to a sudden blast of revival-type religion. One little push is all it would take."

Mauser looked back at Holland. "I still don't get my going to Budapest. How, why, and when?"

Holland glanced at his watch. His manner suddenly became brisk. "I have an appointment with the President," he said. "We'll have to turn this over to some of the other group members. They'll explain the details, Joe. You'll go as a military observer, ostensibly to check on potential violations of the Universal Disarmament Pact." A sudden thought struck him. "And I imagine it would add to your prestige, possibly open additional doors for you, if you carried more status."

He turned to his terminal again, flipped a switch.

"Miss Mikhail, in my office is Joseph Mauser, now Mid-Middle in caste. Please take the necessary steps to raise him to Low-Upper, immediately. I'll clear this with Tom, and he'll authorize it as recommended through the White House. Is that clear?"

CHAPTER TWENTY

Budapest had changed little in five hundred years. The Danube, seldom blue except when seen through the eyes of lovers, still wandered its way between the ancient town of Pest and the still older town of Buda. Where the stream widens, there is room for the one hundred and twelve acres of Margitsziget—Margaret Island to the West-world. Down through the ages, through Celts and Romans, Slavs and Hungs, Turks and Magyars, none have been so gross as to use Margitsziget for other than a park.

Buda, lying to the west of the Danube, is all rolling hills and bluffs, ancient towers, fortresses, castles and walls which have suffered through a hundred wars, a score of revolutions. It dominates the younger, more dynamic Pest, which stretches out on the flat plains to the east so that even if one stands on the Harmashatarhegy hill of Buda and strains one's eyes, it is difficult to find the farther limits.

The shuttle port was on the outskirts of Pest. The craft carrying Mauser and Max Mainz, who had been drafted for special duty at Mauser's request, settled in for a gentle landing.

Max, his eyes glued to the window, said, "Well, it doesn't look much different from a lot of other towns."

237

"What did you expect, Max?"

"Well, I don't know, kind of gloomier, I guess. I've seen this town a dozen times before on telly, and it never looked this good."

"And seeing is believing," Mauser muttered cynically. He glanced out the window as the shuttle taxied toward the terminal. "It looks like we have a reception committee," he said, indicating a group of uniformed men standing outside the building.

Mauser and Max were cut off in the de-boarding tunnel and whisked outside by a junior officer in Hungarian uniform, who seemed to disappear after leading them to those waiting outside the terminal.

In spite of his mission and because he was in mufti and no longer held military rank, Mauser restrained himself from returning the salutes of two young lieutenants from the West-world embassy and a be-medaled colonel in Sov-world uniform.

The lieutenants, who could have been twins so alike were they in size, bright smiling faces, and words of welcome, shook hands, and introduced themselves as Roberts and Anderson.

Then he was introduced to the Sov officer. One of the Lieutenants said, "Major Mauser, may we present you to Lieutenant Bela Kossuth of the Pink Army?"

Evidently they were using Joe's old title and rank as if he were retired. It meant little to him. The Sov officer clicked his heels, bowed from the waist, extended his hand. His grip was dry and firm.

"The fame of Joseph Mauser is well known in the Proletarian Paradise," he said, sincerity in his voice.

"Pink Army?" Mauser said. "I thought you called it—"

The colonel was indicating a hoverlimo with a sweeping gesture that would have seemed overly graceful, had not Mauser felt the man's grip only a moment earlier. Kossuth interrupted him politely, "The shuttle was a trifle late, and the banquet we have prepared awaits us, Major. A multitude of my fellow officers are anxious to meet the famed Joseph Mauser. Would it surprise you to know that I have replayed, a score of times, your celebrated holding action on the Louisiana Military Reservation? Zut! Unbelievable—with but a single company of men!"

Mauser was looking at him blankly. *Celebrated?* He could barely remember the fracas the mincing Hungarian was talking about. That was the one where, as a junior officer, he had held his position in the swamps while his superiors were supposedly reforming behind him, while in actuality they were frantically negotiating terms with the enemy. No, he could barely recall that one; but it was well remembered by anyone else who had seen it, especially military men.

One of the West-world lieutenants laughed at Mauser's expression. "You're going to have to get used to the fact that there are as many fracas buffs over here, sir, as there are back home."

The Sov colonel wagged a finger at him. "But no, you misunderstand completely, Lieutenant Roberts. We *study* the bloody fracases of the West. Following the campaigns of such tacticians as your Marshal Stonewall Cogswell goes far toward the training of our own Pink Army in its own, ah, fracases."

That raised a dozen questions in Mauser's mind. But first he turned and indicated Max Mainz, who had been standing behind, eyes wide, taking it all in. "Gentlemen, may I present Max Mainz?"

The faces of the lieutenants went blank, and one of them coughed, as though apologetically.

The Sov colonel looked from Joe to Max, and then back again. His face assumed that expression so well known to Mauser. The aristocrat looking at one of the lower class. Kossuth said, "But this, ah, chap is a servant, one of your Lowers?"

"I had heard the Sov-world was the Utopia of the proletariat," Mauser came back. "However, gentlemen, Max Mainz is my friend as well as my . . . assistant."

The three officers murmured formalities to Max who, as a Lower born, was not overly nonplussed by the situation. He knew the three were Upper class, and couldn't understand what the major was getting worked up about.

The four, led by Kossuth, climbed into the limo.

Mauser picked up the conversation where it had broken off earlier. "I'm afraid that my background is hazy, Colonel Kossuth. You mentioned the Pink Army. You also mentioned your own fracases. I knew you maintained an army, of course, but I thought the fracas was strictly a Western custom. Your military attachés are usually scornful of them."

The lieutenants grinned, but Kossuth said seriously, "Major, nations which hold each other at arm's length often use different terminologies to say much the same thing. It need not be confusing, however, if one digs a little. Perhaps, for a moment, we four can lower barriers enough for me to explain.

"While in the West-world you hold your fracases to"—he ticked the items off on his fingers—"One, settle disputes between business competitors, Two, train soldiers for your defense requirements, Three, keep bemused a potentially dangerous lower class—"

"I object to that, Colonel!" Anderson interrupted.

The Sov officer ignored him. "—and Four, dispose of the more aggressive potential rebels, by allowing them to eliminate one another in combat."

"That, sir, is simply not true," the lieutenant blurted.

"And your alternative?" Mauser said, evenly. "Under what auspices does the Sov-world maintain its army?"

The Hungarian shrugged. "The Proletarian Paradise maintains two armies, Major. One composed of veterans for defense against potential foreign foes, and named the Glorious Invincible Red Army—"

"Or the Red Army, for short," Anderson chimed in.

"—and the other composed of less experienced proletarians and their techno-intellectual, and sometimes even Party, officers. This is our Pink Army."

"Wait a moment," Mauser said. "What's a proletarian?"

One of the lieutenants laughed dryly.

Kossuth stared at Joe. "You *are* poorly founded in the background of the Sov-world, Major."

Mauser said, "Deliberately, Colonel Kossuth. When I learned of my assignment, I deliberately avoided cramming unsifted information. I decided it would be more desirable to get my information at the source, uncontaminated by West-world propaganda."

One of the stiff-necked twins, both of whom Joe was beginning to find a bit *too* stereotypical of West-world adherents, said, "Sir, I must protest. The West does not utilize propaganda."

"Of course not," Kossuth said, taking his turn at a dry tone. He said to Mauser, "I admire your decision. Obviously, a correct one. Major, a proletarian is, well, you could say, ah—"

"A Low-Lower," Anderson or Roberts said. Mauser kept getting them confused; even their names were similar.

"Not exactly," the Sov protested. "Let us put it in

this way. In the Proletarian Paradise, it is from each according to his abilities. The most useful members of society are drawn into the ranks of the Party, and since they contribute the most, they are the most highly rewarded."

"Sure," Anderson or Roberts said, "but it is strictly hereditary. I doubt if any proles have been made Party members in two generations."

Kossuth, in indignation, unknowingly parroted the lieutenant's earlier words. "That, sir, is simply not true."

Mauser figured it was time to soothe the troubled waters. "And the . . . what did you call them . . . techno-intellectuals?"

"They are the second-most useful members of society. They consist of technicians, scientists—although many of them are members of the Party, of course— teachers, artists, Pink and Red Army officers, and so forth."

Max spoke up, "Well, that sounds just about like Uppers, Middles, and Lowers to me."

The Hungarian was glaring at Max. Mauser cleared his throat and said, "And the Pink Army itself? It is the third class?"

"Don't be silly, my man. There are no classes in the Proletarian Paradise."

"Yeah," Max said, "and back in the West-world we got people's capitalism, and the people own everything. Yeah, we don't have to worry about revolutions against us."

"That will be all, Max," Joe said, getting in before the lieutenants could snap something at the feisty little man. Joe had already decided that they were both Uppers, but was somewhat surprised at their lowly rank.

One of the lieutenants mumbled something about

Afghanistan. It was obviously a leading remark intended for Kossuth.

Kossuth glared at him. "We're almost to our destination, Major Mauser. However, I should add that minorities among some of the more recent additions to the Sov-world, particularly in the more backward areas of southern Asia, have not quite adjusted to the glories of the Proletarian Paradise."

Both of the lieutenants chuckled softly.

Kossuth continued. "So it is found necessary to dispatch punitive expeditions against them. A current such expedition is in the Kunlun Mountains in that area once known as Sinkiang to the north and Tibet to the south, to Afghanistan to the East. Kirghiz and Kazakhs nomads in the region persist in rejecting the Party and its program. The Pink Army is in the process of eliminating these reactionary elements."

Mauser was puzzled. He said, "You mean, in all of these years you haven't been able to clean up such a small disorder?"

Kossuth said stuffily, "My dear major, please recall that we are limited to the use of weapons pre-1900, in accord with the Universal Disarmament Pact. To be blunt, it is quite evident that certain foreign clements—which shall remain unnamed—are smuggling weapons into Tibet and other points where rebellion flares, so that on some occasions our Pink Army is confronted with enemies better armed than themselves. These bandits, of course, are not under the jurisdiction of the International Commission, and while we are limited, they are not."

"Besides," one of the lieutenants added, "they don't want to clean them up. If they did, the Sov equivalent of the fracas buff wouldn't be occupied watching the progress of the Glorious Pink Army against its reactionary foe, on telly."

Mauser, under his breath, mimicked the Sov officer's words. "That, sir, is simply not true."

Joseph Mauser, Low-Upper, Category Government, Branch International Relations, Rank Military Attaché, was ostensibly a military observer, assigned to the West-world embassy in Budapest. As such, he spent several days meeting embassy personnel, his immediate superiors, and his immediate inferiors in rank. As a newcomer from home, he was wined, dined, evaluated, found an apartment, assigned a hovercar, and in general assimilated into the community.

Not ordinarily prone to the social life, Mauser was able to find some interest in all of this due to its newness. The citizen of the West-world, when exiled by duty to a foreign land, evidently did his utmost to take his native soil with him. Sov food and drink were superlative, especially for those of Party rank, but most food supplies for the West-world community were flown in from the West. Home furnishings, clothing, and reading material—all were imported, to make this an oasis of the West in the Sov-world.

Mauser's undercover role as a potential contact for the Sov-world underground—if such existed—was unknown even to the higher-ranking officers of the embassy. He found it easiest to maintain his cover by slipping into the embassy routine.

His Upper-caste rating made little impression on the other embassy personnel, largely because it was the prevalent rank. In dealing with the Sovs, contact was almost exclusively with Party members and the policy was that West-world officials were never put into the position of having to work with Sovs who ranked them. Only office workers were drawn from the Middle caste, and these kept to themselves, except during working hours.

Mauser's immediate superior turned out to be General George Armstrong, with whom Joe had once served some years before, when the general had commanded a fracas between two labor unions fighting out a jurisdictional battle. Although Mauser hadn't particularly distinguished himself in that fray, the general seemed to remember him well enough. Mauser was taken in with open arms, somewhat to the surprise of other attachés who ranked him in caste or seniority.

At first, getting organized in apartment and office, getting the feel of Budapest, its transportation system, its geographical layout, its offerings in entertainment, he came into little contact with officials of the Sov-world. In a way the city was confusion upon confusion. Budapest was the center of world Sovism, and the languages of Indo-China, Outer Mongolia, Latvia, Bulgaria, Karelia, or Albania were as apt to be heard on the street as was Hungarian.

He also had little time to think about Nadine Haer, which was just as well. Now that he had been promoted in caste—had indeed reached what he thought to be his life's goal—there was comparatively little boundary for their romance to cross. But she seemed to be holding him at arm's length. There had been one night, shortly before he left the Westworld, but otherwise she had avoided being strictly alone with him, had cut off any talk involving their future. Their few phone conversations, since Mauser had arrived in Budapest, had been similarly cool.

But Joe Mauser was in no hurry, in romance or in anything else. His instructions were to take the long view. To take his time, feel his way. Somewhere along the line a door would open, and he would find that which he sought.

In a way, Max Mainz seemed to acclimate himself

faster than Mauser. Completely without language other than Anglo-American, while Joe had both French and Spanish, the little man was still of such persistent social aggressiveness that in a week's time he knew every Hungarian of proletarian rank within blocks of where he lived and worked. Within a month he had managed to acquire a present-tense, almost verbless jargon with which he was able to conduct all necessary transactions pertaining to his duties, household and otherwise, and to get into surprisingly complicated arguments. Mauser had to give up attempting to persuade him that discretion was called for in discussing the relative merits of West-world and Sov-world.

In fact, it was through Max that Mauser made his breakthrough in his assignment to learn the inner workings of the Sov-world.

CHAPTER TWENTY-ONE

It was a free evening for Mauser. For once he had no commitments in the embassy social whirl, and he was contemplating staying at home, perhaps reading. But Max had been gushing about a cabaret in Buda, during their inspection tour of an artillery plant that afternoon. He'd discovered a place nicknamed the Becsikapu, where the wine flowed as wine can flow only in the Balkans and where the gypsy music was as only gypsy music can be. Max had developed a sudden affection for wine after only two or three attempts at what was known locally as Sor, which he didn't consider to be beer.

"And what kind of place is it?" Mauser asked, only half interested. "For proles, Party members, or what?"

Max said, "Well, I guess it's mostly proletarians, but in these little places you can see almost anybody. Couple of nights ago when I took off, I saw a Russkie field marshal there. And was he ever drenched."

Mauser shrugged; he was at loose ends. Besides, this was a facet of Budapest life he had yet to investigate. An intimate night spot frequented by all strata of Sov society.

He came to a quick decision. "OK, Max, let's give it a fling. It'll be a switch from the ostentatious clubs Nadine was always dragging me to in Washington."

Max was suddenly belligerent. "Does that mean better?"

Mauser grunted amusement at the little man as he slipped into his jacket. "No, it doesn't," he replied, "and take that chip off your shoulder. When you were back home, you were always beefing about what a rugged life you had being a Mid-Lower. Now that you're over here, you're ready to fight at the smallest hint that someone thinks all is not perfect at home."

"Well, all these characters are up to their ears in curd about the West. They think everybody's starving over there because they're unemployed. And they think the Lowers are, like, ground-down. And that there's lots of race troubles, and all."

As they walked out onto the street, Mauser suddenly realized how much closer Max had gotten to the common people than he had. But he was still amused at Max's attitude. "And wasn't that what you used to think about things over here, when you were back home?"

"Well, you know, that's right. They're not as bad off as I thought. Some of those telly shows I used to watch were a little exaggerated, I guess."

"If international fracases were fought by the news media," Mauser said absently, "the old Cold War might have been won by one side or the other, rather than carried through to this stalemate."

The Becsikapu turned out, for the most part, to be what Max had reported: a rather small cellar cabaret, specializing in Hungarian wines and such nibbling delicacies as turoscsusza, the cheese gnocchis. It specialized as well in a romantic atmosphere dominated by gypsy violins. It came to Mauser that there was more of this in the Sov world than at home. The Sov proles evidently spent less time watching telly than did the Lowers in the West-world.

They found a table, crowded though the nightspot was, and ordered a bottle of chilled Reteasca. It wasn't until the waiter had recorded the order against Mauser's embassy card that it was realized that he and Max were from the West. So many non-Hungarians, from all over the Sov-world, were about Budapest that foreigners were an accepted part of the environment.

"Well, look there," Max said, as usual making no attempt to lower his voice. "There's a sample of this place not being as advanced as the West-world. A waiter! In a beer joint. How come they don't have autobars and all?"

"Sure, sure," Mauser said dryly. "And maybe you'd prefer canned music and a big telly screen, instead of a live show?"

"No," Max protested, taking a half glass of wine in one gulp. "But don't you see how this takes up people's time? All these waiters and musicians and all could be home, relaxing."

"And watching telly and doing trank," Mauser said, not really interested. Several women, alone at the bar, had caught his eye.

"You don't seem to appreciate our entertainment," a voice said in coldly-accented Anglo-American.

Mauser looked for the source of the words. Three officers sat at the next table. Only one, a captain, wore the distinctive pinch-waisted uniform of the Hungarians. The other two wore Sov epaulets which proclaimed them majors, but he couldn't place the nationality of the uniforms. A dozen empty bottles littered the table.

"To the contrary," Mauser said carefully, "we find it quite enjoyable, sir."

But Max had two full glasses of the potent Reteasca in him, and was not backward. "We got places just as good as this in the West, and bigger, too. Lots bigger. This place wouldn't hold more than fifty people."

The major who had spoken first, who, Mauser noticed, wore the boots of a cavalryman, said nastily, "Indeed? I recognize now that when I addressed you both as gentlemen, I failed to realize that in the West gentlemen are not selective of their company and allow themselves to wallow in the gutter with the dregs of society."

The Hungarian captain said lazily, "Are you sure, Frol, that *either* of them are gentlemen? There seems to be a distinctive *odor* about the lower classes from any part of the world."

Mauser came to his feet quietly.

Max suddenly sobered. "Hey, Major, easy. It isn't important."

Mauser picked up his glass of wine. With a gesture so easy as to be almost slow motion, he tossed it into the face of the foppish officer.

The Hungarian, aghast, took up his napkin and began to brush the drink from his uniform. The major to his right fumbled in assistance.

The cavalryman, though, was of sterner stuff. He was up in a flash, grabbing a bottle by its long neck. As Mauser backed off a step, the major broke it off at the base on the edge of the table. In the back of his mind, something told Mauser that this was an old pro, a Russian from the Red Army.

The major came toward him, kicking a chair to one side. Mauser hunched his shoulders forward, took up one of the large cloth napkins from the table, and wrapped it around his hand in a quick double gesture.

The Sov officer advanced, holding the jagged bottle as a sword. His face was working in rage. Mauser, outwardly cool, decided that he was glad he'd never have to serve under this one. This one gave way to rage and temper when things pickled, and there was no room for such luxury in a fracas.

Max was yelling something from behind, something that didn't come through the bedlam that had engulfed the Becsikapu.

The Russian was a second from gutting him with the bottle. At the last possible instant Mauser struck out with his left leg and hooked with his foot the small table at which the three Sov officers had been sitting. A quick twist threw it to the side and into the path of his enraged opponent.

The other swore as his shins banged the side. His momentum carried him on, and for a moment he was off balance.

Mauser stepped forward, quickly, precisely, and chopped down and to the side of the other's prominent jawbone. The Russian went suddenly limp, falling flat on his face

Mauser spun around. "C'mon, Max! Let's get out of here." He didn't want to give the other two time to organize themselves and decide to attack. He and Max just might be able to beat them, but Mauser wasn't sure where the staff would stand in the fray— nor anyone else in the small cabaret, for that matter.

Max, at the peak of excitement now, yelled, "What do you think I've been saying! Follow me—there's a rear door next to the rest room."

Waiters and others were converging on them. Mauser didn't wait to argue. He hurried after the little man, dodging and darting through the tables and chairs like an old-time broken-field football player.

Mauser had assumed that there would be some

sort of repercussion from the run-in with the Sov officers, but he hadn't suspected its magnitude.

The next morning he had barely arrived at the small embassy office assigned to him when his desk terminal lit up with Armstrong's habitually worried-looking face. Without taking time for the customary amenities, he said, "Major Mauser, will you come to my office immediately?" It was not a question.

There Mauser found Armstrong and his aide, Lieutenant Anderson, who Mauser had finally sorted out from Lieutenant Roberts. Also present were Colonel Bela Kossuth and another Sov officer, whom Mauser hadn't met.

The atmosphere was very stiff, very formal, very cold.

The general said, "Major Mauser, Colonel Kossuth and Captain Petofi have approached me, as your immediate superior, to request that your diplomatic immunity be waived so that you might be called upon in a matter of honor."

Mauser didn't get it. He looked from one of the Hungarians to the other, then back at Armstrong, scowling.

Lieutenant Anderson said unhappily, "These officers have been named to represent Captain Sandor Rakoczi, Major."

Bela Kossuth clicked his heels, bowed, said formally, "Our principal realizes, Major Mauser, that diplomatic immunity prevents his issuing a request for satisfaction. However, since honor *is* involved—"

It suddenly snapped into focus—they wanted a duel! Mauser kept his voice as coolly formal as the other's. "General Armstrong, I—"

"Mauser," the general said quickly, "as an official representative of the West-world, you don't have to respond to anything as silly as a challenge to a duel!"

The faces of the two Hungarians froze.

Mauser finished his sentence. "—I would appreciate it if you and Lieutenant Anderson would act for me."

Kossuth clicked his heels again. "Gentlemen, the *code duello* provides that the challenged party choose the weapons."

General Armstrong's face went dark with anger. "Choice of weapons, eh? Against Sandor Rakoczi? If you will excuse us now, gentlemen, Lieutenant Anderson and I will consult with you in one hour in the Embassy Club. I say frankly, I have never heard of a diplomat being subjected to such a situation, especially on the part of officers of the country to which he is accredited."

The Hungarians were unfazed. Kossuth glanced at his watch. "One hour, in the Embassy Club, gentlemen." The two bowed again, and were gone.

Armstrong glared at Mauser. "Damn it, if you hadn't been so quick on the trigger, I could have warned you, Mauser!"

Mauser still wasn't over his surprise. "You mean to tell me," he said, "that these people still conduct duels? I thought duels had gone out back in the 19th century."

"Well, you were mistaken," Armstrong bit out. "It seems to be a practice that can crop up in any decadent society. Remember Hitler reviving it among the German universities? Well, it's all the rage now among officers of the Sov world. It is limited, however, to Party members; the lower proles are assumed, I suppose, to be without honor."

Mauser shrugged. "I'm not exactly an amateur at combat, you know."

Armstrong snorted in disgust, then turned to Anderson. "Lieutenant, wait in the outer office for me until it's time for us to meet those heel-clicking Hungarians."

"Yes, sir." Anderson saluted, shot a look at Mauser as though in commiseration, and left hurriedly.

"What's wrong with him?" Mauser asked.

Armstrong pulled open a desk drawer, brought forth a bottle and glass, poured himself a shot, and knocked it back without offering any to Mauser. He replaced bottle and glass and turned his scowl back to Mauser. "Haven't you heard of Sandor Rakoczi?"

"Should I have?"

"He happens to be the top fencing champion in this half of the world—has been for six years. He is third among Red Army pistol and rifle marksmen. I once saw him put on an exhibition of trick handgun shooting. Uncanny. The man has abnormal reflexes."

Armstrong walked to the room's sole window, stared out for a long moment before turning back to Mauser. "Besides which, Major, you've been set up."

"How's that? We got into a fight in a nightclub last night—the man was drenched."

"Sandor Rakoczi doesn't get into fights—not unless he's been ordered to. Captain Rakoczi is what was known as a hatchetman in the old days." Noting the questioning look on Mauser's face, he added, "Let me explain. The Party no longer conducts purges these days; everyone is supposed to be buddy-buddy. However, that situation is sometimes inconvenient for those at the top. So less direct methods have been devised for removing those who have become an irritant to those at the top. One method is to have them challenged by such as Sandor Rakoczi."

Mauser settled down into a chair. "But that's ridiculous. *Why?* Why should they want me eliminated?"

"You don't have to accept."

"If I don't, I'll be laughed out of town. Remember

that big banquet the Pink Army gave me when I first got here? The celebrated Major Joseph Mauser fling? What happens to West-world prestige when the celebrated Joe Mauser backs down from a duel?"

"If you refuse the challenge," Armstrong mused, "you will be laughed out of town. If you accept it, and are killed, you are still removed from the scene." He frowned. "Somebody obviously does not want Joe Mauser in Budapest."

The pieces were beginning to fall together. Mauser regarded Armstrong carefully. "You're one of us, aren't you? Tied in with Phil Holland and Frank Hodgson." He spread his hands before him. "Why wasn't I told?" he demanded. "Am I a junior member, not to be trusted?"

"You should study up on revolutionary routine, Major. The smaller the unit of organization, the better. The fewer members you know, the fewer you can betray. Here in the Sov-world, back before the Sovs came to power, the size of their cells was five members, so the most any one person could betray was four."

The tic started at the side of Mauser's mouth.

"Don't misunderstand," Armstrong said hurriedly. "Your fortitude isn't being questioned. Bravery doesn't enter into it. There are methods available today against which nobody can hold out." He seemed to come to a sudden decision. "We can't let this take place. You'll have to back down, Mauser. Somehow there's been a leak, and your real purpose here is known. Fine. Holland will just have to send someone else to replace you."

But Mauser had had enough by now. "Look," he said, "everybody seems to be operating on the assumption that I can't take care of myself with this foppish molly. I've had fifteen years of combat."

"The man's a professional assassin. And this is his home field."

"Besides," Mauser finished, "I have a job to do, and it doesn't involve being run out of Budapest."

Armstrong glared at him. "Dammit! Don't go drivel-happy on us, Mauser. I've just told you the man's the best swordsman in Europe and Asia combined, and the third best shot."

"How is he with Bowie knives?" Mauser asked.

To Mauser's surprise, the Sovs actually turned up two genuine Bowie knives. He had expected the duel to end up being conducted with trench knives or some other alternative weapon. But the Sovs, ever great on museums, had located one of the weapons of the American frontier in a Prague exhibit of West-world history. The other was found in Budapest itself, in a military museum's extensive collection of fighting knives.

Formally correct, Lieutenant Bela Kossuth appeared at Mauser's billet three days before the duel, a case in his hands. Max, in his role as batman, conducted him to Mauser, doing little to keep his scowl of dislike for the Hungarian from his face. Max was getting fed up with the airs of Sov officers; caste lines over here were, if anything, more strictly drawn than at home.

Mauser came to his feet on recognizing his visitor, and returned the other's bow. "Colonel Kossuth," he said

Bela Kossuth clicked heels. He held the case before him, opened it. Two heavy fighting knives lay within. Mauser looked at them, then at the other's face.

Kossuth said, "Major, your somewhat unorthodox selection of weapons has been confusing. However, we have located two Bowie knives. Since it is assumed that the two gentlemen opponents are not thoroughly familiar with the weapon, it has been suggested that each be given his blade at this time."

Mauser got it now. Sandor Rakoczi hadn't become the most celebrated duelist in the Sov-world by making such mistakes as underrating his opponents. The weapon was new to him. He wanted the opportunity to practice with it. That was fine with Mauser.

Kossuth clicked heels again. "Our selection, unfortunately, is limited to two weapons. Since you are the challenged, Captain Rakoczi insists that you take first choice."

Mauser shrugged, then took up first one, then the other. It had been some time since he had held one of the famous frontier weapons in his hands. While still a sergeant, he had once become a close companion of an old pro whose specialty was teaching hand-to-hand combat. Over a period of years he and Mauser had been comrades, going from one fracas to another as a team. He had taught Mauser considerable, including passing on to him the belief that, of all blade hand weapons ever devised, the knife invented by Jim Bowie, whose career had ended at the Alamo, was the most efficient.

Mauser ran his eyes over the blades carefully. On the back of one was stamped *James Luther, Van Cleave, Kentucky*. Mauser had found what he was looking for. He pretended to examine the other knife as well, ignoring the Sheffield, England, stamp of manufacture.

The Bowie knife: Blade, eleven inches long by an inch and a half wide, the heel three eights of an inch thick at the back. The point at the exact center of the width of the blade, which curved to the point convexly from the edge, and from the back concavely, both curves being as sharp as the edge itself. The crossguard was of heavy brass rather than steel, and a further brass backing ran along the heel to the point where the curve began. Brass, which is softer than steel, could catch an opponent's blade rather than allowing it to slip off and away.

Mauser balanced the weapon he had selected and shrugged nonchalantly. "This one will do," he said, replacing the other knife.

Kossuth snapped the case closed. He could see no difference between the two; the selection of weapons had been a formality, as far as he was concerned.

Max saw the Sov officer to the door and returned to the main room. "Major, sir," he said worriedly, "are you sure you've checked that thing out? I've been asking around, and they put these duels on telly here, just like the fracases at home. This Captain Rakoczi's got one hell of a reputation. He's quick as a snake and twice as mean. Kind of a freak."

"So they've been telling me," Mauser mused, again balancing the frontier weapon in his hand. It had a beautiful balance, this knife so big that it could be used as hatchet or machete.

Yes, a Bowie knife could be used for more than just a cutting blade—something that he was counting on Captain Rakoczi not knowing.

CHAPTER TWENTY-TWO

The ring, set in the center of some kind of enclosed stadium, measured thirty-five feet across and was floored with sand. Joe Mauser and Sandor Rakoczi stood stripped to the waist, both barefoot. General Armstrong and Lieutenant Roberts stood to one side of the ring and Colonel Kossuth and Captain Petofi on the other, behind their respective principals. A respectably-sized audience was scattered through the stadium's seating facilities.

Kossuth was reciting, "It has been agreed, then, that the gentlemen participants shall be restricted to this ring. Seconds will remain withdrawn twenty feet. The conflict shall begin upon General Armstrong calling *commence*, and shall end upon one or the other, or both, of the gentlemen participants falling to the ground. Minor wounds shall not halt the conflict. This is understood?"

"Yes," Mauser said. He had been sizing up his enemy. The man was almost a duplicate of Mauser in build, perhaps slightly lighter, slightly taller. Like Mauser, he bore a dozen scars about his torso. Sandor Rakoczi hadn't worked his way to the top without taking his share of punishment.

Rakoczi said something, obviously affirmative, in Hungarian.

As Max had said, the Sovs were putting this one on telly. The cameramen were highly evident, with six cameras in all strategically placed so that every phase of the duel would be covered. They were, of course, set well back from the action.

Lieutenant Roberts, his open face drawn worriedly, passed to Mauser his Bowie Knife. Captain Petofi proffered Rakoczi his. The two men stepped into the arena, the dimensions of which were marked with blue chalk. Though nothing had been said, it was obvious that if a combatant stepped over this line he would be declared the loser.

They stood opposite one another, both with arms loose at their sides, both holding their fighting knives in their right hands.

General Armstrong raised a hand. "Ready, Captain Rakoczi?"

The Hungarian nodded curtly.

"Ready, Major Mauser?"

"Ready," Mauser said. Under his breath, he added, "As ready as I'm ever going to be." He was feeling qualms about it now. He'd been too long in the game not to recognize a superlative fighter when he saw one. Somehow, in the heat of the action in the little cabaret, Rakoczi had not seemed so formidable.

The four seconds withdrew the required distance, joining two doctors and half-dozen medical corpsmen standing on the floor of the stadium. Farther back still, Mauser knew, were the emergency facilities. Mauser found it somewhat ironic; two men were going to be allowed to butcher each other, but moments after, all of the facilities of modern medical science would be at their disposal.

General Armstrong dropped his hand and called, "Commence!"

Mauser spread his legs, grasped the knife waist-high so that his thumb was along the side of the blade. He shuffled forward slowly, feeling the consistency of the sand; one slip would be fatal.

The Sov officer had assumed the stance of a swordsman. His smile was foxlike. For the first time Mauser noticed the scar along the other's cheek. It was white, prominent against his swarthy skin. Yes, Sandor Rakoczi had copped quite a few in his time. At least the man wasn't infallible.

As they moved cautiously toward each other, the Hungarian's grin broadened. "Ah, our bad man from the West," he said, "you thought to choose a weapon unknown to me, eh? But perhaps you have never heard of the Italian short sword, eh? Do you think this clumsy weapon is so different from the Italian short sword?"

Mauser had never heard of the Italian short sword, although it came back to him now that he had seen medieval duelists fighting with two swords—one long, one short—in phony fracas films back home. Obviously, his opponent was familiar with them.

They circled, warily, each watching for an opening, each sizing up the other. Once action was joined, things would move fast. The Bowie knife was not built for finesse.

Rakoczi darted in like a striking cobra. His blade flicked, and he leaped back, instantly on guard. Mauser's left arm leaked blood, a long red streak from shoulder to elbow.

Mauser blinked. He'd been told that there was something freakish about this man. His reflexes were indeed unbelievably fast.

He attempted a slashing blow himself. The other danced away, and Mauser found his blade biting empty air.

Rakoczi's mocking laughter rang through the stadium. "Bastard!" he said. "Is that the word? Clumsy, awkward, stumbling . . . bastard. It is well to rid the world of such, eh?"

He was a talker. Mauser had met the type before, especially in hand-to-hand combat. They talked insultingly, hoping to enrage you and provoke you into foolish attack. Mauser was untouched by such tactics, though.

He circled again, his mind working frantically. He had, he realized, no physical advantages. He was neither stronger nor faster than the other, and he had no reason to believe that he had greater stamina. If anything, it might be the other way.

Rakoczi was in again, through Mauser's guard, darting his blade as though it were a foil. A cut opened magically on Mauser's chest from left nipple to navel, and bled profusely.

The Sov duelist slipped back a good six feet, instantly. He laughed. Mauser hadn't had time to move even one foot.

Rakoczi jeered. "Ah, my bad man from the West who throws wine in the face of gentlemen. You grow afraid, eh? Your mouth twitches. You feel in your stomach the fear of death, eh? No longer do you worry about locating the Sov-world undergound and helping the revolution. Now you worry about death."

Mauser wet his lips. The tic at the side of his mouth was in full evidence.

Mauser tried rushing him, plowing through the sand. But the Hungarian danced back, still taunting him. He was obviously comfortable on the sandy floor, as Mauser was not. He had erred in agreeing on a sand arena. For Mauser it was like trying to operate on a sandy beach, but Rakoczi seemed in his element.

Even as Mauser's attack slowed in frustration, the

other darted in, slashed once, twice, scoring on Mauser's left arm, once, twice.

He was a bloody mess. None of the wounds were overly deep, but combined they were costing him blood. He got the feeling that the Hungarian could finish him off at will, that Rakoczi had his number. That it was no longer a matter of the other being careful not to underestimate his foe. Mauser had been correctly estimated—and found wanting. He realized that only by sinking to the sand and throwing the fight could he come out alive.

And then he saw the other's expression. There was to be no giving up in this fight. At the first sign of such intent on Mauser's part the other would dart in and deal the finishing blow. The death blow. Rakoczi was fully capable of such speed.

Mauser knew suddenly what he had to do. Whether it was acceptable or not would be settled later. It was time to use cunning against his opponent's superior attributes.

His heels almost to the chalk line, Mauser dashed suddenly forward. His opponent, slightly surprised at this move from an obviously cowed opponent, darted away to the other end of the ring with blurring speed.

Mauser grinned wolfishly. With a sudden motion he tossed the Bowie knife into the air. It turned in a spin to come down blade first. He caught it with thumb and two fingers.

He stepped forward with his left foot, threw with his full force. The Bowie knife, balanced to turn once in thirty feet, blurred through the air and buried itself in the Hungarian's abdomen.

The Sov officer grunted in agony, stared down at the protruding hilt with unbelieving eyes. He looked up in hate, glaring at Mauser, who stood now in the stance of the karate fighter.

Mauser could see the other's agonized thoughts in his expression. There were medics available and, though the wound was a decisive one, it need not be fatal. The Sov officer glared at Mauser again, his teeth grinding in pain and shock. To move across the ring now would be disastrous, stirring the heavy knife blade in his intestines.

Rakoczi knew that he had only seconds before he would sink to the sand. But perhaps that would be sufficient. He reversed his own knife.

Mauser watched him, anticipating, and moved closer, closer. The other's face was a mask of pure agony, but he was no quitter. He was going to make his own throw.

The throw came too fast to avoid. The heavy frontier knife turned over halfway and the hilt struck Mauser along the side, glancing off ineffectively. Sandor Rakoczi fell to the sand then, and the medics closed in. Mauser carefully staggered to the edge of the ring, arms raised in triumph.

CHAPTER
TWENTY-THREE

His wounds were clean, straight slashes, not overly deep. According to the medics, they would heal readily enough. In his time Mauser had copped more serious ones; but after treatment he was relegated to the small embassy hospital, ostensibly for observation.

He was, so Max informed him, the hero of the West-world colony in Budapest. And the Neut-world, too, for that matter. It was quite a scandal that a diplomatic representative had been challenged to a duel by a known killer of Rakoczi's reputation. Informal protests were lodged, of course, but Mauser could imagine just how effective they would be. Little more than going through the motions.

A hero he might be, but he wasn't allowed visitors during this, his first day of recuperation. Max, as his aide, was permitted, but no others. At least, so it was throughout the morning and early afternoon. Then, so obvious it was that his condition was not critical, General Armstrong bulled his way in to see him.

The general scowled down at him for a long moment, as if trying to read Mauser's mind. He said, finally, "You looked like an overgrown hamburger steak, there for a while."

Mauser grinned wryly. "That's how I felt—like chopped meat," he said. "I've never seen anyone move so fast. I wouldn't be surprised to learn that he was on amphetamines."

Armstrong's expression turned curious. "Tell me one thing, Mauser—if you wanted to use throwing knives, why didn't you just challenge him to a duel with throwing knives?"

Mauser shifted his shoulders. "I figured my only chance with him was to use a weapon with which he wasn't familiar. The Bowie knife was it. It didn't occur to him that a large blade built in that shape was a precisely balanced throwing knife as well as a cutting blade." He twisted his mouth. "If the Sovs think all the Machiavellians are on their side, they're wrong. Captain Rakoczi got sucked in; *I* had a throwing knife, but he didn't."

Armstrong looked at him blankly.

Mauser explained. "The knife designed by Jim Bowie was made by a smith named James Black, of Washington, Arkansas. Bowie made himself so notorious with it that the blade became world-famous. Black and a few other smiths in what were the southern states at the time made a very few exact copies. Others tried to duplicate Black's work, but only those who had been shown by Black himself succeeded in producing the perfect balance needed in such a large knife. It turns over exactly once in thirty feet. All I had to do was get Rakoczi fifteen feet away from me, and he'd had it. When he tried to reciprocate, his throw was off balance." He cleared his throat. "By the way, how is he?"

Armstrong said soberly, "He's dead, Mauser."

"Dead! With all those doctors?"

The general's face assumed its habitually worried expression. "I rather doubt that he died of your knife—not directly, anyway. The Party brass do not approve of failures. I imagine that medical efforts on Captain Rakoczi's behalf were perhaps not as strenuous as they might have been. You were correct when you said you would have lost prestige had you fled Rakoczi's challenge or insisted on diplomatic immunity. As it is, the prestige has been lost by the other side.

"I imagine, by the way, that no further effort will be made to eliminate you. It would be too blatant."

Mauser frowned. "There was one thing I wanted to talk to you about, General. Rakoczi was baiting me, trying to rattle my nerve, while we were in the ring. Called me a lot of names, that sort of thing. But he also said something about my no longer having to worry about locating the Sov-world underground."

Armstrong slumped into the bedside chair. "Damn—that tears it! They're fully aware of your mission, then, though they don't have it exactly right. Your purpose isn't to aid the local underground, but to size it up, get the overview. I'll have to get in touch with our organization in Washington. One thing for certain, we're not going to be able to let you go into the field as a military attaché and observer."

Mauser had been scheduled to observe some of the combat taking place in Turkey with nomad rebels. He had looked forward to the experience, learning first-hand how the Sov forces differed from the mercenary armies of the West-world. "Why not?" he asked.

"You'd never come out alive, them knowing that much about you. There would be an accident, and the nomads would be given the dubious credit for having killed you." He stood. "I've got to think about this. I'll drop in later, Mauser."

Mauser thought about it, too, after the other had

left. Obviously the restrictions on his movements would be a handicap to his ability to serve the organization. Would this be it—this one assignment—and he would be dropped?

Max stuck his head in the door then. "Major, one of the Hungarians wants to see you."

"Who?" Mauser snapped. "And why?"

"Colonel Kossuth. I told him you couldn't have visitors, but he won't leave."

Kossuth, Mauser knew, was assigned full-time to the West-world embassy. It suddenly occurred to him that the Hungarian, privy to the inner workings of the Party, might be able to enlighten him on matters pertaining to Joseph Mauser and his associates, even if inadvertently.

"Show him in," he told Max.

"But the doc—"

"Show him in, Max."

Colonel Bela Kossuth was solicitious. He clicked heels, bowed from the waist, inquired of Mauser's condition.

Mauser wasn't feeling up to military amenities, in light of recent events. He growled, "I'd think you'd be wishing I occupied Captain Rakoczi's place just now, rather than concerning yourself with my health."

The Hungarian's eyebrows went up. Uninvited, he took the chair beside the bed. "But why?"

"You *were* the man's second."

Kossuth was expansive. "When asked to act, I could hardly refuse a brother officer. Besides, my superiors suggested that I take the part." He changed the subject abruptly. "As you probably have ascertained, Major, there was considerable doubt regarding the desirability of your remaining in Budapest. Thus, a method was found of eliminating you."

Mauser was astonished. "You admit that the duel was a planned attempt to eliminate me?"

The colonel looked about the room. "Why not? There is no one here to witness our conversation."

"And you admit that your precious Party, the ruling body of this paradise, actually orders what amounts to assassination?"

Kossuth examined his fingernails with studied nonchalance. "Why not admit it? The party will do literally anything to maintain its position, Major. Certainly, the death of a junior officer of the West-world means nothing to them."

"But aren't you a Party member yourself?"

"Of course. One must be, if one is to operate freely in this best of all possible worlds."

Mauser sank back to his pillow. He could not understand this man, whom he had regarded as a stereotypical Sov officer, speaking in this manner.

Kossuth crossed his legs comfortably. "See here, Major: you are all but naive in your understanding of our society. Let me, ah, brief you on the history of this part of the world and the organization which governs it. Have you studied Marx and Engels?"

"No," Mauser replied. "I've read a few short extracts, and a few criticisms, or criticisms of extracts. That was enough."

Kossuth nodded seriously. "That's all practically anybody reads anymore, even in the Sov-world. The point I was about to make is that the supposed founders of our society had nothing in mind even remotely approaching the current state of affairs when they did their research. It evidently didn't occur to either of them that the first attempts to achieve the—" the Hungarian's voice went dry—"glorious revolution would take place in such ultra-backward countries as Russia and China. Nor did it occur to them that these attempts would be headed by power-hungry individuals out to better themselves under the guise of being 'for the people.' " There was sarcasm in his voice now.

"The revolution of which they wrote presupposed a highly industrialized, technical economy. Neither Russia nor China had this. The, ah, excesses that occurred in both countries in the mid 20th century were the result of efforts to rectify this. You follow me? The Party tried to lift the nations into the industrial world by their bootstraps, to keep itself in power by leading one promise with another."

The colonel cleared his throat. "Let us just say that some elements resisted the sacrifices the Party demanded—the peasants, for instance."

Mauser said, dryly himself, "If I am correctly informed on Sov-world history, you do not exaggerate."

"Exactly. Let us admit it. Stalin in particular, but others too, were ruthless in their determination to achieve industrialization and raise the Sov-world to the level of the most advanced countries."

Mauser said, "This isn't exactly news to me, Colonel."

"Of course not. Bear with me, I was but creating background. To accomplish these things, the Party ostensibly had to, and did, become a strong, ruthless, even merciless organization, with all power safely—from its viewpoint, of course—in its hands."

The Hungarian pursed his lips. "But then comes the rub. Have you ever heard, Major Mauser, of a ruling class, caste, clique, call it what you will, which stepped down from power freely and willingly, handing over the reins of government to some other element?"

Mauser vaguely remembered hearing similar words from another source in the not too distant past, but by now he was fully taken up by the Sov officer's presentation. He shook his head, encouraging the other to continue.

Kossuth nodded. "They tell me that in ancient Greece and Rome tyrants or dictators would assume full power for a period long enough to meet some emergency, and would then relinquish such power. I do not know. I would think it doubtful. But whether or not such was done in ancient Greece, it has since been a rare practice indeed.

"A ruling caste, like a socio-economic system itself, when taken as a whole, instinctively perpetuates its life like a living organism. It cannot understand, will not admit, that it is ever time to die. This is what happened with the Party. It came into existence to satisfy the greed of its founders, and now perpetuates itself to feed its members."

Mauser was astonished still at the words of this supposedly staunch supporter of the Communist philosophy.

"Thus," Kossuth concluded, "the dreams of Marx and Engels, misguided as they were, have been prostituted in their realization to a sad parody of a social system. It has been that way from the beginning."

The Hungarian seemed to switch subjects slightly. "As Marxist philosophy expanded its frontiers, so to speak, a new development manifested itself. At first, Russia alone was the guiding light of the Communist philosophy. But as she became increasingly powerful, she exported her revolution, taking over such advanced countries as, let us say, Czechoslovakia and East Germany. Here, supposedly, would have been the conditions under which the original ideas of Marx and his misguided collaborator would have flourished, but experiences in these countries were the ultimate disproof of the validity of those ideas. Such expansion did, however, serve its purpose in keeping the Party in power."

Mauser started to speak, but Bela Kossuth held up a hand and laughed gently. "Ah, the ironies of fate, my friend. As the Sov-world expanded its borders, it assimilated peoples of far more, ah, sharpness, shall we say, than our somewhat dour Russkies. In time, bit by bit, inch by inch, intrigue by intrigue—"

"I know," Mauser said. "The capital of the Sov-world is now Budapest, rather than Moscow."

"Correct!" the Hungarian beamed. "At the very first, we Hungarians tried to fight them. When we found we couldn't prevail, we joined them—to their eventual sorrow. However, the central problem has not been erased. We have finally advanced to the point where we have the affluent society. But we have also reached stagnation thanks to the Party, which, like a living organism, refuses to die."

He held his hands out, palms upward, as though at an impasse.

Mauser said suddenly, "What's all this got to do with me, Colonel Kossuth?"

The Hungarian pretended surprise. "Why, nothing at all, Major Mauser. I was but making conversation. Small talk."

Mauser didn't get it. "Well, why come here at all?"

"Ah, yes, of course." The Sov officer came to his feet again and clicked his heels. "My superiors have requested that I deliver this into your own hands, as well as copies to the West-world Ambassador and General Armstrong." He handed a document to Mauser.

Mauser turned it over in his hand, blankly. It was in Hungarian. He looked up at the other.

Lieutenant Colonel Bela Kossuth said formally,

"The government of the Sov-world has found Major Joseph Mauser and General George Armstrong *persona non grata*. As soon as your health permits, Major, it is requested that you leave Budapest and all the lands of the Sov-world, never to return."

He clicked his heels, bowed again, and started for the door. Just as he reached it, he turned and said one last thing to Joe Mauser.

"You have quite a bit in common with Colonel Arpad, you know."

In spite of Max's protests, Mauser insisted on abiding by the Sov government's expulsion order on the following day. A special plane took them to London, where General Armstrong left them, and Mauser and Max caught the regular shuttle to Greater Washington.

The flight itself was largely uneventful. Mauser retreated into his thoughts. He had a great deal to think about. Not only was the collapse of his mission on his mind, but the future, as well. There was a new element in the revolutionary equation now, involving Arpad. And, in his personal equation, there was Nadine Haer.

He had come to several decisions since yesterday, decisions involving both his public and personal futures.

Max, looking out the plane's window as they took off from Budapest, seemed to be steeped in an air of nostalgia. "Look there," he pointed. "Can you see that big statue of the Magyar warriors, there in front of the Szepmuveszeti Museum?" He sighed. "I had a date with a Croat girl, to meet her there tomorrow night. She thought it was romantic, me being from the West, and all."

"Max, my friend," Mauser said, "save me the lurid details of your romances."

But his voice hadn't really borne irritation, and Max went on, "You know, you kind of get used to these people. They aren't much different from us. Take fracases, for instance. They don't have them like we do, but they got their telly teams out there in Siberia, with the boys that go chasing the cerebels and all. And they got their duels they cover on telly. But I was thinking, why don't they get modern and have real fracases, like us? And then we could have, like, international meets, and they'd send a division, and we'd send one, and have it out. Zen! That'd be really something to watch!"

Mauser winced.

"Max, it took the human race ten thousand years to put even a temporary halt to the international war. Now you want to bring it back for the sake of a sadistic telly show?"

"Yeah, but—"

"Max, don't worry over it. War will always be with us, as long as there are free men who want to stay that way." He chuckled. "But it is rather ironic to encourage it. Let's have a drink."

Mauser and Max Mainz parted ways as they deboarded at the shuttle port in Greater Washington. Max was taking off immediately to find a recruiting station. There was little for Mauser to say to the man other than to express his thanks; he left with a wish that they might work together again in the future.

He shrugged as Max strode off in the direction of the vacuum tube terminal, then turned and—

Nadine Haer was in his arms.

Their initial reunion was silent, physical.

After a few minutes, he found himself grinning, grinning at the very personal revelation that the old saw about absence making the heart grow fonder was indeed true.

"I've missed you," he murmured into her ear, "and—"

She shushed him with a kiss.

When he could speak again, he said, "We can be married tomorrow, open contract, your terms . . ."

Her eyes widened, "Well, don't you think you might consult me about it?" There was humor in her voice.

"Yes, my dear," he replied playfully. Then, his tone more serious, "Nadine, my love, will you marry me?"

It turned out that Nadine had met him in official, as well as personal, capacity. Holland and Hodgson wanted to see Mauser immediately, and she had been sent for him—not that she wouldn't have met him, anyway. After taking the time for Mauser to make a quick phone call, they were on their way.

It was but a short drive into the city proper, and before long they were retracing the route over which Nadine had taken him that day that seemed so long ago. Through the long corridor, eventually to the small office with the receptionist.

Miss Mikhail said brightly, "Dr. Haer, Major Mauser. Mr. Holland is expecting you. Go right in."

Just before pressing through the door, Nadine put her hand on Mauser's arm and looked into his face ruefully. "Darling, you've had so much hard luck in your time, I'm sorry this first assignment for the organization had to be a failure."

Mauser smiled at her. "What makes you think it was?" he said, opening the door.

Nadine's brow furrowed in thought as he ushered her into Phil Holland's presence.

That efficient operator made the same motions he had the first time Mauser had met him here, greeting Nadine and shaking hands briskly with Mauser and motioning them to sit. While they were getting settled, Frank Hodgson sauntered in, seemingly as lackadaisical and disinterested as ever. After a minimum of exchanged pleasantries, he settled onto the couch and fished for pipe and tobacco.

Holland took in Mauser's arm, still immobilized in a sling, and the other signs of his wounds. He said crisply, "I thought that we had removed you permanently from the field of combat, Joe."

Mauser said sourly, "Some of the Sovs thought otherwise."

"It is hard to understand how you could have revealed yourself so quickly," Holland said, irritated.

Mauser pursed his lips and looked at Nadine. He said, "I think I've figured that out. It's practically impossible for Nadine to dissimulate. And I've never seen her and her brother together but that they weren't arguing."

Nadine was frowning at him. "What has Balt to do with it?"

Mauser said, "I have a sneaking suspicion that, in the heat of one of your arguments with your brother, you revealed my mission and its real purpose."

Nadine's hand went to her mouth.

Mauser finished with, "And he is, after all, a member of the Nathan Hale Society. I have no doubts that the organization has some connections with their equal number in the Sov-world."

Holland grunted. "Very possible. However, it's done now. The thing is, Joe, what is your opinion on sending other operatives on the same mission?"

Mauser shook his head. "Unnecessary."

Frank Hodgson paused in lighting his pipe, to peer through the smoke.

Mauser said, "In fact, it was unnecessary to send me."

Holland's voice was testy. "I assure you, Joe, that particular assignment was quite important. We simply cannot afford to move until we know what the Sov-world will do. Your task was obviously a delicate one. There are strong elements in not only the Upper Caste, but even the Middle and Lower ones, here in this country, who would spring to the defense of present West-world society if they thought an attempt was being made to alter its structure. If the Sov government reported that it had been approached by elements of a revolutionary group, the fat would be in the fire."

Mauser nodded. "I realize all that."

"You were expected to worm your way into their circles, to feel them out. To contact their own underground, if one exists. To ferret out definite information on how they would react if we began definite changes in the status quo here."

Mauser continued to nod.

Holland was increasingly irritated. "Then why in the hell do you say your mission was unnecessary?"

"Because they had already sent a mission over here to contact us," Mauser told him, evenly.

Had he suddenly gotten up from his chair, walked up the wall, across the ceiling, then down the other wall, they could not have been more amazed.

The terminal on Phil Holland's desk squeaked something, and he took time enough to snap, "No. I told you, Miss Mikhail, I was not to be disturbed by *anyone*."

But Mauser said, "If that's Colonel Arpad, I suggest you let him in. I took the liberty of phoning him and asking that he meet us here."

Frank Hodgson was the first to recover. "Arpad! I've just about gathered enough on him to have him declared *persona non grata* and shipped back to Budapest."

"As I was shipped back to Greater Washington," Mauser said dryly. "Colonel Arpad and I seem to duplicate each other's activities in almost everything."

Phil Holland rolled his eyes. "Ask the colonel to come in, Miss Mikhail."

Ever the correct Sov-world officer, Colonel Arpad came to attention immediately upon entering the room, clicked heels, bowed from the waist. Except for Mauser, none of them had met him, but he evidently knew them all, greeting them by name.

The men had come to their feet. Mauser said, "Meet Colonel Lajos Arpad, high in the ranks of the Sov-world Party, and at present on secret mission from the Sov-world underground revolutionary organization." Smiling, he took in their expressions before finishing, "His mission being to determine what action the West-world might take if the secret group which has determined to make basic changes in the Sov-world socio-economic system was to take action."

It was the Hungarian who stared now. His eyes bored into Mauser's face. "I do not, of course, admit that, Major Mauser. But where in the world did you receive that strange opinion?"

Mauser sat down again. The blood he had lost still bothered him, and he was tiring.

He said, "From Colonel Bela Kossuth, in Budapest. No doubt another high-ranking member of your group." Mauser's eyes went back to Holland and Hodgson. Quick-minded these two might be, but they were being asked to assimilate some shocking information.

Mauser brought it all out. "I don't know why it didn't occur to any of us that the problems of the West-world and those of the Sov-world have become similar, almost identical. The West-world's socialist turnings brought it down much the same path as the Sov-world. Both have achieved a so-called affluent society. But in doing so, both managed to inflict upon themselves a caste system that perpetuates itself, under the banner of being 'for the people,' to the detriment of progress.

"In the past, revolutions were accomplished by the masses. A starving lower class, pushed beyond the point of endurance, would violently change the rules of society so as to realize a better life. But now neither West nor Sov-world has any starving. The majority of Lowers and Proletarians are well clothed, fed and housed, and bemused by fracases and trank, or its equivalent over there."

Mauser shrugged, the weariness growing. Possibly he shouldn't have traveled so soon. "The best elements in both countries have finally realized that changes must be made. These elements—the more capable, more competent and intelligent—are already *running* each country, though they are not necessarily Uppers or Party members. Phil Holland here, supposedly a Middle secretary to the Foreign Minister, actually has performed that worthy's work for several administrations. Frank Hodgson is the working head of the Bureau of Investigation, though only a Middle. I assume a similar situation prevails in Budapest."

Arpad still stood. He shrugged in resignation. "It does."

Mauser came to his feet, looking to Nadine. He

said, "Gentlemen, I evidently have not recovered from my recent wounds as much as I thought. I had better retire. Meanwhile, I suggest you exchange some notes."

Nadine hurried to his side, worried.

Holland, Hodgson, and Arpad were staring at one another, suspicious, their manner akin to that of small boys or strange dogs at first meeting.

Hodgson grumbled, his voice for once not lazy, "Our records show you to be a Sov espionage agent."

The Hungarian nodded, equally suspicious. "That is my official position. But I am also secretly a member of the executive committee of the organization to which Major Mauser alludes. I have been attempting for some time to get in touch with the West-world underground, if one existed. I had almost come to the conclusion that no such group was in existence."

Joe Mauser stood in the doorway now, grinning. He said, "Relax, boys, and let down your hair. You've got a lot in common. It looks as though, at long last, the Frigid Fracas is fading away."

KEITH LAUMER

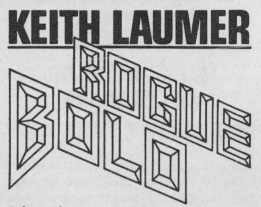

ROGUE BOLO

The Bolo Mark XX is a landgoing battleship with brains and enough firepower to destroy continents. Nothing in the universe can stand against it. Usually, it does what it's told . . .

Spivey's Find was a backwater planet, not very exciting, but a good place to live and bring up kids. Things hadn't always been that good. A few decades back, during the war with the Deng, it had seemed that the Deng might overwhelm humanity on Spivey's Find—until the Federation reinforced the colonial forces with a brand new kind of weapon: a Bolo Mark XX. After the war, the Bolo remained, shot-torn but still conscious, a memorial to the war. What thoughts brooded in its mechanical mind?

Now the Deng have returned, and humanity's only hope is that Mark XX. But the Bolo seems to have a war plan of its own, one that doesn't take humanity into account . . .

Of all Keith Laumer's works, his Bolo stories are perhaps the most eagerly awaited by hardcore SF fans, because there are so few of them. *Rogue Bolo* is the first new Bolo book in years, and it's Laumer at his best, writing about humanity's greatest weapon turning rogue!

DEATHWISH WORLD

MACK REYNOLDS
with DEAN ING

HEADS YOU WIN, TAILS YOU DIE

Life under a Deathwish policy was fun while it lasted, but for Deathwisher Roy Cos it was far more than that. For him, gaining access to great wealth in exchange for becoming a target for hired killers was a political act: You can buy a lot of media attention with a million pseudobucks, and Roy had a cause worth dying for.

Already Roy has survived twice the term of the average Deathwisher, and people are getting interested in what he has to say. That's why Worldgov has labeled him a Special Case and put Mercenaries Inc. on his trail. No matter how smart and tough he may be, no matter how just his cause, even flight to High Orbit can't save Roy now . . .

FEBRUARY 1986 ★ 65552-3 ★ 384 pp. ★ $3.50